Oranges
in the Sun

Oranges in the Sun

Short Stories from the Arabian Gulf

edited and translated by
Deborah S. Akers
Abubaker A. Bagader

LYNNE
RIENNER
PUBLISHERS

BOULDER
LONDON

Published in the United States of America in 2008 by
Lynne Rienner Publishers, Inc.
1800 30th Street, Boulder, Colorado 80301
www.rienner.com

and in the United Kingdom by
Lynne Rienner Publishers, Inc.
3 Henrietta Street, Covent Garden, London WC2E 8LU

Library of Congress Cataloging-in-Publication Data
Oranges in the sun : short stories from the Arabian Gulf / edited and
translated by Deborah S. Akers, Abubaker Bagader.
    p. cm.
  Includes bibliographical references.
  ISBN-13: 978-0-89410-893-8 (hardcover : alk. paper)
  ISBN-13: 978-0-89410-869-3 (pbk. : alk. paper)
  1. Short stories, Arabic—Persian Gulf Region—Translations into English.
I. Baqadir, Abu Bakr Ahmad. II. Akers, Deborah S., 1955–
  PJ8000.82.E5O73 2007
  892.7'301—dc22

                                                        2007026837

British Cataloguing in Publication Data
A Cataloguing in Publication record for this book
is available from the British Library.

Printed and bound in the United States of America

 The paper used in this publication meets the requirements
of the American National Standard for Permanence of
Paper for Printed Library Materials Z39.48-1992.

5   4   3   2   1

For

Nur Bagader
with love and gratitude for her
unstinting support to Abubaker

and

Alia Shubaily,
Deborah's first child—I love you dearly

———————————

Contents

Acknowledgments

This book is the result of nearly five years of arduous collecting. We would like to thank the many individuals who contributed to the project in various capacities. First and foremost, we wish to express our most sincere appreciation to our esteemed sponsor, Ahmad Badib, for his kindness and enthusiasm for the book, and for the generous grant he provided. We would also like to express our warmest appreciation to Abdul-Aziz al-Sebail, not only for providing us with advice on story selection, but also for generously taking the time to review the introductory overview to the collection and offering numerous helpful comments and suggestions.

We wish to convey our deepest appreciation to the authors of the stories collected here for supporting our project and for generously contributing their works to the endeavor.

We would also like to offer our sincere thanks to the members of the literary societies of Saudi Arabia, Yemen, Oman, United Arab Emirates, Bahrain, Qatar, and Kuwait, who received our proposal for this project with great enthusiasm and spared no effort in helping us identify and collect stories from authors in their respective countries. We are grateful as well to the staff of the Jeddah Literary Cultural Club for their painstaking work in assembling the stories from which the pieces in this volume were selected, as well as for attending to the laborious task of seeking copyright permissions.

We continue to be grateful to all other individuals and institutions that have contributed to the successful completion of this book. In particular, Raad Shubaily for his help in typing and formatting the manuscript and Larry Downes and the Information Technology staff of the College of Arts and Sciences at Miami University for their technical advice and support during the preparation of the manuscript. We would also like to thank the staff of the Ohio State University library and especially Dona Straley, Middle East subject and collection specialist, for her help and advice regarding transliteration.

Finally, we would like to thank all the other individuals involved in the project, who are far too numerous to name; without their help, the completion of this project would not have been possible.

—Abubaker A. Bagader and Deborah S. Akers

The Short Story in the Arabian Gulf Region: Origins and Development

Deborah S. Akers

———◆———

The short story as a genre in the Arabian Gulf region is a relatively recent development. Diverse regional and historical factors stimulated the emergence of magazines and newspapers in which stories could be published, thus increasing rates of literacy among the general public. The oil boom of the 1970s was one factor that spurred considerable economic expansion throughout the region, initiating a period of significant infrastructural changes that contributed to the growth of the publishing industry. Another factor that prompted interest in the short story was the establishment of literary clubs and state-sponsored organizations that hosted conferences and other events, enhancing literary output through the publication of collections.

Initially, the short story was used as a thinly veiled medium for the expression of sociocultural and political issues that were otherwise too sensitive or controversial to be dealt with directly. These early stories were often more social commentaries than art form, and from the Western perspective they frequently lacked the character and plot development deemed to be necessary elements of the genre. Over time, however, changes took place in authorial styles, and short stories in the region assumed greater literary complexity.

The stories in this collection, all translated from the Arabic, come from Saudi Arabia, Yemen, Oman, the United Arab Emirates, Bahrain, Qatar, and Kuwait. Organized by country (the order of the countries is roughly geographical, moving from west to east), they were chosen to provide a representative sample of the broad spectrum of the genre; thus, they encompass the works of both established authors and those in the early stages of their careers. (To the extent that information about the authors is available, that information is included in a note at the end of each story.) Some of the stories are humorous; some are impressionistic; some pertain to socially significant issues, such as class distinctions, warfare and terrorism, and the clash of cultural values.

These stories reflect the recent history of the Arabian Gulf region. They epitomize a conflicting attraction and resistance to the rush of modernity, covering themes that range from migration and political unrest, to the Iraq War and terrorism, to the materialism and social injustice that accompanied the differential increases in wealth following the discovery of oil. Moving from pearl diving and fishing to modern-day oil fields and glass-and-steel office buildings, the stories show that there is a price to be paid for modernization: the characters, nostalgic for the simpler ways of the past, lose touch with their core values and become alienated in their rapidly changing societies.

Given the still-evolving nature of the genre in the region, some stories in the collection are more developed and complex than others. Following is a brief discussion of the development of the short-story genre by country, as well as a review of the stories themselves.

SAUDI ARABIA

Short-story writing in Saudi Arabia dates back to the 1930s (Shamikh 1984), with the publication in 1932 of "al-Ibn al-'Aqq" by 'Aziz Diya' (al-Hajri 1987). However, the short story as a genre did not emerge until after World War II. The initial collection of short stories, *Urid an-Ara Allah*, was published in 1946 by Ahmad 'Abd al-Ghafur 'Attar, and the newspaper *al-Bilad*, which began circulation in 1946, was instrumental in spurring on the development of short-story writing in the kingdom (al-Hajri 1987).

By the 1950s, foreign classic literary works, both novels and short stories, were being translated from French and English into Arabic. Saudis who lived outside of the kingdom or were educated abroad in other Arab countries began to write stories that imitated literary styles in those places (al-Hajri 1987; al-Sebail 1991). Other newspapers also began to provide space for short stories, and by 1960 hundreds of stories had been printed. But the papers did more than just provide an outlet for these stories; they also organized writing contests and solicited submissions from their readers.

With the oil boom of the 1970s came the expansion of education, professional specialization, and increasing importation of specialists from abroad, including those in literary fields (al-Sebail 1991). Works of both nonfiction and fiction greatly proliferated. Newspapers continued to facilitate the development of literature, with many providing weekly sections for the publication of literary pieces. Short stories produced during this period were more significantly influenced by these important changes than by the works of authors of the previous generation.

Another important development that took place beginning with the oil boom was the availability of higher education for women. As a result, many female writers emerged, adding their own perspective to the genre (Bagader, Heinrichsdorff, and Akers 1998). Other significant developments included the expansion of publishing houses, the opening of new bookstores, and the formation of literary clubs in various cities (cf. al-Sebail 1991).

A number of the Saudi authors whose works are presented in this collection address themes of traditional life. The late Ahmad al-Siba'i was a highly regarded short-story writer whose works acquaint us with a time in Mecca before the many changes brought about by the oil boom. In his "Auntie Kadrajan," included here, we meet a young Meccan woman who expects her father to select a husband for her as dictated by Saudi custom. She is disappointed, however, and the story ends sadly with Auntie Kadrajan in old age, still waiting for her suitor.

Nostalgia for a way of life that has passed is the theme dealt with in Zahra S. al-Mu'bi's "Suq al-Nada," the story of a former prisoner who returns to the old bazaar to find glaring electric lights and modern innovations; everything has changed in two decades—not only the marketplace but also the people who frequent it.

Social issues, and particularly women's issues, are a theme in many Saudi short stories. In "The Jewelry Box," by Badriyah al-Bashar, we meet a motherless young girl, al-Nuri, whose father marries a woman who is unkind to her. Al-Nuri finds love and solace in Layla, her beloved aunt, who becomes her guiding force even after Layla's death. "The Impossible," by Najat Khayyat, one of the earliest female short-story writers in Saudi Arabia, opens with the protagonist's wedding ceremony. During the ceremony, she contemplates the wasteful opulence of the aristocracy into which she is marrying, as evident from the lavish jewelry and extravagant dresses worn by the guests. In "I Was Betrayed with a Single Golden Pound," by Munirah A. al-Ghadir, a young girl from a poor family is forced to marry a wealthy old man. She likens her situation to the "slavery of the marriage market," where parents from poor families sell their daughters to grooms who can pay the highest dowry. "Knowing His Secret," by Sharifah al-Shamlan, is also about Saudi women's experiences in marriage. The story concerns the devastating quandary a wife faces upon discovering her husband's secret love affair; she must decide whether to stay for the sake of her children and family or leave.

The next two stories touch upon the theme of war. Saudis have been affected by a number of regional conflicts, including the first Gulf war when Saddam Hussein's Iraqi forces fired missiles into Saudi Arabia. "The Shelter," by Ibrahim Nassir al-Humaydan, depicts a father who must comfort his frightened young children when they hear bombs exploding nearby. In "An Encounter," a sentimental piece about a loved one and loss by 'Abd Allah Husayn, we meet a heartbroken old man who maintains the routine of making *shawarma* sandwiches for his satisfied customers while staring at the Gulf waters and hearing his dead son, whom he lost in the war, call to him with the tides.

Turning again to social issues and the dilemmas of modern life, in "Bloodstains on the Wall," by Ahmad Bogary, a young boy's father is run over in a tragic accident. Here we witness the abuse of the poor by the aristocracy, when the boy is asked to wash his father's bloodstains off the marble wall of a villa for a mere ten riyals. 'Abd Allah Bakhshawayn's "The Silver Polisher" depicts a traveling businessman who is grappling with the fact of his father's death. The protagonist in the last story in this section, "Reaching You Through the Letter Carrier," by 'Abd al-'Aziz Mishri, laments the need for laborers to go to foreign lands to make a living; these sad men live in neither their home country nor their host country, but someplace in between.

YEMEN

Short-story writing in Yemen began in the 1940s (Ibrahim 1977). One of the first stories to be published was Ahmad al-Barraq's "Ana Sa'id," which appeared in 1940 in *al-Hikmah* magazine, then two years in circulation (al-Sebail 1991). The genre developed along with the advent of various magazines and newspapers, notable among them the newspaper *Fatat al-Hijaz* (Ibrahim 1977). The first collection of short stories, *Anta Shuyu'i* by Salih ad-Dahhan, was published in 1956. Stories written during the late 1950s and 1960s reflected the broader political and social issues confronting Yemeni society at the time.

Increasing contact with other literatures as a result of writers spending time abroad had a major influence on Yemeni literature. Muhammad 'Abd al-Wali (1940–1973), who was educated in Egypt and the Soviet Union, was considered the leading short-story writer of his time (Weir 2002). As a result of efforts by al-Wali and others, short stories started to move from being loosely structured social commentaries to a more structured realistic style of prose. The stories collected in this volume represent some of the more recent works.

In many of the Yemeni stories in this collection, we see a resistance to modern life and nostalgia for the simpler ways of traditional life. For example, in Wajdi al-Ahdal's "To Return by Foot," we meet a young man for whom walking symbolizes a silent rebellion against modern forms of travel. The protagonist stands for his convictions—to keep his life simple and not depend on others—even at the cost of losing his love, Dahlia.

We witness a similar resistance to the rush of modernity in "The Nightmare," by Hamadan Dammaj. In this story, the protagonist appears to be terrified by the modern ways of life that encroach on him. His fear manifests itself in a recurring nightmare in which he is struck by an automobile; when the dream's misfortune nearly befalls him in reality, however, he is saved by a stranger.

The appeal of traditional ways of life is reflected in the colorful story "The Corn Seller," by Zayd Muti' Dammaj, in which the interlocutor shares with us his romantic fantasies about the beautiful young woman who sells corn in the qat market. Modernity, however, is boldly encroaching on traditional ways of life as depicted in "A Parting Shot," by Muhammad O. Bahah. In this provocative tale, an abandoned wife takes control of her life by becoming literate and finding a job; ultimately, this allows her to write a shocking final letter to her husband.

Quite a different contemporary issue is illustrated in Yassir 'Abd al-Bagi's "Bus #99," in which a radical young man attempts to blow up a bus. 'Abd al-Bagi brings the coldheartedness of terrorism to the forefront when he depicts a grandmother and her grandson innocently holding a briefcase with a bomb in it while the terrorist watches from a distance.

Romantic love is the focus of two of the stories from Yemen, but with quite different outcomes. "Sanaa Does Not Know Me," by Muhammad al-Gharbi 'Umran, is a touching narrative of a man who mistakenly believes he has found love in his classmate, whose elegance reminds him of a palm tree from the coasts of Tuhama. A happier turn of events rewards the shopkeeper in Zayd Salih al-Faqih's "The Veiled One," in which the shopkeeper's stories captivate the neighborhood children, especially the shy Zarga, who comes from a wealthy family.

"Trilling Cries of Joy," by 'Ali 'Awad Badib, examines a young man's conflicted feelings of love and resentment for his mother, a professional triller, who ululates at weddings, holidays, celebrations, and other special occasions. This lyrically written tale speaks of the experience of missing a parent in death, a feeling so acute that even her irritating trilling gains favor in her son's memory.

OMAN

The development of short-story writing in Oman is relatively recent. In 1970, political change brought a new government that instituted extensive modernization programs and ended the country's years of isolationism (al-Dahab 1987; Allen and Rigsbee 2000). These political changes resulted in the establishment of schools and literacy programs, as well as the appearance of newspapers and magazines that provided venues for literary endeavors. The first newspaper in the country, *al-Watan*, established in 1971, carried the earliest Omani short stories. The newspaper *'Uman* was also a vehicle for such efforts. During the 1980s, a number of collections were published—including *Wa-akhrajat al-Ard* (1983) by Ahmad Bilal and *Intihar 'Ubayd al-Umani* (1985) by Ahmad az-Zubaydi—further boosting interest in the medium (al-Sebail 1991).

At present, the combination of a literate audience and the continuing development of media outlets for the publication of written works serves to stimulate interest in the short-story genre. Despite these changes, however, Oman remains a society that is highly bound by tradition, and the distinctively traditional style of the Omani authors is reflected in the moving stories in this collection.

A predominant theme in the stories from Oman is social injustice due to socioeconomic inequality. Many of the stories depict the sense of futility and unfairness that the lower classes experience as the world around them changes beyond their ability to cope. "Oranges in the Sun," by Yahya bin Salam al-Mundhri, tells of a crippled father's efforts to provide for his family, as symbolized by his struggle to cross busy city traffic carrying a sack of oranges. It is this father's sense of powerlessness against his fate that defeats him. Likewise in "The Disaster," by Muhammad ibn Sayf Rahabi, we witness the bewilderment and frustration of a young tea server in an office as he is dragged to court for picking up a discarded pen from a wastebasket and is pronounced guilty of stealing.

Two stories, "A Crisis at Sea," by 'Ali Muhammad Rashid, and "Sounds of the Sea," by Saud Bulushi, reflect the importance of the sea in the lives of many Omanis. Rashid's "A Crisis at Sea" takes us back to the days when many depended on pearl diving for their livelihood. In this story, a young boy must grow up fast following the unexpected death of his father, the captain of a pearl-diving ship. Bulushi's sentimental "Sounds of the Sea" relates the musings of an old man who longs for the sea as the sun slowly sets on his life. All around him he hears the sea's insistent seductive call, feels its cool, humid breeze, and even longs for its suffocating wind, until he surrenders and dies.

"Ghomran's Oil Field," by Su'ad al-'Arimi, is a poignant story about an Omani guard who works in an oil field alongside expatriate laborers from Asia and Africa. Similar to pearl diving, in which earning one's livelihood requires risking one's life, working in an oil field, too, comes with extreme hazards. The author romanticizes the sacrifice that the protagonist makes to save his coworkers when a fire engulfs the field.

Omani writers also bring us stories of romance. In "A Voice from the Earth," by Ahmad Bilal, the protagonist, Ahmad, finds legal documents and a clay jar filled with gold coins tucked away under the floorboards in his family's home. From these papers, he learns that his father had secretly married and was supporting a second wife; and through this turn of fate, he meets the girl with whom he falls in love. Sulayman al-Ma'mami's "The White Dog" is a fantasy about the search for romantic love and the disappointment that can follow. The young man narrating this story has to deal with more than one kind of loss.

UNITED ARAB EMIRATES

The history of short-story writing in the United Arab Emirates (UAE) begins with the establishment of the country in 1971. The first short stories appeared sporadically in magazines and newspapers that began circulating in the early 1970s. At that time, several collections were published, including *al-Khashabah* (1975) by 'Abd Allah Saqr Ahmad and *ash-Shaqa'* (1977) by 'Ali al-Sharhan. A major influence on the genre was the appearance of new magazines and newspapers in the 1980s, a number of which devoted sections to short stories and literary topics. Following the oil boom, there was an expansion of state-sponsored education, resulting in an overall increase in the literacy rate that further established the importance of literature in Emirati society (on education in the Gulf regions, see Misnad 1985).

Many of the stories from the UAE address social and economic problems that confront modern-day Emiratis, as in 'Abd al-Hamid Ahmad's short story "The Plight." Muhammad al-Murr brings issues of alienation to the forefront in "An Idyllic World," his Kafkaesque rendering of the reveries of a low-ranking civil servant who is fired when he asks his boss for a raise.

The fate of a couple's children when their bicultural marriage fails is the subject of the shocking "Surprise at the Airport," by Asma' al-Zar'uni. In a more romantic vein, 'Abd al-Ilah 'Abd al-Qadir "A

Bouquet of Jasmine" tells of a divorced mother who finds love, but whose chance of happiness is ultimately thwarted.

BAHRAIN

Short-story writing in Bahrain began in the 1940s—the first short story, Mahmud Yusuf's "Ha'irah" was published in 1941 (Ghlum 1981)—but its development was sporadic for the next two decades. Newspaper and magazine publication during the 1940s and 1950s was intermittent due to government shutdowns (see Al-Rumaihi 1975), which limited outlets for short stories. It was not until the mid-1960s that there was finally an uninterrupted publication of periodicals, allowing the re-emergence of the short-story genre (Ghlum 1981). The first major collection, *Sirat al-Ju'wa as-Samt*, was published in 1971, and short-story writing has continued to develop in Bahrain since then. The stories included in this volume represent the more recent contributions to the genre.

Material wealth, or its lack, is central in the stories of Muhammad 'Abd al-Malik. In "That Winter," the story of a devoted nephew and his ailing Auntie Norah, al-Malik shows the extremes of what money can and cannot buy.

"The Dogs," by 'Abd Allah Khalifah, reflects a troubled painter's feelings as his fellow artists threaten to destroy his reputation if he continues to paint in his unique style rather than like the rest of his contemporaries. Khalifah shows the protagonist learning from a stray dog about how to stand his ground. Also a story of survival, Hasan 'Isa al-Mahrus's "Al-Assadiah" displays folkloric elements as an ancient *sidr* tree with mystical powers survives in the hearts of the villagers against the threats of a landowner who wants to build a villa where the tree is planted.

In the final story in the section, "The Siege," by 'Abd al-Qadir 'Aqil, we meet a father and his six-year-old son out for a drive. The car and its passengers appear to have become trapped in a dead zone. As he tries to drive out of this zone, the father sees a figure beckoning to them but wonders whether she means to help or harm them.

QATAR

In Qatar, short-story writing developed relatively recently (Kafud 1982). A number of political and economic changes occurred when Qatar became an independent nation-state in 1971 (McCoy 2004). The nationalization of petroleum production in 1974 led to the creation of a modern infrastructure, which facilitated the appearance of newspapers, magazines, and the publishing industry. And as with other countries in the Arabian Peninsula, the short story in Qatar is associated with the development of journalism and publishing.

One of the first short stories published in Qatar was Ibrahim al-Muraykhi's "al-Hanin," which appeared in 1971 in the magazine *al-Urubah* (al-Sebail 1991). However, the primary vehicle for the establishment of the short story as a distinct literary genre was the magazine *al-Ahd*. First published in 1974, *al-Ahd* specialized in Qatari culture and literature. In addition to individual stories, the magazine also published a collection of short stories entitled *Anta wa Ghabat as-Samt wa at-Taraddud* (1978), by the noted female writer Kultham Jabr. Two other collections were published during the 1980s: *Sab'at Aswat fi al-Qissah al-Qatariyyah* (1983), which contains stories by seven Qatari writers, and *Bai al-Jaraid* (1989), by Nurah as-Saad. In contrast to what is found in other countries in the region, the majority of the writers in Qatar are women, which is perhaps a reflection of the relatively high rate of literacy among Qatari women (Misnad 1985).

In the 1990s, the National Council for Culture, Arts, and Heritage was established in Doha, Qatar's capital city, with the stated objective of actively cultivating the country's cultural heritage and enhancing its literary output by publishing collections and organizing literary events. In 2002, the council published an English-language volume, *Selected Qatari Short Stories*, edited by Hasan Rashid and Abbakr al-Nur Uthman. The collection showcases stories by many well-known Qatari writers, some of whom are featured in the pages that follow.

Widad 'Abd al-Latif al-Kuwari reflects in her story "Layla" the central place that children hold in Arabian society. Here we see the extent to which parents can pressure their son to divorce his wife if she cannot produce heirs to carry their bloodline and family name. In "A Woman," Huda al-Nu'aymi describes a sixteen-year-old girl who was given by her father to an older man in exchange for money. When the girl discovers she is pregnant with twin girls, her joy is of a different nature than that of a grown woman: now she can play with her own babies instead of with dolls. "A Night of Sorrow," by Kultham Jabr, is about the dilemma that a professional woman faces in her supposedly modern relationship with her boyfriend.

In "The Prize," Jamal Faiz shows how ambition leads an office worker to win the "Employee of the Year" prize. The protagonist feels much pressure to excel in the workplace, but his excessive eagerness has disastrous consequences.

In Nasir al-Hallabi's amusing tale "The Alley," we meet a meticulous engineer who prides himself on being organized and cannot tolerate the chaos that is routine on the streets and walkways of Cairo. The author skillfully describes the broken sidewalks, narrow alleyways, and incessant traffic jams that the protagonist must endure—leading to a violent confrontation and a surprising conclusion. In "The Checkpoint," by Muhsin al-Hajiri, a modern hero suffers the consequences of his long hair: he must prove to a belligerent police officer that he is indeed the man who is pictured in the ID he carries.

Hasan Rashid writes about a mischievous and feisty youth, Ahmad, in the humorous tale "The Storyteller." Ahmad tells countless stories about *jinns* and devils, exaggerating his victories over all challenges. His colorful imagination and zest for life catch up with him, however, when he almost drowns after making a two-rupee bet.

KUWAIT

Short-story writing in Kuwait has one of the longest histories in the Arabian Gulf region (see Abd Allah 1973; ash-Shatti 1989; Ghlum 1981). The first Kuwaiti short story to be published was Khalid al-Faraj's "Munirah," which appeared in 1929 in *al-Kuwayt* magazine. The genre received a significant impetus during the late 1940s, when there was an expansion of journalism and the appearance of a number of newspapers and magazines, such as *al-Ba'thah* and *Kazimah* (al-Sebail 1991), that published short stories. A collection of short stories, Fadil Khalaf's *Ahlam ash-Shabab*, was published in 1954, and the decades that followed saw work that demonstrated increased sophistication and artistic development. By the 1990s, there was already a third generation of authors who had devoted themselves to writing short stories.

A number of the stories in this collection stress the significance of the 1990 Iraqi invasion in the lives of Kuwaitis. Layla al-Uthman's "The ID Card" focuses on the first Gulf war and the strong feelings of nationalism that the Iraqi occupation provoked in Kuwaiti citizens. The trauma and anguish of the war and its aftermath are also addressed in the stories by Muna al-Shafi'i ("Hunger"), Hamad al-Hammad ("The Return of a Captive"), and Layla Muhammad Salih ("Guns and Jasmine"). These tales, written by those who experienced the invasion firsthand, personalize the war, making its impact all the more real and poignant.

The other stories from Kuwait included in this collection are an eclectic sampling, ranging from a fantasy piece to stories that address social issues, matters of the heart, remembrances of lost loved ones, and the passage of time. The destructive forces of modernization are considered in Muna al-Shafi'i's "The Age of Pain," in which a young girl poignantly reminisces about the death of her beloved grandfather. In "New Wrinkles," Badr Abu Raqabah explores sentiments about the passage of time and loss. Al-Uthman's "The Homeland Is Far Away, the Roads Are Many" deals with the socioeconomic tensions that exist between privileged indigenous Kuwaitis and working-class Palestinian immigrants, highlighting the frustrations and disappointments that follow the latter. In "Bashrawi," Talib al-Rifai relates a tale of a foreign worker who, allowed his first vacation after being away from his home country for a number of years, is anxious about the customary gifts he must bring home with him for the countless members of his extended family.

◆ ◆ ◆

The stories that follow capture and embody a distinctly unique vision of the world, as well as the emotional and material concerns of the people of the Arabian Gulf.

BIBLIOGRAPHY

Abd Allah, Muhammad Hasan. 1973. *al-Harakah al-Adabiyyah wa al-Fikriyyah fi al-Kuwayt*. Kuwait: Rabitat al-Udaba fi al-Kuwayt.
Abdullah, Muhammad Morsy. 1978. *The United Arab Emirates: A Modern History*. London: Croom Helm.
al-Ahdal, Wajdi. 1998. *Ratanat al-Zaman al-Miqmaq: Majmu'ah Qisasiyah*. San'a, Yemen: al-Hayah.
Ahmad, 'Abd al-Hamid. 1982. *al-Sibahah fi 'Aynay Khalij Mutawahhish: Qisas*. Beirut: Dar al-Kalimah lil-Nashr, bi-al-ishtirak ma'a Muassasat al-Khalij al-'Arabi lil-Dirasat wa-al-Nashr.
———. 1987. *al-Baydar: Qisas*. Beirut: Dar al-Kalimah.
———. 1992. *'Ala Haffat al-Nahar: Qisas*. al-Shariqah, UAE: Ittihad Kuttab wa-Udaba al-Imarat.
———. 2003. *Juyub Anfiyah li-Ihlal al-Salam*. Damascus: al-Mad'a.
Ahmad, 'Abd Allah Saqr. 1975. *al-Khashabah*. Dubai: Matba'at Dubay.
Allen, Calvin, and W. Lynn Rigsbee. 2000. *Oman Under Qaboos: From Coup to Constitution, 1970–1996*. Portland, OR: Frank Cass.
al-'Ammah lil-Kitab. 2001. *Harb Lam Ya'lam bi-Wuqu'iha Ahad: Majmu'ah Qisasiyah*. San'a, Yemen: Markaz 'Abbadi lil-Dirasat wa-al-Nashr.

al-'Arimi, Su'ad. 1990. *Tuful: Qisas.* al-Shariqah, UAE: Manshurat Ittihad al-Kuttab wa-al-Udaba al-Imarat.

Badib, 'Ali 'Awad. 1984. *as-Safar fi adh-Dhakirah.* N.p.

Bagader, Abubaker, and Deborah Akers. 2001. *They Die Strangers: Selected Works by Abdul-Wali.* Austin: University of Texas Center for Middle Eastern Studies.

Bagader, Abubaker, and Ava Heinrichsdorff. 1990. *Assassination of Light: Modern Saudi Short Stories.* Washington, DC: Three Continents Press.

Bagader, Abubaker, Ava Heinrichsdorff, and Deborah S. Akers. 1998. *Voices of Change: Short Stories by Saudi Arabian Women Writers.* Boulder, CO: Lynne Rienner Publishers.

Bakhshawayn, 'Abd Allah. 1985. *al-Haflah.* Jazan, Saudi Arabia: Nadi Jazan al-Abadi.

Bilal, Ahmad. 1983. *Wa-akhrajat al-Ard: Qisas Qasirah.* Oman: Matabi' al-'Aqidah.

al-Dahab, Muhammad. 1987. "The Historical Development of Education in Oman: From the First Modern School in 1893 to the First Modern University." PhD dissertation, Boston College.

Dammaj, Zayd Muti'. 1973. *Tahish al-Hawban.* Bani Suwayf, Egypt. np.

———. 1982. *al-'Aqrab.* Beirut: Dar al- 'Awdah.

———. 1986. *al-Jisr.* San'a, Yemen: al-Jumhuriyah al-'Arabiyah al-Yamaniyah, Wizarat al-'Ilam wa-al-Thaqafah.

———. 1994. *The Hostage: A Novel.* North Hampton, MA: Interlink Publishing Group.

———. 2001. *al-Midfa' al-Asfar: Qisas.* San'a, Yemen: al-Hayah al-'Ammah lil-Kitab.

Ghlum, Ibrahim 'Abd Allay. 1981. *al-Qissah al-Qasirah fi al-Khalij al-'Arabi: al-Kuwayt wa al-Bahrayn: Dirasah Naqdiyyah Tahliliyyah.* al-Basrah, Iraq: Marka Dirasat al-Khalij al-'Arabi. Baghdad: Tawzi' al-Dar al-Wataniyah.

al-Hajiri, Muhsin. 1996. *al-Balagh wa-Qisas Ukhrá.* al-Dawhah: M. al-Hajiri. Doha, Qatar.

———. 1997. *Banat Iblis: wa-Qisas Ukhr'a.* Amman, Jordan: Dar Usamah.

———. 1998. *Haram 'Alayka—wa-Qisas Ukhrá.* al-Dawhah: M. al-Hajiri. Doha, Qatar.

al-Hajri, Sihmi Majid. 1987. *al-Qissah al-Qasirah fi al-Mamlakah al-'Arabiyyah as-Su'udiyya Mundhu Nash'atiha Hatta 'Am 1964.* Riyadh: an-Nadi al-Adabi.

al-Hammad, Hamad. 1991. *Layali al-Jamr: Qisas.* Kuwait: H. Al-Hamad.

Husayn, 'Abd Allah. 1989. *as-Sayd al-Akhir.* Dammam, Saudi Arabia: Dar al-Yawm.

Ibrahim, 'Abd al-Hamid. 1977. *al-Qissa al-Yamaniyyah al-Mu'asirah.* Beirut: Dar al-'Awadah.

Jabr, Kulthum. 1978. *Anta wa Ghabat as-Samt wa at-Taraddud.* Qatar: Mu'assasat al-'Ahd.

Kafud, Muhammad 'Abd ar-Rahim. 1982. *Al-Adab al-Qatari al-Hadith.* Qatar: Jama'at Qatar.

McCoy, Lisa. *Qatar.* 2004. Philadelphia: Mason Crest Publishers.

al-Mishri, 'Abd al-'Aziz. 1979. *Mawt 'ala al Ma'.* Riyadh: an-Nadi al-Adabi.

————. 1986. *Asfar as-Sarawi.* Riyadh: Jam'iayyat ath-Thaqafah wa al-Funun.

————. 1987. *Bawh as-Sanabil.* Taifs, Saudi Arabia: Nadi at-Taif al-Adabi.

————. 1987. *az-Zuhur Tabhath 'an Aniyah.* Jazan, Saudi Arabia: Nadi Jazan al-Adabi.

Misnad, Sheikha. 1985. *The Development of Modern Education in the Gulf.* London: Ithaca.

al-Murr, Muhammad. 1991. *Dubai Tales.* Boston: Forest Books.

————. 1994. *Wink of the Mona Lisa and Other Stories from the Gulf.* Dubai: Motivate Press.

————. 1997. *Banat Iblis: wa-Qisas Ukhr'a.* Amman, Jordan: Dar Usamah.

Netton, Ian Richard. 1986. *Arabia and the Gulf: From Traditional Society to Modern States.* Totowa, NJ: Barnes and Noble.

Rashid, Hasan. 1996. *al-Mawta la-Yartadun al-Qubur: Majmu'ah Qisasiyah.* Doha, Qatar: Hasan Rashid.

————. 2001. *Aswat min al-Qissah al-Qasirah fi Qatar.* Doha, Qatar: al-Majlis al-Watani lil-Thaqafah wa-al-Funun wa-al-Turath.

————. 2001. *al-Hidn al-barid: Majmu'ah Qisasiyah.* Doha, Qatar: al-Majlis al-Watani lil-Thaqafah wa-al-Funun wa-al-Turath.

Rashid, Hasan, and Abbakr al-Nur Uthman, eds. 2002. *Selected Qatari Short Stories.* Doha, Qatar: al-Majlis al-Watani lil-Thaqafah wa-al-Funun wa-al-Turath.

al-Rumaihi, Muhammad Ghanim. 1975. *Bahrain: A Study on Social and Political Changes Since the First World War.* University of Kuwait.

al-Sebail, Abdulaziz. 1991. "The Short Story in the Arabian Peninsula: Realistic Trends." PhD dissertation, Indiana University.

al-Shafi'i, Muna. 1992. *al-Nakhlah wa-Raihat al-Hil: Majmut'at Qisa.* Kuwait: Dar Su'ad al-Sabah.

————. 1994. *al-Bid—Marratayn: Majmu'ah Qisasiyah.* Kuwait: Sharikat al-Rubay'an.

————. 1995. *Dirama al-Hawass: Majmu'at Qisas.* Kuwait: Sharikat al-Rubay'an lil-Nashr wa- al-Tawzi'.

————. 2002. *Ashya Gharibah—Tahduth.* Kuwait: Dar Qirtas lil-Nashr.

————. 2005. *Nabadat unthá.* Kuwait: Dar al-Watan.

al-Shafi'i, Muna, Layla Muhammad Saleh, and Hamad Hamad. 2004. *Arrivals from the North: A Collection of Kuwaiti Short Stories.* Kuwait: Ministry of Information, Government Printing Press.

Shamikh, Muhammad 'Abd al-Rahman. 1984. *The Rise of Modern Prose in Saudi Arabia.* Riyadh: University Libraries, King Saud University.

al-Shamlan, Sharifah. 1989. *Muntaha al-Hudu'.* Riyadh: Jam'iyyat ath-Thagafah wa al-Funun.

al-Siba'i, Ahmad. 1980. *Khalati Kadrajan.* Jiddah, Saudi Arabia: Tihamah.

al-Shatti, Sulayman. 1989. "Tarikh al-Qissah al-Qasirah fi al-Kuwayt." *Al-Adab* 2–3: 66–105.

al-Uthman, Layla. 1987. *Fathiyah Takhtaru Mawtaha: Majmu'at Qisas.* Cairo and Beirut: Dar al-Shuruq.

————. 1987. *al-Hubb la-hu Suwar.* Cairo and Beirut: Dar al-Shuruq.

————. 1987. *La Yaslahu lil-Hubb: wa-Qisas Ukhrá.* Beirut: al-Muassasah al-'Arabiyah lil-Dirasat wa-al-Nashr.

———. 1990. *Halat Hubb Majnunah: Qisas.* Cairo: al-Hayah al-Misriyah al-'Ammah lil-Kitab.

———. 1996. *Zahrah Tadkhul al-Hayy: Mukhtarat Qisasiyah.* Beirut: Dar al-Adab.

———. 1998. *Yahduthu Kull Laylah: Qisas.* Beirut: al-Muassasah al-'Arabiyah lil-Dirasat.

———. 2003. *Yawmiyat al-Sabr wa-al-Murr: Maqta' min Sirat al-Waqi'.* Kuwait: Layla al-Uthman.

———. 2005. *Laylat al-Qahr: Qisas Qasirah.* Cairo: Dar Sharqiyat.

Weir, Shelagh. 2002. "Introduction." In *They Die Strangers: Short Stories by 'Abd al-Wali,* translated by Abubaker Bagader and Deborah Akers. Austin: University of Texas Center for Middle Eastern Studies.

Zahlan, Rosemarie. 1989. *The Making of the Modern Gulf States: Kuwait, Bahrain, Qatar, the United Arab Emirates, and Oman.* London: Unwin Hyman.

al-Zubaydi, Ahmad. 1985. *Intihar 'Ubayd al-Umani.* Beirut: Dar al-Haqa'iq.

Saudi Arabia

Auntie Kadrajan

Ahmad al-Siba'i

◆

Auntie Kadrajan wasn't her real name, but a nickname that people called her, which means "poor thing." You'll feel sorry for her when you learn how she got it and found that she would never be called anything else.

Some neighbors claimed she was only a little over fifty, while others insisted she was older than Amm Idrous, the traveling saffron peddler. Idrous himself assured everyone that "She was a teenager, already covering her hair, when I was just a little boy learning to read at Al-Maghrabi's Quran School. The school was next to her mother's house." Idrous was convinced she was only two or three years shy of sixty.

Auntie Kadrajan didn't care about all of this, for counting years was a bother. She could remember the year of the great flood, as well as the elephant that came to town when she was a little girl. She even attended receptions for the sharif of Mecca. But when she was told that these events were separated by long years, she said, "Hush! Those kinds of details give me a headache."

As for herself, she considered herself not much older than thirty, with only a few years in between that she forgot to count. She said that with the utmost confidence and affirmed it by walking elegantly on her wooden heels, between the guest room and the hallway of the small room she had converted to a kitchen, swinging with a coquettish gait as though she were a young woman in her twenties.

When I was a young boy, my friends and I played hide-and-seek in our alley behind her house. I was her pampered favorite. When our game reached the peak of its excitement, I would hide in her home. Whenever she saw me running toward her, panting and out of breath, she would think I was afraid of someone chasing me to beat me. She would tell me to run to the front hall and hide under the fringe of the couch. There I would regain my courage and catch my breath, then creep out on my hands and knees. She would stand in my way and try to

17

prevent me from leaving, repeating: "How many times have I told you, son, not to let the other children gang up on you? These boys are rotten, and you are very young." She didn't know, out of her naïveté, that it was part of the game that whoever was the seeker had to find those hiding or at least tag one of us in order to win the game.

I used to notice how Auntie Kadrajan took great care of her *kohl* pot. She would keep a small box near it and frequently stretch her hand to dip into it and, using fingertips, rub some cream onto her face. I was too young to understand what she was doing.

Quite often, I saw her sitting at the tea table. After finishing her tea, she would put away the tray stacked with teacups and sit still looking intently into a mirror. Using a pair of tweezers, she would pluck a strand of gray hair from here and there. And because she took me for a child, she would ask me to come and sit with her to help find the gray hairs. I used to tell my mother this story on evenings when she got together with the neighbors. They would laugh and wink at one another and one of them might sigh and say, "Poor thing!" Then they would all raise their eyebrows and collectively sigh saying that she was indeed a poor thing.

I couldn't figure out their reasons for calling her a poor thing, or why they felt sorry for Auntie Kadrajan. I felt that she was kinder and sweeter in her relations with people than any of her neighbors, including my mother. I saw in her a keen desire to take care of herself and others, a concern I did not find in any of the neighbors I frequently visited. Her home was very small, but so clean that it frequently invoked compliments. The cushions of the guest sofa were decorated with glittering sequins, while the pillows in the middle of the sofa were embroidered with flowers that sparkled in blue and yellow. Along the fringe was a poetic verse of some kind. I liked the way it looked, though I couldn't read but one word: "Oh."

She used to clean her home dressed in her best, wearing a gown made of a flowing transparent fabric, her hair tied back with a comb that was decorated with glittering gems. The slippers she wore looked as new as the day that she bought them.

I remember, whenever I told this to my mother she'd say, "Poor Auntie Kadrajan. She is such a sorry woman!"

I don't recall whether at that young age anything about Auntie Kadrajan's situation fascinated me more than trying to make sense out of her life—which was elegant and graceful in the eyes of a child—and the pity I saw from my mother and her neighbors. I grew older, no longer a child to visit the guest room of Auntie Kadrajan. I didn't hear much about her anymore, until one day I heard she had a mental problem and had to move in with her relatives where she died shortly thereafter.

I finally learned her story from one of the old women who used to be my mother's neighbor. I begged her to tell me about Auntie Kadrajan, to explain why she and her friends moaned and sighed despite the refined life Auntie Kadrajan used to live. Only then did I come to understand the many things that were incomprehensible before.

◆ ◆ ◆

Auntie Kadrajan grew up in her father's home, becoming a beautiful, willowy young woman. She lost her mother early in her life and continued to live with her father and her sister in the big house. After her sister died too, when Auntie Kadrajan was just a teenager, she and her father were all that were left of her family. She took care of her father, and in turn he would spoil and pamper her. Her father, a rich landlord, was an old man. She received many offers for marriage, but her father would not agree to any of them. He said she was his only child, the only one who could look after him in his old age. But those who knew him better said he feared his property would fall into a stranger's hands.

Auntie Kadrajan lived in her father's home until he died, when she was still in the radiance of her full youth. After the days of mourning passed, her cousin, who was also her legal guardian, asked for her hand in marriage. But she refused. He was older than her, with children her age. When he asked again, she stubbornly rejected his offer. And from then on, he abused his position as her legal guardian and refused all those who wanted to marry her. For each of the suitors he invented a defect that left her in the end a spinster in her own home.

Her income was guaranteed from her share of her inheritance, but despite that, she lived feeling a void, like every young girl who fills her heart with the dream of a knight waiting for her.

As her waiting stretched longer and longer, the mansion became too big for her in her solitude. She moved some of the furniture to the quiet room on the ground floor and rented out the rest of the house. She passed her time there, suffering from loneliness.

Days passed. One day, she woke to the sound of a knock on her door. Standing there were three guests from Indonesia who had come for a pilgrimage that year. They were a man and two women carrying a letter from some relatives of her late father. Auntie Kadrajan received them in the guest room, wearing a thin veil in accordance with the fashion of Meccan women when they received pilgrims. She felt these pilgrims were trustworthy. After they were greeted and had been served coffee and tea, she felt the eyes of the young man furtively following her around. It didn't bother her that he paid attention to her, and in fact she surprised him by letting her eyes rest on his gaze for a moment or two.

A few hours after the guests had said farewell, someone knocked on her door. This time it was the head of the pilgrims, the *sheikha*, who had come to tell her the wish of the guests' son to ask for her hand in marriage.

She was taken with the idea and told the *sheikha* the story of her cousin, her legal guardian, how he used all sorts of tricks to keep her unmarried.

But the *sheikha* was a shrewd woman, and as she left she said encouragingly, "Look, my daughter. After the pilgrimage the boy will return home with his mother and sister, whom you met. When he is back home, he will ask his father's permission and get the necessary money for the dowry and other expenses. Then he will come back to us. His father would like for him to study here, get married, and settle down. Don't worry about your cousin not agreeing. You are not a young girl. When the boy returns, you can go off with him to the judge, who will marry you, since you do accept and you are not a minor. Do we agree?"

"Whatever you say, ma'am."

"Then it is agreed!"

"Whatever you say. You are just like my mother."

♦ ♦ ♦

The pilgrimage ended and the last ship for Indonesia left port. Auntie Kadrajan counted the months of the year with tense nerves. It was the one chance in her lifetime. "I will not let this chance slip through my fingers," she thought. "I don't care about the dowry, how big or small it is. What a great woman the *sheikha* is. How wonderful are her ideas. Yes, I'll go with him to the judge's home and declare my willingness to marry him since the first day he knocked on the door of my house. How wonderful to find my match, a person who will fill my home after years of loneliness! May Allah have mercy on you, Father. During your life you shackled me to your own wishes. Then after death you passed on to me this bitter loneliness and let your nephew, that villain, shackle me for his personal interests. I'll break these chains regardless of how strong they are . . . So come, come, my love, my soul mate. I hope to Allah you hear me!"

But it seems he did not hear her. In the next year, the ships loaded with Indonesian pilgrims started to land at Jeddah. More ships came, one after the other, but she did not hear anything. The season ended and was followed by another. Still, she waited and refused to lose hope.

Auntie Kadrajan lived on this hope for years and more years to come. She began to age, and the signs of passing years etched wrinkles along her cheeks. She admitted that she was getting older, but she continued living her daydreams, waiting for her suitor at every noise in the alleyway in front of her home. She would listen carefully to every knock, even if it was on her neighbors' doors, out of fear that he might have lost his way to her house. This was why she was always dressed, with her makeup on, even when she did her housework, picking up things with her fingertips with the elegance of a bride on her wedding night!

Her neighbors would laugh at the care she took to maintain her appearance even during inappropriate occasions or in a fashion not suitable for her age. But those who understood such matters, since they themselves had experienced such loneliness, pitied her and blamed her father bitterly for preparing her for such a delusion. Others, such as those foolish neighbor women who had no understanding of such things, found her eccentric behavior comical. And so they called her "Auntie Kadrajan."

♦

AHMAD AL-SIBA'I *(1905–1984), a native of Mecca, taught in traditional quranic schools and completed his studies at the Fa'izeen School, where he became principal. He was also editor in chief of the daily newspapers* Sawt al-Hijaz *and* al-Nawda, *and established the first theater in Mecca. Highly regarded as an essayist, short-story writer, and social critic, he was posthumously honored in 1984 with Saudi Arabia's State Award for Merit in Literature. His works include the novel,* Fikra (An Idea) *(1948), a collection of short stories,* al-Murshid ila 'l Hajj wa 'l-Ziyara *(The Guide to the Hajj and the Visit) (1948), and "Khalati Kadrajan"(My Aunt Kadrajan) (1967).*

Suq al-Nada

Zahra S. al-Mu'bi

◆

Ma'atouq's head swims as he searches out new areas of hope. He wants to touch the cool breeze of the outdoors and breathe in freedom—to cover the wounds of his soul and purify his spirit. After years, today is the day of his release from prison. His thoughts turn eagerly toward childhood memories, toward remembrances of the past.

In his mind he floats as lightly as air toward the open gates of the world.

When the heavy prison door finally opens, he quickly steps out to open the portals to the past. He embraces the daylight in sleepless anxiety, feeling as if the light were awakening his dreaming eyes.

He shuffles down the road, well aware of all the landmarks. His worries accompany him. He drags his feet. He wants to go faster, much faster. But how can he? He depends on his cane. He feels his way with an open mind and a strong desire.

Ma'atouq hails a taxi, eager to meet up with the life from which he was snatched more than twenty years ago.

He says to the taxi driver, "Suq al-Nada, please."

The driver doesn't understand him and asks for his desired destinations.

"I said, take me to Suq al-Nada."

Finally, it is clear that the taxi driver doesn't know where Suq al-Nada is.

He is obliged to get out of the taxi to look for another driver.

Many taxis stop, but before engaging any of them, he asks, "Do you know where Suq al-Nada is?"

It takes him more than an hour, after the sun has burned his shaved head, to find a taxi driver who knows the old downtown area.

◆ ◆ ◆

Finally, after two decades, his feet touch the soil of his youth and of old friends for whom he has yearned. He looks toward the *suq*, smiling, smiling as he walks toward his old hangout—the café where he used to sit every afternoon, drinking tea, smoking *shisha*, and listening to *On the Road* and *Listener's Choice* on the radio.

Unfortunately, he doesn't recognize the place at all. He can't even find remnants of what he remembers. He looks carefully but still can't recognize anything. There's nothing to indicate that the café ever existed in this spot. He stops a passerby. "Isn't this where Café al-Izzi used to be?"

He doesn't get a satisfactory answer.

As he enters the *suq*, his steps slow and falter. What did he expect, to meet his friends and loved ones?

His feet take him toward the mayor's office, but he sees no signs to indicate the existence of such a gathering place. He mumbles to himself, "It would be great if I ran into some of my old friends." So he continues checking out the storefronts on both sides of the alley.

Much has changed—actually, everything has changed. There is al-Massri's store, by the gate of Mushtaha's corner, where he used to fix stoves. Here is the egg seller, and there is the yogurt and milk vendor. Assayed, the seller of herbs, used to stand here; the fruit seller used to sit there, the vegetable seller here.

Ma'atouq feels his way, looking intently at faces that pass by, hoping perhaps that he will recognize somebody. Or that somebody will recognize him. But all the landmarks of the *suq* are changed, and all these faces fail to evoke his past.

"*Ya* Allah, even the *suq*'s dirt floor has changed. Even *it* doesn't recognize me. I, the son of this land. I grew up here. My fingers were torn here."

Now the *suq*'s ground is covered with pieces of tile instead of dirt. Store owners used to sprinkle water in front of their stores to keep the dust down. One could smell the earth then. Even the shops have changed. Now there are air-conditioned grocery stores.

Pictures of the past crowd his memory. "I wonder when this tall building was built?" he says to himself. He knows this area. It was an empty lot surrounded by some humble stores.

Ma'atouq conjures up the sight of his friend the butcher when he used to cut the meat, surrounded by many roving hungry cats. He'd throw some fat to one of the cats and a bone to another. He would kick another, after it bothered him with its continuous meows. In his memory, the noise of the cat fights mixes with the voices of the passersby and the cries of hawkers selling their wares. But now he is surprised by the silence of the *suq*.

"How can that be?" The *suq* used to sing with many intertwined tunes. Everything used to move with the same rhythm. He even misses the dewy fragrance of al-Nada. Suq al-Nada was named after that scent—from the morning dew running down the shop doors.

He remembers the al-Nada barber, the first modern barber. Only the young boys who wished to have special haircuts would go to him.

Ma'atouq walks in astonishment, occasionally leaning on the walls of stores. In a daze, he looks at the sun as it says farewell to the *suq*'s silent expanse. Suddenly, the bright lights that glare down from everywhere surprise him.

He remembers how the *suq* used to turn dark at sunset. Only a few merchants hung lanterns near their stores to expel the ghost of darkness or to win a small number of clients, since only a few people went shopping at night in those days. Now, he sees hordes of people swimming along the waves of crowds. The buying and selling continues, even after the retreat of the sun.

His feet walk ahead of his dreams. Here he is, trying to recover from shock, going toward the women's welfare hostel near the *suq*. He asks about the *sheikha* of the hostel, but he is told that she died some time ago.

The *sheikha* was the only person who knew the whereabouts of his blind mother—his mother who was stricken at the hour she heard of the allegations against her son that put him in jail. He was thirty years old then; today he is fifty and free from prison, but despair and sadness weigh him down.

He walks toward one of the mosques in the *suq* to ask about the imam—his teacher, Shaikh Ali Hillal—but they tell him that he, too, is dead.

At that moment, the sound of the *azan* calls for prayer. Ma'atouq stands to pray. The prayers of his teacher walk with him in this dark moment. His teacher taught him to recite the *surahs* of the Holy Quran. He does so now. Even though Ma'atouq is very much alone in this time and place, still he feels the spirit of his shaikh and the old *suq* alive within him. When he finishes praying, he heads back toward the shops. This time he is determined to find a face from the past among all the new faces.

"God is great," he mutters. He marvels at the newly tiled sidewalk and studies the bright faces of the children.

◆

ZAHRA S. AL-MU'BI *is both a writer and an educator. She is the author of numerous short stories.*

The Jewelry Box

Badriyah al-Bashar

◆

My stepmother is a harsh woman. But she is not like stepmothers in the familiar bedtime stories, who are clever and hide their cruelty from others. When I was a child, she would answer our neighbors' questions bluntly and threaten to hit me in front of them. "It doesn't matter how much I beat the child because strictness is what makes girls behave; it's what makes real women out of them," she'd say to justify her actions. In the final analysis, the neighbors would say, "Muna is a stepmother, and what can one expect from a stepmother?"

One day my father tried to explain why he married this woman and brought her into our home. He sat in his favorite chair, sipping a small glass of sweetened black tea, and drew me near.

"Listen, daughter. Muna is incapable of having children of her own. This will work to your advantage. It is because she misses the blessing of being a mother that she will envelop you with her love. The love you lost when your mother died. I only want the best for you, my daughter, and this is all I can do."

Now that I am grown and a mother myself, I still remember that conversation.

"No, my father. I think being a good mother is an ability from God; it is not learned and especially not by someone who has no heart for it."

The reality of the situation is that I was young, and he needed someone to care for me. When father gave up childrearing, abandoning those responsibilities to his wife, he chose to overlook how she overburdened me with chores greater than I was capable of undertaking at that age. He stayed out of it because his wife would not tolerate any kind of interference. I was trapped like a fly in amber.

In my lonely existence, I looked forward to visits with my father's sister Layla. Auntie Layla had a beautiful carved wooden box she kept in her bedroom. It was decorated with small copper studs; its golden handle clanked with a thud when she opened it. She called it Saharah, the jewelry box, and kept inside it all kinds of precious delights, including candy for me and other children.

When I was young, I was never so bold as to look inside. I would never reach for a piece of candy until my aunt handed it to me. Even the candy from the box had its own magical scent, a scent with hints of musk, saffron, and frankincense. The sour gumballs she handed out would melt in my mouth, but the flavor would linger on my breath until the next morning. Inside her box were also several small velvet pouches tied with ribbons. Each held the rich scent of henna, *sidir*, and other Arabian aromatics.

When Auntie Layla dug deeper, I caught a sparkle of hidden gemstones. I do not know how many there were, but each time I saw a necklace it had different stones in it—topaz, lapis, or amber. The stones were arranged like prayer beads except that in the middle there would be a golden pendant with engraved images like I had never seen before. The pieces were so exotic, I liked to imagine they were the jewelry of princesses from foreign lands. It wasn't until much later that I learned they were Indian, Arabian, and Bahraini.

At prayer time, Auntie Layla would get out her prayer rug to pray and, when finished, would pull me toward her. Opening her large Holy Quran with its worn black cover, she would say, "al-Nuri, could you read this for me?" She was the only one who called me by my proper name. Her kindness always brought tears to my eyes. I would look in the holy book and read the difficult words she could not read. Sometimes I lay by her warm, sweet side and listened to her beautiful recitations. After a while, I would find myself falling swiftly to sleep.

Then the harshness of time—a command from my stepmother—would carry me to our home where I'd be ordered to clean the yard, wash the dishes, and do my homework, which I could never finish without giving in to sleep.

As I got older my aunt encouraged me to be strong and wise. I learned how to resist Stepmother's ill treatment. One way I did this was to spend part of my day at Aunt Layla's, doing homework, napping, and filling my stomach with her hot food. I left the housework and chores for my stepmother.

Muna got mad. She threatened me and argued with my father to stop me from going to my aunt's home. When he did not respond, except to close the bedroom door in her face, she refused to sit with him at meals. Soon my father joined me for lunch at Auntie Layla's house, then later he began—like me—to come for the entire afternoon. His wife was left at home, eating alone with nothing but misery and loneliness for company. Life is ironic, for instead of finding a safe refuge for me, Father followed me to a refuge of his own.

As my aunt grew older, I could not accept the inevitable signs of her aging. I noticed no difference in her physical appearance because I loved her for what was inside. When she asked me to put henna on her hair to cover the gray, I thought it was because all women in our family grayed prematurely. When she asked me to stand next to her, to support her while she stood with her shaking legs, I thought that rheumatism left no one untouched. Even when my aunt would nod off to sleep while sitting with us, I would tease her, "Auntie, go to sleep. Leave staying up late for young ones!"

She used to murmur to herself, "May my final days be kind and merciful!"

Eventually Auntie began to stay in bed longer and longer, and her weak voice whispered shorter sentences. All of this wakened in me a fear, feelings of loss I could no longer hold back. Breaking into tears, embracing her, I begged her not to go. "Auntie, for whom are you leaving us? Are you, too, leaving us like my mother?"

"My daughter, everyone will die sometime."

She pointed toward the jewelry box. "This is for no one but you, al-Nuri. It used to fascinate you when you were small. It was your hiding place from your stepmother, do you remember? Your tears would dry when you saw the candy. It is yours now to enter and hide from the troubles of the world." She patted my hand and added, "Inside this jewelry box is my secret. I'll be there, listening and watching. Whenever you need me I'll be close by and take care of you. If life gets difficult, open the box, but only at night. If you look carefully, you'll find my face looking out at you. If you find me smiling, then you'll know I agree with what you are asking."

The loss of my aunt was devastating. Alone, I went through the formalities of the condolences, as if I was her only child. While her sons took care of the male visitors, I moved slowly through the desert of loneliness.

In my grief, I pulled out my aunt's jewelry box, but only in the darkness of the night, just as she requested. I stared into the box, fascinated by Auntie Layla's things. I smelled her saffron, the henna mixed with musk. Whenever I wanted to test a matter that perplexed me, I sought refuge in my aunt's face.

So I did when my father came to tell me that our neighbor's son, Salem, had asked for my hand in marriage. Though Salem was the only man to whom I felt close, I knew I must consult my Auntie Layla, to ask her how to choose my salvation. I said to my father, "I'll seek advice from my aunt," and rushed toward her room.

Perhaps my father thought I had lost my mind, crushed by the loss of my aunt whom he knew I loved so very much. Perhaps he thought I was trying to cover my shyness by running to her room and crying. There I saw my aunt's countenance, lighting up the box's lid with her gentle smile. I knew that I had my aunt's blessing, so I married Salem.

When I moved to my husband's home I took my aunt's jewelry box with me. Since our life together was happy, my husband and I had two sons early in the marriage. I packed the jewelry box away and forgot about it. There were no reasons for me to need my aunt's counsel.

One day, my sons came running toward me screaming, each keen to win the race and blame the other for his childish misdeed. Abdullah shouted, "Mother, he did it!"

I walked toward the room from which they'd come. The closet was open; my aunt's jewelry box lay upside down on the floor, her henna scattered all over the place, its smell filling the room as it used to, her necklaces jumbled in a knot in a corner of the box.

With a broken heart, I picked up the box. I heard glass break as it fell from the lid of the jewelry box. The inside cover was gone. Instead there was only a piece of black board. Nothing shone from within the box. There were no eyes. I crouched on the floor and carefully picked up a broken piece of the mirror. I laughed for my childhood and the warmth of my aunt who had so comforted me every time I opened the jewelry box. For it had never been her face I'd seen, but my own.

♦

BADRIYAH AL-BASHAR, *from Riyadh, holds a PhD in sociology. She is the author of three collections of short stories—including* Nihayat al-Lu 'Bah *[The End of the Game] (1992) and* Masa' al-Irbi 'a *[Wednesday Evening] (1994)—as well as the novel* Kahrif Sharis *[Vicious Fall].*

The Impossible

Najat Khayyat

◆

Today is my wedding day. The hall's marble columns shimmer in a lake of lights and people parade in a marvelous festival of colors. The place is crowded, full of movement and life.

Earlier, when my gaze met yours, a sudden happiness shone in your eyes, then was lost in the crowd. I escaped into the throng, to the faces filled with colors. I forgot the sight of your shining eyes and began to calculate the cost of such a fabulous event. How much did the perfume seller make, I wondered, and the hairdressers, fabric sellers, florists, cigarette exporters, hotel managers, and the electric company? If this amount was collected, how enormous it would be. What would we do with it? My imagination wandered among several projects that could push my community forward. I returned to reality with ideas that would displease these painted faces in the crowd.

By chance, I came back to you. Our eyes met, and this time our encounter was long. Your eyes asked to know the secret of my evasive, wandering mind. I tried to control my urgency, but it broke its chains and was clearly drawn on my lashes. I forgot all my projects for that moment, and your question got lost in my eagerness. I became oblivious to the noise around me; the colors paled, and your beautiful amber eyes evoked in me a longing, warmed me and quenched my desert dryness. My eyes embraced you for a long moment.

Noise took me again from you, and between us stood a wall constructed of women with made-up faces. I was bored with those faces and wished to be alone with you so that nothing could interrupt our conversation.

I saw your thin tan hand holding something white burning between your nervous fingers. I feared for your hand, afraid of the crumbling ash. I remembered a poem by Nazar Kabani about a burning cigarette.

The faces moved, and I saw that your eyes searched for me. My heart moved in ecstasy. A smile appeared on your lips, inviting me to a date with an unknown destiny. Your tanned hand collected the curls that spilled over your bronzed forehead. I liked the excitement of your hand; I wished I could take it between my own. If only I could hold it and relieve it of its fatigue. It told an interesting tale, narrated a mysterious history full of secrets. Maybe one day I will write about what your hand told me.

I turned back to the people and looked at them without any emotion. They were moving pictures, playing a role in tonight's play. Our expressions of joy are so stupid and tiring! These people act so artificial, I thought. Even their smiles seem feigned.

The most beautiful thing about the hall was that it swam in light, and the colors flickered like multihued butterflies. Don't be angry, I thought. I will come back to you. Whenever I escape from you, I find you in front of me, like the determination of fate. Whenever I see your unruly hair curling over your neck, it reminds me of a dark forest of coffee plants rich with Arabian aromas. I gaze at your tanned face, trying to penetrate its tender façade. It seems to me that beneath your brow hides a kindness. Does the face express the reality of the self? My thoughts point out that I have lost faith in what people show to each other. Except your amber eyes, which always seem to speak the truth.

I return to the hall and sit on the chair near you. My memory brings a moment back to me; it is the silent conversation of waves, the sound of a sea breeze. It is ironic that in my search for reality, I find myself remembering a day that has passed from my life.

The car runs slowly along a long road by the sea. No, it is not this sea, and the night covers the horizon. City lights extend to the zigzagging coast like a necklace of shining jewels around the neck of a beautiful African woman. At the edge of the horizon is a silver crescent that looks like an innocent child smiling for us. The emerald banana trees produce an exciting sound in the sea breeze . . . and he was by my side. I was in love with him. His hand was in mine, and each of us told the other that we had suffered from longing for the other and about what feelings ran in our blood. How foolish am I, when I recall that the motion of life stood still to witness the conversation of our hands, the whispers of our souls. Sometimes, actually often, I do not know why moments of overwhelming love obliterate us to the degree that we forget we are two.

When I found the reality—the reality of my relation with my love— I saw myself as an independent person with her own world, earth, sky, and we were separated. I alone came back, searching for nonexistence.

◆ ◆ ◆

I opened my eyes and returned to reality. Noises came to me from within, and a warm yearning crept into my blood, for you and your amber eyes.

Your smiles ask questions. Don't ask me; I don't know the answers. Let me live again in the amber perfume. Its fragrance makes me dizzy, puts me in a whirl. I don't feel myself anymore; my body melts and vanishes. How beautiful is that feeling! I read a story in your face. I read its lines over your tired forehead. They draw my attention toward you. You wonder about my silence.

You're used to people talking when they want something. They all talk, but I am not one of them. By my silence, I say things you don't understand. By my silence I think of things words do not communicate. In my silence I build an abode for you, oh great-grandson of Belquis.

My thoughts take me away from you and your eyes. I get lost among the glittering butterflies. One passes by me, carrying the wealth of the father on her wrist. Yes, incredible wealth frozen in a diamond bracelet around her wrist. The price of this bracelet is enough to open a small factory. What good is frozen wealth? It is a heavy burden on life, but these women are glittering aristocracy in the eyes of those who look at them.

I close my eyes for a moment. When I open them, I see your hand point to something. I don't know what. As I search the dark night that comes from your eyes, I ask myself if our skies and earths will unite. Will our two individual personalities melt together and obliterate our existence? Impossible! So cries our age. So let us then live. Maybe we will be able to achieve together this impossible task.

◆

NAJAT KHAYYAT, *one of the earliest female short-story writers in Saudia Arabia, was educated in Beirut. Her collection* Makhad as-Samt [Pain of Silence] *was published in 1966. She also writes about social issues for local newspapers.*

I Was Betrayed with a Single Golden Pound

Munirah A. al-Ghadir

◆

I sat in front of the mirror, looking at my tired face, exhaustion and poor health wearing away at my soft features. My hair was musty with the smell of the night, and fatigue lay heavy on my shoulders.

Slavery. Youthfulness. Gold. Refusal. These words reverberated through the room like echoes in a deserted cave. It was all so impossible. I never thought it could happen to me, but it did.

I stared up at the ceiling for a while. Then I shook my head as if dismissing something frightening from the edge of my memory. I let my eyes wander over a wall covered by garish wallpaper and velvet curtains that sagged passively from the rod. An ornate mirror reflected a large gloomy picture hanging on the opposite wall. It drew my attention like a feather wet with unhappiness. Slowly, I sailed far away from this place.

I returned to a small house in the old part of the city. The street was dusty, and the children were scattered like stones in a narrow alley, playing with a dirty, ragged ball. Looking out from one of the wooden windows, I watched them and was possessed by a strange emotion, like a raging river filled with feelings of love, and dreams filled with torrents of despair.

These small children were excused for their playfulness, and as I had learned from a psychology book, their quick bodies and lively intelligence would fade with the dust of the alleys and ugly scenes of the street.

Oh! It's a savage world. I'm better off here. Some don't even find a bit of bread to eat. They said I was a role model. Someone to aspire to. Perhaps I am. Or was.

As I returned to the reflected painting in the mirror, I pushed back an escaping tendril of black hair from the fading glow of my pale face. Silence envelopes the room, standing in stark contrast to the alley filled with noisy children, loud conversation between neighbors, and the din of bustling carts. A solitary bird might come searching for love in the garden trees, but it would fly away as if escaping the growing loneliness that shrouded this house and its captive.

I stood there waiting, without answers, without interpretations. I remembered waiting for the school bus, dreaming of a special world in which I was its hero. When I took the bus, I felt there was some sort of strange connection between the seats and the color of the school uniform. Some sort of longing existed between the two, like a mother feels for her newborn baby. When I held a book in my hand, I'd start a journey full of dreams. I thought all things were possible. (How naïve and stupid I was. I used to believe that the world was a ball of rubber that I could turn as I liked.)

I skipped the distance between my eyes and the mirror several times. A small moan escaped my lips. I turned and saw a gold-embroidered *abayah* and a short wide *thobe*. It was the face of an old man. Mixed dyes blurred the color of his wiry hair. Wrinkles tried to hide under the folds of fat on his face. His lips were tied with a thread of greed, and from between them came the malice of an old man looking at a beautiful young woman. His mouth was drawn in the smile of an old wolf.

The old man turned toward my house in the alley, his huge potbelly leading the way. I saw another man walking next to him, with the look of a naturally good person, kind and loving. But greed was painted on his good face, too. When I saw him, I shivered in fear; and when I tried to steal a look at his eyes, I found a strange glittering, a look of satisfaction. The good man tried to talk to me, but I sensed he was holding something back.

The look in Father's eyes spoke more than a thousand words, but his sincerity hid a feeling of guilt. I wish you had not spoken, Father . . . I wish the wild animals had snatched and eaten me. All of that would have been easier to bear than your speech that terrible afternoon, when the sun beat its whip upon our small house. When I sat by your side and you brought me the news, it was like a mine planted in my pounding chest.

A rich man who knows nothing but the tinkling of gold and the smell of money came to us from far away with wealth, fortune, all the dreams and hopes we could envision. Oh, whoever said that I loved wealth; it will never own even a small spot in the vast space of my dream. I never searched for it like my friend Muna who announced that she would like to marry a rich man. When we told her the rich man will be married to another woman, too, she said, "So what?"

We told her, "He will be an old man, as old as your father."

She answered, "It doesn't matter. I don't like the foolishness of young men. I prefer a mature man."

Even then I did not understand Muna's logic. How could she trade her dreams for a handful of coins? I remember how she would examine the gold pieces in her jewelry box and ignore the envious look of others at the expensive necklaces she wore.

I hated the color of gold. Except for the color of gold, my family would not have dragged me into the slavery of the marriage market where I was sold, without any wealth and without any privileges.

I was not even twenty, yet I was buried between the sheets of a sixty-year-old man. Half a century separated us. A cavity in the heart of the earth separates any world of mine from his. Like a sacrifice, they pushed me to him. I was betrayed by a single golden pound.

My passive mother said, "Oh, Layla, good luck came your way. How fortunate you are. Thanks to Allah . . ."

My poor mother was very happy. She was so happy that she gave friends and neighbors presents. Poor Mother. Luck was part of your tradition and rituals and did not extend to marriage. Luck is with the man. All that mattered to you was that a man could come and take this headache of a girl from your hands.

But I used to think of my groom differently than you did. I dreamed of him in a way that money did not matter. How stubborn was I. My bed in that small room was planted with rebellious ideas. As a high school girl driven by dreams, I clung to rosy visions of a handsome groom whom I would personally choose.

Events reproduced themselves in my head. Grief grew in my heart, accumulating like clouds that fell as hot tears from my eyes. I reflect on my grief and remember the yellow school bus, the black *abayah*, the navy blue uniform, the wedding gown, the black Mercedes that carried me to that deserted palace in the middle of the night. All these memories mix and collide.

I opened the window and looked at the sky as if broadcasting my tragedy. I considered driving into its blueness. Maybe I would forget this conflict somehow. The sun melted on the horizon, turning into a blood red disk. The evening was a black knight, knocking on the doors that summer evening.

Time stopped. I had become like a beautiful doll, a dumb plaything thrown around carelessly while the old man ran after money.

I was startled by the sound of the doorbell. It had been days since anyone rang it. Minutes later the maid knocked on the bedroom door and said, "There's a letter for you, madam."

I bit my lips in surprise and accepted the envelope. Looking at it in my hands, I was plagued with fear. Who was it from? My family? A friend? Who would remember a forgotten woman living in a secluded house? I opened the envelope, pulled out two pages, and unfolded one of them. It was covered with signatures and black letters. Divorce papers. Freedom! My limbs froze, and I became like a chunk of ice. I quickly opened the second page. It was from my husband, the old man, asking me to leave the house. He was due to arrive tomorrow with another bride, a new victim.

◆

MUNIRAH A. AL-GHADIR, *from Saudi Arabia's Eastern Province, is the author of numerous short stories.*

Knowing His Secret

Sharifah al-Shamlan

◆

It is not my habit to inquire into his work. My husband's work is a private and vast space filled with all the problems of the legal world. I'm merely a woman working hard as a journalist at the newspaper, trying to line up an interesting piece for an article, do an interview, or perhaps fill my reverie by publishing a poem. I hate answering telephone calls, though my work involves a lot of time on the phone. But I don't like to ask about my husband, Ahmad's business, nor do I pay attention to the names of people who call for him. He has his own world and I have mine. Although we do meet occasionally, it is as rare as the coming together of two magnetic poles.

In my busy office, where I am sometimes happy, sometimes nervous, I have a coworker, Suad. We spend much time together, attending meetings and planning reports. One day after we finished our work, she confided in me her problems with her husband.

"Layla, it is impossible to continue this way. He sees other women. Then he has the nerve to be jealous of me, though I am not the one at fault. He makes my life a mixture of *jinn* and *affarit*, fear and terror. Each day I hope for something better, but that day has yet to come."

As she told me the details of his abuse, my heart warmed toward her. But what she told me about her husband was still very hard to believe.

"If he is that cruel, how could he let you work? Especially in journalism, where you are constantly traveling and constantly meeting people! Doesn't that inflame his jealousy and make it worse for you?"

"He lets me work for the money. Even though when I come home each night he makes me a nervous wreck."

Suddenly, my respect for my own husband soared. Ahmad had never once asked how much I earned. Nor did he ask what I do with my money. In comparison to Suad's husband, he was a good and loving spouse.

However, I didn't realize that Ahmad was to be the topic of the conversation until after a few indirect queries when Suad finally got to the point and asked about his law practice. She leaned forward in her hard wooden chair and met my eyes, asking intently, "I want to divorce my husband. Do you think Ahmad would agree to handle my case?"

I read such urgency in her expression that I knew I would have to talk to Ahmad about her case. Never before had I intervened in Ahmad's work, nor had I ever asked him to help someone. But I knew I could not refuse her request.

That evening, I told Ahmad about Suad's problems. As I drew out her sad story, I may have embellished a bit to win his sympathy. I knew he did not typically take on domestic cases. In fact, he had often stated his aversion to handling family-related matters. He did not surprise me now. A crease formed between his brows, and a dark cloud of annoyance overshadowed his features.

"Why should I waste my time with a woman whose case will take years in court? And she has children, which means there will be juvenile matters to deal with. Those can only complicate matters." He sighed and searched my eyes for understanding. "Layla, these kinds of cases can burn out an attorney in a short period of time. They are nerve-racking. It just isn't worth the effort."

"I know. But it is only one case, and she is a special friend. Please, Ahmad, just this once."

"All right. But I will do it only because you asked."

Relief flooded every inch of my body. Taking his hand in mine, I thanked him and smiled.

Shortly thereafter, Suad started to occupy Ahmad's time with many personal things. It began with her asking him for a ride to court. Then the many telephone calls related to her case. I began to feel suspicious when I encountered Suad and Ahmad together near her apartment. But I reassured myself that Ahmad had more integrity than to fall for a woman with a passing legal case.

In a matter of months he had gathered the documents and witnesses to litigate her case. He used his skill and legal talent to successfully show that Suad was a victim in her marriage. Not only did he win the case but he also won alimony in the amount of fifty thousand riyals.

It was an incredible victory, for most women lose their youth waiting for a divorce to be granted. Then if the judge does pass sentence, it is for the woman to pay an amount that requires her to spend half her life making installment payments to her ex-husband. But Ahmad was careful to win the case, and Suad ended up victorious. I asked him if he would take on more domestic cases, but he refused.

Home life returned as usual. Suad's calls became less frequent. I thought to myself that it was because she was free now and had time to relax. Although we still worked at the same paper, our work rarely brought us together. I was relieved because I had been wishing to work independently for some time. But some instinct warned me things were not the same. Ahmad would leave at random times in the evening and seemed to say very little to me or the children. I was accustomed to his quiet nature, but not this new silence, which was not normal. I began to worry, especially when the telephone would ring twice and then go silent.

On the day my husband left on a business trip, Suad did not come to work. I cursed the devil for the black thoughts that obsessed me. I tried to expel such ideas but to no avail.

My fingers trembled as I phoned Suad's home number. The Filipino maid answered, "Hello."

"May I please speak with Suad?" I whispered in a nervous voice.

"She's not here. She is out of the county, ma'am," answered the woman with a broken Arabic accent.

As I put the phone in the cradle my world turned upside down. I could not relax, I felt so agitated. Was Ahmad with her? I could not think straight. Or had they simply gone separate ways? Oh, Allah! How could I stand it until he came home?

When he returned he entered the door wearing a grin. He kissed the children and embraced me. But his arms felt like a prison. I didn't want to face my own feelings, the turmoil or the confusion, but I had to know what happened.

After putting down his bags, Ahmad went to take a shower. I could hear the water running in the adjacent room. Seeing his canvas suitcase on the bed I snapped open the latches. My hands trembled as they swiftly searched through his folded clothes to find anything out of the ordinary. Then my fingers met something cold and feminine. It was a small thing, her golden comb. A chill raced through my body. I heard him opening the door. I swiftly hid the comb and turned to him with a smile. I tried to control my nervousness. The timing was delicate. I did not want to do something that I would regret later. God had given me strong nerves and the power to control my expressions.

"I have dinner waiting for you," I said hoarsely, my heart thumping furiously all the while.

"Good. It's been a long flight, and I didn't eat anything on the plane," he replied, smiling with the charm that had first captured my heart. Leaving before my face revealed its pain, I joined the children in the kitchen.

"Baba is home," I said, trying to release the tension constricting my throat. "Help me put the food on the table."

In the morning, I went to my office. I jotted down my options and studied them carefully: home, husband, children. My beautiful world had started to fall apart. A painful breach had begun to tear my family into pieces. Could I mend it? It was up to me to do so or else let things fall apart. I felt feverish. I trembled and suddenly retched everything that was in my stomach. Trying to stand I grabbed the back of the chair before everything turned black and I slid unconscious to the floor. My colleagues took me to the hospital where I discovered I was pregnant. How could this be? Around me sat the children and their father. I could feel the fear and concern in his eyes. Suad did not inquire about me; she didn't even call.

At home the telephone rings twice and then becomes silent, but Ahmad doesn't even move. He doesn't even leave home for his work. His phone calls are not whispered anymore.

My husband talks about the desire of his widowed brother to remarry. He is the father of three sons and wishes to marry a good wife who will take care of them. I feel a wicked urge and so I say with a gesture of innocence, "Suad would make a good match for your brother."

My husband sighs, "May Allah give me salvation!"

I say, "You seek salvation from Allah, but why? She is a good woman and her divorce does not mean her end!"

"It is you who are a good woman. You have good intentions, but please leave her alone. She has her world, her life. Don't let her enter yours."

I want to shout at him, "But what about you?" But concern for my home and my children keeps me silent. I am just one of millions of women who must swallow her pain to protect her home and children. I know that, just as I know I have him back. But our love is like a cracked crystal vase, only the crack is etched deep within my heart. I only wish, from the bottom of my heart, that my husband never learns that I know his secret.

◆

SHARIFAH AL-SHAMLAN *was born in Iraq but emigrated to Saudi Arabia, where she received a B.A. in journalism. In addition to being a prolific writer—her published collections of short stories include* Muntaha al-Hudu' *[The Utmost Calm] (1989),* Maqati min Haayat *[Episodes of a Life] (1991), and* Wa Ghadan Ya'ti *[Tomorrow Will Come]—she has served as director general of Women's Social Affairs in the Eastern Province.*

The Shelter

Ibrahim Nassir al-Humaydan

◆

My smallest daughter, Layla, came close and looked at me with tearful eyes. Tentatively, she touched my sleeve. On her face danced a question, "Baba, what is happening?"

The clock pointed to one after midnight. She was not used to staying up this late, but the emergency sirens had woken her.

I put my arms around her and was about to speak, to comfort her, when a huge explosion broke out somewhere in the night. Layla cried in fear and grabbed hold of me, her hands balling into fists. I wrapped my arms around her more tightly and murmured some reassuring words.

As I checked the faces of the rest of the children huddled near me in the living room, I saw that the blood had left their cheeks, leaving them stonelike, ashen. My wife, Hussa, tried to gather them all close to her, as if they were in danger of being stolen away from her. She looked at me through a tendril of hair that had escaped down her cheek. Her brows creased in worry, framing her large, luminous eyes. "Ahmad, what are we to do?"

What should I tell my beloved wife? That things would be fine? That tomorrow we would wake up to find it was all a bad dream? That there really was no war? She knew differently and so did I.

Layla interrupted my response, sobbing her words through clenched teeth. "Baba, don't leave me . . . hold me tight. Don't let me go."

I felt weak and shaken, like a warrior who had lost his weapons on the battlefield. I could do nothing, not even defend myself. How cheap life seems when one is helplessly swept away like a feather in the wind. We were told that we must prepare a shelter. We must be ready for an emergency, for a surprise attack.

Everyone had busied themselves with taping plastic curtains on the windows and sealing the air ducts. We had even taped up the backs of doors. Hussa piled up pillows, blankets, covers, and whatever else we needed for sleeping. Then I brought canned food, bottled water, and fresh fruit that we could stockpile for some period of time. How long would it last, I wondered. I could not even guess.

Now we listened to the static of the small television set. We waited for the news announcer who appeared from time to time, blurted out some new information, and then faded behind the snow and static of the television screen. We nervously followed the reports and listened carefully for noises coming from outside.

"Why are they bombing us, Baba?" Layla asked innocently.

I was tense from my daughter's questions, and from the long night of waiting and jumping at every sound. I tried to answer calmly, to satisfy her curiosity, at least for the time being. "It's because people make mistakes when dealing with each other."

Layla could not understand what I meant, so she gazed at me, trying to extract an answer from my expression. Then she turned to the window covered with plastic curtains as if she was expecting something surprising to happen.

I tried to calm her. "Come on, Layla. Relax, sweetheart. Nothing will happen, except that which God has already decided."

Her face shined suddenly, as if what I said comforted her. Or maybe I'd simply reminded her of God's protection and care. She asked, "Doesn't God love everyone?"

I nodded as I covered her with a blanket so she might sleep. A religious program came on the television. We listened attentively. The turbaned shaikh recited from the Quran. When he finished we all said our prayers. There was nothing left for us to do.

Mai, my middle daughter, suddenly said, "Baba, I'm not scared anymore!"

"Me too," I replied.

It was true. I felt as if a weight had been removed from my shoulders. My family was facing the situation with less fear because we were together. But then I felt sad for the thousands of children who did not have anyone to provide them with love or comfort. How did they manage to face such a fate alone?

I sat down on the floor with my family and pulled Layla onto my lap. She rested her head against my shoulder, her fears forgotten. At that moment the radio announced the danger was over. I took a deep breath and said, "Oh, God, this terrible time has made children its first victims."

Hussa touched my arm and said, "That is part of the ugliness of war—it leaves children orphans."

I nodded and looked at the faces of my children. I thanked God for my family and prayed for the end of the war. I hoped that all of the other children, the ones who had lost their homes and their parents, would find love and comfort someday, the way we had found it, here in this shelter.

◆

IBRAHIM NASSIR AL-HUMAYDAN *(b. 1932) is a native of Riyadh but was raised in southern Iraq and lived in Kuwait before returning to Saudi Arabia. Considered one of the country's pioneering writers, al-Humaydan has received numerous awards for his literary work. He is the author of eight novels and six short-story collections, and has written extensively for magazines, newspapers, and television. Among his works are the short story collections,* Ard bilaa Matar *(Land Without Rain) (1967) and* Ummatna wa-al-Nadhah *(Our Mothers and the Struggle) (1962), as well as the novel,* Safinat al-Manta *(Ship of the Dead) (1969).*

An Encounter

'Abd Allah Husayn

◆

Abu Saad sharpened his long knife with a swinging motion and then left it by his side as he stood watching the passersby walk to the beach. Children ran along the edge of the waterfront. The Gulf water was placid; the park was packed. Red light from the neon sign outside his restaurant fell on his silver hair. His white uniform and sharpened knife gave him the appearance of a great marine captain who was not fortunate enough to lead the world standing fully erect, for his back was hunched, which destroyed his looks. His long arms reached to his knees if he kept them by his sides. If he moved them, they gave the impression that they were like the wings of a seagull about to fly.

Abu Saad was always busy, either preparing a *shawarma* sandwich or looking quietly at the sea. He jokingly told his customers that he came from the sea, which explained why he looked at it with such longing. But the fact was that he could not bear to part from the blue waters, for his son, who was taken by the waves, called to him with the tide. Abu Saad swore that when he was tired of living and felt it was time to die, then he would walk into the sea. But it seemed he was not finished yet, for he continued each day with extraordinary energy and hummed under his breath, "I would like to get married in time for the Eid."

He was proud of the sharpness of his vision and his hearing. What he was most proud of was the astronomical number of sandwiches he had prepared in his long life. What he regretted was that three-fourths of that number was eaten by thieves and murderers. Just a few went to good people.

"Like your good self . . ." This was the phrase he used with whoever bought his *shawarma*.

If we can believe his claim that his son was calling him, then we must believe, too, the reason he worked hard in preparing *shawarma* sandwiches and the secret of taking such care in their preparation—he added to it lemon and garlic—it was for the good of the soul of his son.

"I'd like one chicken *shawarma*," a new customer said, leaning eagerly on the counter. Abu Saad took a piece of pita bread, cut into the middle, and heated it on the blue flame. He personally prepared the sandwiches; the war had not changed that. He spread sesame seed paste inside and filled it with green salad. Then, waving his knife, he diligently sliced the meat from the rotisserie, the white chunks falling off easily once the succulent meat was fully cooked. The blue flames sizzled and cracked from oil splattering. The smell of the barbecue was pungent with the garlic that distinguished his *shawarma*. He stuffed the sandwich with meat and the satisfied customer said, "You live far away from the war."

"Nothing's changed. I sell fifty chicken sandwiches each day. There is nothing better than that." Abu Saad paused and checked the number of cars filling the beach. "But one's true self emerges during time of war," he continued. "And war is like donating blood. It's scary but it gets the blood circulating."

The customer was surprised by Abu Saad's comments. "That's a big price to pay to get your blood circulating."

"Look, it's a change of a routine. It makes us get rid of the surplus in our population. And, sir, without that event our society would have gotten rotten."

The customer tried to understand. Was the old man fed up with life? Or had he perhaps lost his mind? How could he minimize the dangers of war in a world where there was modern technology that could wipe out a country?

Whenever Abu Saad felt his customers were displeased by what he said, he changed the subject. He would talk of other things, but he always returned to the same point. "What can we do? Our fates are not in our hands; life is in the hands of Allah." With that he jumped to another customer, a fat young man who it seemed had stored a large number of *shawarma* sandwiches in his belly.

"What is bad about war is that it only consumes men who are young." Then Abu Saad gestured to his hunched back, adding, "It does not want an old man like me, with dry bones and little meat, not enough even for one sandwich."

The store's red neon light and the glow of the barbecue flames danced on his wrinkled face, giving him the appearance of a loaf of bread covered with olive oil. When he caught his breath again, war had become merely an eaten-up smile. "War is drums, poems, and medals."

Abu Saad was no different than most of the old men who would like to maintain their right to talk. As he danced with his knife on a make-believe stage, the glittering of oil on his face and the glittering of the sharp end of his knife combined with a third glittering escaping from his eyes. He laughed. The customer did not like his laughter.

"Look, war with its weapons of mass destruction is not like a person committing suicide. They are not comparable," the customer said.

"Don't worry, we've got our methods for survival."

"But the loss is too great."

"But people lose, even at games."

The customer stopped arguing with him; there was no point in debating the old man. He took his sandwiches and left.

Abu Saad stood still again, warming up the flame of the barbecue, gazing at the water, listening to the sound of the tide. Then he turned and watched the customer go. If customers were not ready to listen, the words will stay, hanging over their heads until one day they will harvest them.

He remained standing still, feeling the heat of the barbecue, gazing at the sea, listening to the tide. He ventured one step forward, then stopped. Today was not the day. Another customer was coming and another *shawarma* sandwich had to be made.

◆

'ABD ALLAH HUSAYN *is the author of the collection* as-Sayd al-Akhir *(The Last Sayed) (1989).*

Bloodstains on the Wall

Ahmad Bogary

Every morning at eight o'clock, Uthman al-Takrouni sat on the hard sidewalk in the shade of a lone cinchona tree that even the birds had abandoned. Its gray trunk was thick and its branches rested on the edge of a high marble wall surrounding a luxurious villa. To Uthman, it was like a glorious castle.

The villa overlooked two streets. One of them was a main thoroughfare, the other a secondary road with trees on both sides. Newly built villas perched behind both streets.

Uthman leaned against the trunk of the cinchona tree, waiting for the bus. Between his legs rested a red plastic jug. Inside were two pieces of white cloth, the remnants of an old woolen dress.

Two Mercedes cars—the white and black ones he washed every day for the owner of the villa—were nowhere to be found. Perhaps they've gone away, he thought. It is summertime, the season of travel and less income.

Uthman settled back and quietly watched the wide two-way street shimmer as cars streaked by, sunlight reflecting off their mirrors and windows.

Adam, his good friend, arrived to greet him. "Good morning."

Uthman turned to his friend and replied, "Good morning. Where were you yesterday after evening prayers?"

"I was praying in the mosque," said Adam. "Afterward I was very tired and sat suffering near the door until luck brought me Ibn Halal, the owner of a pickup truck, who gave me a ride home."

Both of them gathered their tools by their legs. They talked together for a while, just to pass the hot morning hours.

From time to time, Adam stood to check the horizon for the bus, his right hand shadowing his eyes. Always, though, he looked in vain.

"*Ya* Uthman, the bus is late today."

Uthman said nothing. He took out his pocket watch and looked at it for a while. He spat on it, then used a dirty handkerchief to wipe the stains from its glass casing. He put it back in his pocket, assuring Adam, "It'll come anytime now."

A car screamed by. Adam shouted above the noise, "Where is Mahmud today?"

"How should I know? He lives closer to you."

Mahmud arrived, his hair uncombed, his beard unkempt, and his eyes bloodshot. "*Salam alaikum.*"

"*Wa alaikum assalam,*" they both answered.

Adam turned toward Mahmud and asked, "What's happened to you today, Hajji Mahmud?"

"Nothing. I was upset last night and couldn't sleep."

"Upset? Is it the mother of your children who doesn't give you peace to sleep?"

Adam winked at Uthman, who had a broad smile on his face.

"Oh, man, don't go that far," Mahmud hissed shyly. He turned his face away from Adam and began to laugh, an intermittent laughter that sounded like the ignition of an old car its owner struggled to start. He squatted on the sidewalk near them, turning upside down an old worn straw basket with two handles. The basket looked like a huge hat without a head. A hat for the pavement. Still the bus didn't come. The three of them sat in the scalding sun, waiting.

Every morning the three of them left their homes—shanty huts made of flattened tin canisters, their ceilings and walls stuffed with dry palm fronds—and traveled all day and part of the evening through winding alleys, searching for their basic needs in the arteries of upper-class neighborhoods. They hungered in the midst of the markets and noise and labyrinths, hoping to make enough money to secure their existence for one day.

On that dusty summer morning, they sat as many others sat in the shade of many other trees, on other hard sidewalks. They waited, as they did every morning, for the bus to take them downtown, where coins were like fish in a wild sea. In the evening they returned from downtown to the nearest bus station, then walked for an hour on torn feet back to their dark, humid huts. Their wives would meet them, carrying their newborns on their backs. Those sleepy infants dangled with limp necks while the other children played naked. The women were eager for baskets of meat, vegetables, sugar, and tea. They usually received nothing but empty hands.

◆　◆　◆

The men sat silently in the shade, frowning, their dark skin glistening in the soaring heat. Half an hour passed. The bus did not arrive. They stood and sat down again—restless in their waiting.

"Let's walk to another bus stop," suggested Adam.

"No," Mahmud said. "The nine thirty bus will come soon." It was nine fifteen. The relentless heat from the morning sun brought beads of sweat on their foreheads. They waited for something to pull them away from the silence of the sidewalk.

Two cars whizzed by as fast as lightning. The sidewalk shook beneath them. Even the leaves of the big trees moved with the hot breeze that suddenly slapped their faces. The men covered their ears, then stood up to watch the exciting early morning race.

As they looked toward the right, Adam shouted, "*Ya* Allah! It looks like those cars are going to collide. Look over there!"

Two small black clouds billowed behind the cars as they became dots on the far horizon.

The men sat down again and forgot what they saw. They became involved in other subjects.

Time passed slowly, in a mass of light, heat, and humidity. Suddenly, Adam shouted as he jumped up to get to the sidewalk across the street. "Uthman! Mahmud! Move quickly! There are now three in this race. How terrible!"

With a similar mad scramble, Mahmud escaped and joined Adam on the opposite sidewalk. Uthman, stumbling with hesitation, was surprised by the third car coming from the right. It struck him as it swerved sharply toward the sidewalk where Adam and Mahmud had been sitting.

Uthman's eyes widened with terror as the car flung him high. He crashed with murderous violence against the marble wall of the villa and collapsed in a bleeding ball onto the sidewalk.

Poor Uthman. He had been sliced into three chunks. His head was split and hung down the wall. His neck and its veins stuck to the wall, blood blooming beneath like a deathly flower. The car severed his right leg before colliding with the trunk of the cinchona tree and exploding into flames. The rest of his body lay limp on the sidewalk, quivering under a thick foam of hot blood.

Police cars arrived immediately. The ambulance came wailing, as did fire trucks heavy with water.

Many left their cars and others came in their wrinkled sleeping gowns to be entertained by the terrible spectacle of the accident.

Adam wept over his friend, howling terribly; he held his head with shaking hands. He walked in circles, shocked, unable to believe that

Uthman was dead. Delirious, he began shouting, "*Ya* Allah, Uthman's gone. He's gone, simply gone." He circled again, his body shaking.

A bearded man, wearing a *thobe* shortened to his ankles and cleaning his teeth with a *miswak*, approached him and said, "Have fear of Allah. This is his destiny."

"Does Allah order people to kill innocent men?"

"Ask Allah Almighty for forgiveness. Ask Allah for forgiveness," the bearded man said and departed quickly.

Adam slumped on the sidewalk near Uthman's torn body. His head disappeared between his legs, and the sound of muffled crying welled up from his sides. Mahmud fainted and was carried unconscious into the ambulance, while firemen struggled to pull the body of the young driver from the burning car.

◆　◆　◆

An old woman put a long white scarf over her head and watched the bloody scene from the balcony of her nearby villa. She shouted and waved her hand, then walked down the hall of her apartment, crying "*Ya* Allah, we ask your protection . . . *Ya* Allah, be kind to Your creatures."

She entered her only remaining son's bedroom and whispered softly in his ear, "Ibrahim, please wake up. Go and see what has happened in the street. Please get up. May Allah keep you safe."

Alarmed, Ibrahim sat up in bed and asked, "What? What's happened, Mother?"

"A terrible car accident. May Allah spare you, my son. Go and find out what's going on. I'm worried that there might be people we know in the accident. I saw a car that looked like your cousin Salah's. Please go. And may Allah keep you safe."

"Don't worry, Mother. What a calamity! Summer has come and brought with it an awful car accident. Lucky for car mechanics."

"Don't say such unkind things," his mother scolded him. "Say how unhappy the mother will be, how sorry I am." She wept bitterly.

Ibrahim slipped from his bed, dressed, and departed. When he returned to the apartment later, he reported to his waiting mother, saying, "It was a Takrouni, a black man. He was sliced into three pieces! Can you believe that?" Then he tucked himself in bed again. He shrank under the bed covers, turned over, and put his hand over his eyes as if to hide the scene. He slept.

His mother sat alone, weeping and praying, recalling bitter memories. The first thing that came to mind was the death of her eldest son,

Abdullah, in a car accident on the road to Jeddah. Her body shivered, and she wept silently as she recalled what they told her: "The police found Abdullah thrown over a mountainside. He slid down the slope after being flung through the front window. They found his car broken into pieces at the bottom of the mountain."

A fountain of hot tears began to fall. Her grief intensified when she remembered that she had seen the accident with her own eyes. It had been ignored by others in the car with her as they drove home from Jeddah. She didn't know then that the victim was her beloved eldest son. She prayed, wept, and between prayers was ravaged by her private pain.

◆ ◆ ◆

The police cars, the ambulance, and fire trucks disappeared, as did everybody else. Life returned to normal on the street. Nothing remained at the scene of the accident except the large bloodstains on the shiny marble wall. The morning shadow of the huge cinchona tree vanished from the luxurious villa. The stains became proof of Uthman's death. His tragic end became the talk of the neighborhood and conversational grist for evening teas on the balconies of nearby villas. It was also the topic of conversation for those who passed in their cars and for pedestrians who walked by the corner. Moments after dusk, the wall became a wailing wall for groups of black women.

These women came every evening and stood apprehensively in front of the wall. Cautiously, they moved closer to the bloodstains until they knew the exact position, then wept painfully as they put their foreheads on the cold wall. During the day, a few young boys stopped by, led by a black youth who pointed his finger and explained how the accident had occurred. They stood still for a few moments, quietly observing the wall. For a whole week Uthman al-Takrouni's relatives visited the location of his death. After a while, though, the residents of the neighborhood began to forget the accident that had once been the center of daily conversations.

The black boys, however, continued to pass by and touch the wall where the big bloodstain remained. Though the stain slowly faded in the sun each day, they touched the wall as the women had. They stood, totally absorbed, their skinny bodies shivering unconsciously, and then went their way.

Just before sunset on the seventh day, a white Mercedes stopped in front of the gates of the marble wall. From the car emerged two young girls laughing behind their black *abayahs*, followed by three children.

A fat old woman, who had removed her sweaty scarf from her face, struggled to lift herself out of the Mercedes. She finally freed herself and walked slowly, her chest heaving. A young man was the first to lead this family march. His arrogance was obvious as he looked past the crowd of black children.

A middle-aged man with a big belly was the last to step out of the car. He was obviously annoyed to see the boys in front of his marble wall. In a loud voice he ordered, "You, boys—get out of here. Go away!"

But as he drew closer, the pale stain on the wall surprised him and his jaw dropped.

"Who did this? Who stained my wall with this blemish?" The boys scattered in fear, some falling on each other as they scuttled away. Only one boy stayed behind. His eyes were fearless, ready for any challenge.

"This is blood . . ." the boy said.

"Whose blood?"

"The blood of a dead man. A car accident killed Hajji Uthman a week ago."

"Uthman? Is that the man who cleans my car? Are you a relative of his?"

"I'm his son, Mussa."

"*Ya* Allah, will you tell me how the accident happened?"

Speaking calmly, as if he were an adult, Mussa reported the details of the accident.

"*Ya* Allah. There is no power but Allah. It is this world that will eventually decay anyway, my son! In any event, I don't want to see this stain here after today. Will you clean it for ten riyals?" asked the man with the big belly.

Mussa felt something like glass breaking inside his mouth. "But that is too little, Uncle Abdulrahman. I'll clean it for fifty riyals . . ."

"What? Are you going to clean five cars at once? No, no."

"But this is my father's blood, and it'll take me a long time to clean it," he pleaded.

"I said only ten riyals. Did you hear? Now start cleaning!" Abdulrahman disappeared inside his villa. Mussa collected soap and water and began to clean the marble while his heart leaped like a frightened bird inside a cage. As he labored to wipe away the stain, tears froze inside his eyes.

The stain of your blood, my father, falling on the street as your body fell. The stain of your blood, my father. Where are you now to see how your blood became a shameful stain on the wall of this beautiful villa?

Oh, my father. And I'm ordered to clean this shame. Where are you, Father?

Mussa wept as he spoke to his father's spirit. Wiping and pouring water, he stopped to touch the cold marble from time to time. He finally sat on the sidewalk—waiting to receive his paltry salary. Abdulrahman was late; Mussa grew uncomfortable waiting.

"Why don't I ring the doorbell?" he said to himself. "At least I'll be able to steal a quick glimpse of the gardens that surround this huge villa."

A small girl came from the villa and shouted, "You, Takrouni boy, take this." She dropped an old ten-riyal bill, then slammed the door before Mussa could have his desired look.

Mussa's anger boiled like a caldron on a hot stove. He jumped twice, like a monkey, and landed in the middle of the street. He jumped again, landing inside the big black garbage Dumpster. There he immersed half his body, like a hungry cat searching for an unspoiled piece of meat.

Mussa found nothing worth his effort and climbed out of the dump. He grew angrier, picked up a long stick, and began hitting the ground with it. The caldron inside him grew hotter. With rough black fingers he felt the ten-riyal note, making sure it was there. Inspired, he bent toward the ground and selected a stone the size of his fist.

Stretching his thin body, he rolled up his sleeve, backed up a few steps, and then threw the stone in the direction of the villa's glass windows. The glass shattered, and a woman shouted from a dark window, "Come help me, Abdulrahman! Quick, I've been hit by a stone on my head."

Abdulrahman's wife started to cry in the darkness of her room, touching her head where blood gushed over her soft skin. She stumbled and started to fall, almost unconscious.

Abdulrahman was taking a shower in the bathroom. His wife leaned against the wall, her hand bloodied. Bloodstains appeared here and there as she fumbled for the light switch. When the light was at last found and turned on, it revealed blood-covered walls everywhere.

◆

AHMAD BOGARY *is both a civil servant and a published short-story writer. Born in Mecca, he now lives in Damman.*

The Silver Polisher

'Abd Allah Bakhshawayn

◆

He stopped me at the entrance of the building, stiffly waving his short walking stick in my direction. He was tall and skinny and the same age as my father who died before I moved into that building.

He said, "You're the new resident. What's your name?"

It was a hot day, and I was in a rush to get away after the noon prayer. I told him my name.

He smiled. "Son of whom?"

I mentioned my father's name and surname.

"Good family," he said, as if he knew my father well. His evasive look gave me the impression that he was searching his memory for a name. "Where is he? Let me greet him."

His question took me by surprise. Trying to get rid of him, I replied, "He's at the mosque; he hasn't yet returned from prayer."

As he was about to go up, the old man said, "Greet him for me and tell him that Uncle Jabir salutes him. Don't forget that." Before he had walked away, he added, "Tell him that I want to visit soon!"

I stood in astonishment. I didn't know what got into me to lie to the shaikh who now climbed the stairs, repeating, "Blessed be this residence. Blessed be this residence."

I went to my car, blaming myself but not feeling terribly guilty.

Three months earlier, I had received the news of my father's death. I was unable to see him one last time and was unable to walk in his funeral procession, for the news of his death reached me only hours before his burial. I was traveling and couldn't reach my family home in time. Sorrow and anger blinded me when I realized that I would arrive there only in time for condolences. I decided that the ones who buried him should receive the condolences. That didn't mean I did not love my father. I just didn't want anyone to know how much I suffered because of his death.

◆ ◆ ◆

It was my habit to wake early. I took my wife to work and my children to their schools and then went back to bed again to wake up after the noon call to prayer, when it was already time for them to come home. Although I almost always left home without running into any of my neighbors, this time I saw the old man to whom I had lied. I blamed myself and felt remorseful about lying to him. Perhaps it was because it didn't seem as though my father was dead. Many a nostalgic night found me thinking of him, speaking to him as if he still lived.

The last time I had seen him was on the night of my departure, when I went to him to say good-bye, taking my children with me. I looked for him in the cafés where he used to sit and play dominoes with his friends. They all turned when the car stopped. My father stood up, happy to see me.

I kissed his hand and head. "I'm going on a business trip," I told him.

A look of disappointment came over his face. "Have a safe trip, and may Allah protect you," he said. Then he turned to the children, played with them, and tried to avoid answering their insistent question, "When will you visit us, Grandpa?"

We left following that exchange, feeling empty and giving a farewell promise that he could visit us in a week or so. Three days later I received the dreadful call.

I forgot about the shaikh during my shift, which starts at sunset and goes on until late at night. The next day I woke to the sound of insistent knocking on the door. I looked at the clock hanging on the wall in front of me; it was eleven in the morning. When I opened the door, I was surprised to see the shaikh, his gray hair looking like my father's. He was well dressed, as my father had been the last time I had seen him, and he looked like my father, in the way that the old look alike.

I retreated hesitantly and, in a worried tone, asked, "Welcome, uncle, what is it that you want?"

He smiled, saying, "*As-salaam alaikum.*"

I answered, still astonished, "*Alaikum As-salaam!* Yes, what is it?"

"Is he in?"

"Who?" I replied.

The shaikh kept his smile. "Your father."

I held myself together, remembering yesterday's encounter, and said with irritation, "No, he left."

He was astonished. "Left to where? It isn't yet time for prayers!"

"He sometimes sits at the shops in front of the mosque and does not return until after the prayers have finished."

His smile vanished for a moment. His complexion changed, and his face filled with strange sorrow and despair. "What a loss. I thought he was at home, so I said to myself, 'I'll come see him and we'll talk for an hour before going to the mosque.'"

Regret and guilt possessed me. I was about to apologize to him, to tell him that my father had died several months ago and that part of me did not want to believe the story of death that came through a quick phone call. Instead, I heard myself say, "If he knew you were coming, he would have waited for you for sure."

The shaikh was upset. "Didn't you tell him that I met you?"

Hurriedly, I replied, "Oh! I did."

"But you did not tell him that I'll visit him soon," he said, as if apologizing on my behalf. "It's typical of a young man's forgetfulness, isn't it?"

I smiled, avoiding more explanation. "I was busy; I was very busy."

He stood with a broken spirit. I felt an acute ache in my chest. He turned and was about to go down the stairs, when he stopped for a moment to say good-bye. "Don't forget to tell him that I came and missed him!" I can't remember what I answered, but I stood by the door until he disappeared.

I tried to sleep after that, but couldn't. The shaikh's image came back to me as he stood by the door, his hair uncombed, frail like a ghost. I felt so guilty. How could I put myself in such an awkward position? How deep was I hurting over the loss of my father? Long nights my wife sat by my side, observing me silently as I reflected on the news of my father's death. My wife used to interpret my unspoken grief and, trying not to irritate me, would say, "Go home and verify the matter for yourself!"

I would gaze at her, heartbroken, then angrily say, "If he didn't actually die, I might kill my brother for putting me through this torture. If he did die, I still might kill someone. Leave me alone."

My wife objected. "If you don't close the issue, you will keep thinking about it and kill yourself with doubts and worries."

Days passed. I was lost in my sorrow but didn't want to travel to verify the matter. I couldn't accept that my father had died. His presence was still strong in my heart, and the memory of our last good-bye lingered in my mind. Why did I turn my life inside out for the shaikh? I had lied about my father without thinking for a moment that the shaikh might knock on my door to ask me about him with such eagerness. Was

I waiting for someone to ask me about my father so I could answer that way? Or was it the trusting look of the shaikh that compelled me to lie because I did not want to bother him with news of death? I felt confused.

On Thursday morning my children told me about a guest who had visited while I was asleep. The youngest sat on my lap and said, "Father, my grandfather was here, while you were asleep."

Before I could reply, the middle son said sarcastically, "He is not our grandfather, you idiot, he just looked like him!"

I opened my mouth in surprise; my wife looked at me knowingly. She took the children out of the room, saying, "Play in your room for a while, don't upset your father." She looked at me and said, "One of our neighbors visited us. He is an old man around the age of your father. He sat with the children for a while and left."

"What did he tell them?" I asked with fear. "What did they talk about?"

"I do not know, I did not sit with them. Ask your son. He received him and talked to him."

My fear increased and I shouted, calling my eldest son nervously. "What did the shaikh ask you? What did you answer?"

As if gauging my reaction, my son replied, "He asked me about Grandpa. I told him he is not here, but left and will come days later. He sat down and played with my brothers for a while, then left."

I sighed with relief, remembering that I had kept the news of my father's death from my children.

"He was very happy when we called him Grandfather," my son said confidently. "He is a very nice shaikh."

"Is that all?" I said calmly.

He replied nonchalantly, "We said good-bye. He said he will come back when Grandfather returns from his journey."

◆ ◆ ◆

The weekend over, I resumed my usual routine. But one thing had changed: the picture of the shaikh was imprinted in my memory. It penetrated my mind, following me everywhere, despite the fact that I didn't see him for three days. Once I even imagined hearing the doorbell and went quickly to open the door, but no one was there. I tried to go to sleep again, but I woke up frightened when I heard the shaikh's voice talking to someone in the living room. My anxiousness was becoming unbearable: I felt lonely and afraid. I imagined the sound of my father's laughter coming from all directions. Certain that he had actually come back, I quickly searched the rooms. There was nothing but my children's toys carelessly scattered about. I felt ashamed that I had lied to the shaikh and wished I'd never see him again. Unconsciously, though, I felt that I had really lost him.

Time passed. One day I asked the doorman about the shaikh. He said that the shaikh lived in the apartment above mine with his daughter, her husband, and their children, and that he owned a small silver-polishing store at the Gold Market. The shaikh sat there every day from afternoon prayer until sunset prayer. I was surprised that he and his family had lived in the same building all this time.

I thought of my father who was once very late coming to visit my children. I felt angry as I recalled our telephone conversation. It was a painful anger, increasing with days. It stopped me from going to see him. Then later I found out the truth of the matter. Following my mother's death, my father lived alone, refusing to move in with one of my brothers, even though they had invited him to do so. He told them that if he wanted to live with any of us it would be with me, but I lived far away, in a place where he had no friends and would be alone.

My father had a small store near the café where he used to go and meet his friends. The store sold very little. He filled it with discarded items he gathered during his walks through old neighborhoods, mainly copper and aluminum, which he sold to buyers who passed by from time to time. He polished and fixed stoves, kerosene lanterns, and torches, and then hung them in front of his store, though they were commodities no one wanted because everyone nowadays has modern appliances. So he left his store unattended and spent most of his days in the café with his friends.

I went to the Gold Market. The shaikh's shop was located on an isolated corner in one of the back streets. He sat behind a dusty table cluttered with bottles filled with abrasive powders and buffing cloths for polishing silver. Between his feet sat a copper tub of tarnish-removing chemicals that emitted a strong odor. I greeted him. His hands were inside the tub, working actively. He raised his head, glanced at me quickly, and went back to what he was doing. I sat on the empty chair by his side and quietly watched him as he worked. From time to time he would take out the piece he was cleaning and examine it carefully. When finished he would place it in another tub. The color of his hands surprised me. Though his complexion was brown and full of life, his fingers were an ugly white, bleached by the harsh chemicals he used. His fingers were long and skinny, the tips eaten up and disfigured.

The afternoon passed while I sat there watching the old man. Outside, the street was filled with children playing soccer. Cars drove by, raising clouds of dust, making it difficult to breathe. He worked intently without raising his head or talking to me.

When we heard the afternoon prayer, I accompanied him to the mosque. Afterward, the shaikh picked up discarded metal pieces he found on his walk back to the store and threw them in a big tub filled with abrasives. When there were enough, he started to polish them, seemingly indifferent to the hot chemical burns on his fingers. He put the pieces that he thought might be gold into a small bag and sheepishly showed them to one of the gold vendors. They threw them in the street, telling him that they were worthless. Before sunset prayers, he closed his store for the night. We walked home silently, as if we had not acquired the power of speech. The shaikh's hands moved by his side and his head dropped as if by habit or force of age. I clasped my hands behind me and tried to say something, but was unable to speak. In front of the building we parted ways; I left him talking to the building guard and started up the steps without saying good-bye.

The following morning I decided to drive to my father's old house. If I did not find him, I would ask someone what really happened. But I left without seeing anyone. I reached the café after evening prayers. My father's friends were starting to gather the chairs from the sidewalk so they could sit together. When they saw me, some of them rushed forward and shook my hands and said, "Here you are, my son. May Allah forgive your deceased—"

"Then my father did die, uncle?"

"He's been dead for some time. Didn't your brothers tell you the news of his death?"

"I don't know, uncle," I exclaimed, at the peak of my despair. "I just don't know."

He could see I was perplexed, so he pulled me by the hand to an empty corner and kindly said, "Please sit down, my son. Sit down." There were no chairs nearby, so we sat on the sidewalk. "Thanks be to Allah, you've come. Your father left something for you in my trust." I looked at him curiously, as he put his hand inside the leather belt tied around his waist, took out a small velveteen pouch, handed it to me, and with relief said, "Now, I've handed over what he entrusted to me, may Allah forgive him."

I opened the small pouch without curiosity. It was filled with some coins and a simple silver ring that I had given him before I left. I put the ring in my pocket and handed the money to my father's friend, but he refused to take it, saying, "I seek forgiveness from Allah, my son. It is not permitted to take the money of the deceased. Even you can't give it away; it belongs to the heirs."

I choked back tears. "Take it and give it to the poor. I don't have time to do that."

"You may give the poor your share only, but what about the shares of your brothers?" he replied. "What could I do with those?"

"Give them to the poor too, for none of us needs it," I said hurriedly.

I learned that my father died in the café after morning prayers. On the previous day, my brothers had visited him. He looked sick then, and they offered to take him to the hospital, but he refused. They sat with him for an hour, then left, hoping to come back the next day.

My father returned to sit with his friends, tired and absorbed. He took out of his belt the pouch with his money and pulled off the silver ring from his finger. He asked his friends to give them to me. When my brothers arrived the next day, they saw an ambulance and police cars. The café owner recognized them in the midst of a crowd that had gathered. He pointed to the officer and led them toward a bamboo chair where Father was lying, covered with a sheet.

The café owner exposed his face and asked my brothers, "Is this your father?"

They looked at each other in anguish. One of them said, "Yes."

The officer looked at them, surprised for a second, then angrily said, "And you left him to die like this?" He ordered the corpse to be carried to the ambulance and told my brothers to follow him to fill out the funeral papers.

It was noon when they called me, saying that they would bury him during afternoon prayer. After I learned the details of what happened, I drove back home. Outside of town I stopped in front of a gas station, filled the tank, and drove for a while. But tears filled my eyes and I could not see anything. I pulled over on the side of the road and began to cry.

◆ ◆ ◆

I woke in the afternoon, tired and sad. Quickly, I put on my clothes and went directly to the shaikh's store. It was as if I had never seen him before. I stopped and looked at him; the store was empty except for a small table covered with tools of his trade. There were no pieces of silver.

I pulled up the chair by his side and asked curiously, "Where is the silver you're polishing, uncle?"

He stopped working. Looking at me modestly, but with a smile on his face, he replied, "These days nobody uses silver as jewelry." His modesty disturbed me. I was embarrassed, for I was touched by how he explained the matter. He returned to work in that wonderful way of his. I noticed after a while that the movement of his quick hands inside the chemical-filled tub had awakened a lot of pain. It showed on his face. He resisted it stubbornly and did not take his hands from the container. It was like a punishment he imposed on himself. My eyes were glued to the sight, observing the pain on his face, perplexed and uncertain of what to do.

After a moment, as if against his will, he removed his hands from the tub and dunked them in a sink of cold water to douse the fire burning in them. He raised his hands to his forehead and sighed.

Turning to him, I said, "Uncle, my father has left on a journey from which he will not return. I fear you will never meet him. But my house and my family are open to your visits. There is much my sons and I can gain from your presence."

"What does that mean, my son?"

"It means, where there is loss, there is gain. Let me make right the way in which I have erred. Say you will come to have dinner with us."

As my heart trembled, he smiled. I knew then there was a chance to make amends. I would start today.

◆

'ABD ALLAH BAKHSHAWAYN, *from Jeddah, has published two collections of short stories, including* al-Haflah *[The Party] (1985). He is considered one of the leading short-story writers in Saudi Arabia. He is also a professional journalist.*

Reaching You Through the Letter Carrier

'Abd al-'Aziz Mishri

◆

Life on the street was so busy that the silence failed to spread its stillness on the gray asphalt.

Tonight was like any other night on the street. The asphalt bustled with the hubbub of the stomping feet going to and fro. Slowly, however, the pedestrians thinned out. I sat watching the square.

Near the light pole sat a fellow in his usual spot, dictating a letter to his friend who leaned his head over a blank page stretched across his knee. The man focused on the fountain pen clasped between his friend's twitching fingers. He dictated in a Yemeni accent, using a stilted, formal Arabic.

"Greetings to my dear mother and to my brother Murshid and his wife, to my Aunt Riffah and her children, and to my sister, Hijjah, and my dear brother Hameed. As for me, I'll be with you, *inshallah*, next month in Shawal.

"You will receive the amount of six hundred Saudi riyals from the carrier of my letter. Please, my dear father, accept it. There is little work these days because foreign laborers are plenty and we do not know English. My dear father, we ask you to pray for us. With best wishes, your son."

The man said to his friend, "I'll give you six hundred riyals when we go back to my place. Please by Allah, hand deliver it to my father, embrace him four times, and kiss him on the cheek and over the head and on the tip of his nose for me."

I was very alert. I focused all my attention on trying to pick up snippets of their conversation without them realizing I was eavesdropping. I was filled with homesickness to the point of crying. My sight stretched to a field of moist glittering streetlights, cars, and reflections of light that shone from the heavens.

◆

'ABD AL-'AZIZ MISHRI *has published four collections of short stories:*
Mawt 'ala al Ma' *(Death on the Water) (1979),* Asfar as-Sarawi *(1986),*
Bawh as-Sanabil *(Secrets of Spikes of Grain) (1987), and* az-Zuhur
Tabhath 'an Aniyah *(Flowers Searching for an Urn) (1987).*

Yemen

The Corn Seller

Zayd Muti' Dammaj

◆

She stood at the gate of the *qat* market, selling barbecued corn. Even from a distance, I was startled by her bright eyes. I was attracted to her with all my senses and with emotions built on romantic infatuation, without which I have no life.

She chose a place on the edge of the main street at the entrance to the *qat* market. Next to her sat the fava bean seller, the pea seller, and the lentil seller. The *qat* market was filled with hundreds of people who loved chewing *qat*. In her right hand was a fan made of palm leaves, which she waved over the charcoal to stoke it; with her left hand she turned over the corncobs. Sweat trickled down her high forehead and ran like dewdrops down her full cheeks. They were reddish and filled with delicious charm. Her demeanor carried a mixture of pride and arrogance tempered with an endearing cheerfulness. All sorts of people asked her questions; they paid up front and she gave each what he asked for.

Every day I stole hours just to be near her. I'd sit directly in front of her if she was in a good mood. Other times I'd sit by her side, enjoying her biting answers to her many customers.

"How much?"

"One riyal."

Her right hand worked diligently, fanning the coals under the corn.

"How much?"

"One riyal and a half."

"Really?"

"Don't you see? It's fresh, ripe, and delicious." She worked even harder, using her right hand to fan the coals.

"How much?"

"Two riyals."

"Two riyals is a very high price."

"Its mother nursed it while she was pregnant."

"If I count the kernels, I'm sure to find I am paying two fils per kernel."

"Do you count the kernels?"

"Why wouldn't I?"

"Greedy!"

◆ ◆ ◆

Though a veil covered most of the lower part of her face, I knew well her beautiful profile from all the days, months, and years of gazing at her.

Beautiful! She truly was. I remember once, during one of my many holidays as a civil servant, I came to her place very early, even before she arrived. I sat in my usual spot directly in front of her stall. Before long the *qat* vendors and sellers of cheap vegetables arrived. Each fought for his place. They battled each other as birds fight for their territory or wolves for their prey in the wasteland. Each vendor wished to set up in a busy spot or grab a better location from a weaker competitor. The fight was quick and intense, but it always ended the same way. The strong imposed their will on the weak, who accepted their fate and prayed to the heavens for justice next time.

Her spot on the crowded sidewalk was the only one vacant, and no one fought over it. Nobody even came close to it, as if it were a sacred shrine guarded by some invisible force. Then she arrived, swinging over her head a sack filled with corn. In her other hand she carried a piece of pottery, a colorful palm frond fan, and a small bag filled with charcoal.

To me, she was as elegant as a tall palm tree and as graceful as a Yemeni grape vine. She had wrapped a bright blue cloth around her middle that accentuated her slim waist.

She was eager to put her things down. Moving quickly, like a fierce flood, she sat down and unloaded her sack and pottery. I thought she saw me, I was sure of it, for I was the only one at the neighborhood gate facing her place on the opposite side. She inspected her goods and looked around. She seemed upset that the fava bean seller, the pea seller, and the lentil seller had yet to arrive. I became worried when she glared at me with shaded apprehension.

Finally, the rest of the vendors rushed in, one after the other, carrying their loaded sacks. She seemed to relax. But my presence disturbed her, or so I thought. My dear lady, this beautiful corn seller, knew I was one of her regular customers! Why wasn't she happy that I was watching over her?

"How much is the corn?" I asked indifferently.

"It hasn't been grilled yet!"

"Yes, but I like it that way."

"Two riyals."

I dropped the money in her lap and took the ungrilled cob.

♦ ♦ ♦

One depressing day she said to me, "Is corn all you eat?"

On hearing this I felt wounded beyond imagination. "I eat other things as well, things that are more important."

"Nonsense," she retorted.

At that moment I swore deep in my heart that I wouldn't come back to her again, and I wouldn't buy any more corn from her. I wouldn't even pass by her place, this neighborhood, this market, or this street, for that matter. There were other places in the city.

♦ ♦ ♦

It was a rainy day. I had only my small black umbrella as I hurried toward my usual spot. Thinking about how my umbrella opened so quickly, like magic, upon pressing a special button on its handle, I said to myself, "Allah is great, mover of clouds . . ."

She had set up a big colorful umbrella that reminded me of those on Western beaches. I pondered for a moment on how Allah has blessed those countries with the bounties of this world and the next and has deprived us so greatly because we're so backward.

The umbrella protected her and the corn roasting over the fire. She was clearly bothered by the rain. She knew that people had to buy *qat* under any circumstances regardless of the weather, but with the rain they would do it quickly and not stop by her stall.

That day she offered me some of her grilled corn and I paid her with a large bill. She apologized for not having any change. But when I tried to return the corn, she became angry, perhaps because I was the only one aside from her who was eating it. I noticed her busy hands decorated in henna with well-drawn geometric shapes. On her wrists she wore delicate golden bracelets, flashing and matching the rings on her full fingers.

♦ ♦ ♦

I stayed by her side one winter day, warming my hands with the heat from her grill. She said, as if she wanted my advice, "I wish I could sell *qat* instead of . . . this." What she said surprised me. As she looked at me, her hand stopped waving the fan. "I love adventure . . ."

I couldn't find any counterargument other than to say that selling *qat*, which was sold mostly by corrupt businessmen, required a lot of capital.

"I've got that," she said.

"You will lose it."

"But there is no loss in selling *qat*."

"You will lose other things, more important things."

"That? Don't worry about me!"

"I fear everything for you!"

"What pleasant flirting!"

"The most pleasing thing is that I'm at your service . . . by the road-side."

"What road?"

"The road of love."

"You exaggerate."

"You're haughty."

"Allah saves us from pride."

◆ ◆ ◆

She was coerced into selling *qat*. I found that out later. The one who convinced her to try it was a big, fat-bellied man with a full beard and sleepy eyes hidden behind large sunglasses. He wore a greedy smile full of cunning, and strange and exotic clothes. He was disliked by her customers and the rest of the *qat* market shoppers. I knew he had acquired his wealth through shady practices and that he had no family or friends to benefit from it. I used to feel that what worried him most was my presence around her and that of her friends, the sellers of fava beans, lentils, and green peas. He could not bear them.

◆ ◆ ◆

Later, whenever I sat at the abandoned corner of the main street, I was overtaken by longing. Noise from the electricity and telephone wires reminded me that my lady was my heaven and a kind, cool shelter. I didn't feel that magic emanating from her anymore. What a wonderful passion it had been.

I didn't tell her of the magic and wonders of her sidewalk and mine, her street and my street, and the alleys leading to the neighborhood and the market. I was touched by an image of her melodic voice gently changing the echo to a dreamy tune.

I tried to forget her, to forget the main street, the alley, the entrance to the market. But one autumn day my feet led me there once more and I was overtaken again by my longing to see that seductive face.

And I found it. She was sitting cross-legged in the back of a small cart near the entrance to the market.

"How much?"

"Fifty riyals."

"Honestly!"

"Buy it and trust in Allah."

"Forty riyals."

"Here, this is how much it's worth."

"Fear Allah!"

"Well, it's up to you."

She took the money and tied the bundle with a rubber band. She argued a lot but without the courtesy or manners of old. She had recognized me but pretended that she didn't care. I started to move away but she pulled me back saying, "I have more security now."

"That's strange!"

"What's so strange?"

I didn't answer so she said, "Everybody is congratulating me on my decision."

"Except me?"

♦ ♦ ♦

Everything remained the same. Amm Saleh, the green bean seller, said the season was near its end. Ali Naqeeb, the dimwit boy, was still selling his lentils; and by his side Hajji Mushally was still selling green peas. His days were almost over.

♦ ♦ ♦

A new girl has been occupying the place of my beloved ex–corn seller. My lady now is a younger girl, also selling grilled corn. Though her beauty is clear and she is young, she has few customers. She doesn't yet possess the feminine charms of that woman who now sells *qat*. Still, I have decided to love her, this young new maiden. I have taken it upon myself to accept this new challenge.

◆

ZAYD MUTI' DAMMAJ *writes both short stories and novels. He has published a number of collections, including* al-'Aqrab *(The Scorpion) (1982) and* al-Jisr *(The Bridge) (1986), and his novel* The Hostage *(1994) has been translated into English.*

Trilling Cries of Joy

'Ali 'Awad Badib

◆

Whenever I heard my mother's trillings, I felt the walls of our home buzz and whistle. Her voice was huge and husky; it echoed even after she was silent. Our neighbors used to call my mother whenever there was an occasion for trilling. She was such an accomplished triller that no woman matched her in it. Once, before sunrise—when a small boy knocked on our door and told her that his mother gave birth and that his grandmother sent him to ask her to come—she put on her clothes, covered her face with her veil, and rushed out. Moments later her voice reached us from far and near. That sweet voice of hers!

I looked over from the window as if I wanted to see my mother's voice cross the neighborhood alleys and embrace the windows of the nearby and faraway houses. Soon she returned home and went to the kitchen right away to prepare our breakfast.

When the pilgrims came back after the *hajj*, the children, sent by their parents, lined up to ask my mother to come to their homes. My mother rushed from house to house, trilling day and night. Her beautiful voice echoed between walls. The children ran toward the pilgrims' homes to receive gifts for the safe return. My mother returned home loaded with presents, some sweets and nuts, and distributed them as soon as she was back.

As for the wedding parties, my mother was the first and the last to trill. She trilled actively during all of the wedding days. She used to repeat, "To know whose wedding it is, listen to the wedding's trillings."

May Allah bless you, Mother. I can still see before my eyes your beautiful mouth with its lips turned round, your tongue rotating and playing inside your half-opened mouth, your voice buzzing in my ear. How great you were, dear Mother. How much did I hope, as you did, too, that we would live together the happiness of this day. But we buried you in that sad tomb. We buried you too soon; we can hardly remember you, except as a person who was once our mother. Now we have nothing more than memory. May Allah bless you, Mother. You used to love weddings; with your trillings you used to announce happiness.

◆ ◆ ◆

My mother was not a tall, well-built woman. To the contrary, she was thin. She was beautiful, however. She was neither sharp-tongued, nor easily angered. She was very social, an excellent conversationalist with a sweet smile. Her laughter was free and always present. It started suddenly and ended slowly and lovingly. My father always admonished her, "I wish that you just laughed but didn't trill." Allah bless him, her trillings irritated him. He was so annoyed by them that he even disliked her giggles. He would reproach her, saying, "What kind of a woman are you? You bark at every occasion like a donkey, either trills or giggles. Be reasonable, woman!"

He used to scold her in front of us as we drank coffee or tea after dinner. She always kept silent. When we grew older, we the sons would join our father's position. The exception to this was my sister Saada. She used to stand up for my mother. When father went too far in ridiculing her, Saada would say, "So what? All women trill. Our mother is the best at it. I'm proud of her."

Mother would smile, and father would drink his coffee and murmur to himself, "Any dolt can trill, too. Your mother will teach you."

After that, Saada would keep quiet. My father would spend the evening talking to himself. Whenever he heard my mother trilling again, he would make a comment, she would laugh at it, and we with her. But whenever someone knocked on our door and asked her to trill, she would rush, and moments later, her voice would reach us through the air. It was the familiar reply to all my father's reproaches.

When I was younger, I was happy, proud of my mother and her trillings. I used to accompany her to wedding parties and other happy occasions, but that did not last long. I grew older and soon I became ashamed of her trilling. The return of the pilgrims started to irritate me, summer vacations—the wedding season—scared me from time to time. I used to walk and feel as though people were calling me names and making jokes about me. I imagined them sitting down in cafés, listening to women's trillings and saying, "This trilling is Mohsen's mother's." Another would answer, "It is she. She trills where there are trillings. She is created to trill!"

I got older, and as I did, my shyness increased, as did my irritation with Mother's trilling. May Allah bless you, Mother. I remember that day when someone scoffed at me for the first time about your trilling. That day, I was so upset that I reacted violently. I was a strong teenager at that time. During high school, every fight with a schoolmate was over Mother's trillings. They were the cruelest comments to have to bear.

I finished high school and worked as a teacher for a year. Despite all our objections, she continued to trill, carrying out what she considered to be her duty. Nothing changed, except that my sister Saada began to accompany her wherever she trilled.

It was decided that I'd travel abroad to Sudan for my university education. The first thing I thought of were the trillings with which Mother would see me off. My father jokingly said, after we finished dinner, "May Allah help you with your mother's trillings on the day of your departure!"

The night I was to leave, Mother sat by my side and advised me to take care of myself. She talked to me for a long time. We packed everything and closed my suitcases together. Her eyes began to tear and she murmured, "I'll trill until you disappear down the street."

I looked at her face for a long time and wondered what would happen if I asked her not to trill. I thought of threatening her by saying that if she did, I would not leave. She would probably have said, "Then don't leave!" I wanted to say to her, "Look, if you've got to trill, don't overdo it." But I kept silent.

She asked me to look three times back toward our home as I crossed the road. She recited prayers and then said, "May Allah make your way easy, that you'll travel and come back in good health, get married, and we will all be happy." To cheer her up, I said, "Would you trill at my wedding party?"

Her face glowed, her eyes glittered. "Yes, I'll trill at your wedding, unlike the trills of any mother on her son's wedding!"

Is it true that we buried you at dawn that day?

♦ ♦ ♦

In the beginning of my stay in Sudan, I worked hard to push away any thought of trilling from my life. I was satisfied to be free of it. But after a year, I found myself keenly listening that I might hear a trill, even a faint, distant one. When I heard one far away, I instantly recalled my childhood, accompanying my mother, holding the end of her dress as I followed her from house to house. I remembered the alleys of our town, its sea, its mountains, family and friends. Everything kept appearing and disappearing, surrounded by buzzing and echoing, the sighs of trills . . .

One year later, in the middle of my university studies, I decided to visit home. I was eager to go home, to hear my mother's trilling. I decided to make it a surprise. As I started to see the horizon of the town in front of me, I felt that terrible dislike for the trills again, those that I dreamed of in Sudan, coming all at once to the surface.

I walked down the nearby alley. All the residents of these homes could hear my mother trilling at parties, weddings, birthdays, and when people returned from travels. Here I was back from travel. Let my mother trill as she likes, I thought, even as my dislike of trillings erupted inside me. Whenever a son returned to his mother, she would trill, but I dreaded the neighbors' gossip and the nearby café customers saying, "I heard Mohsen's mother awakening me from sleep with her trilling today."

"Didn't you hear the mother of our friend Mohsen today as she was trilling? I thought she would never be silent this time."

"She is crazy—it's the craze of trilling; she's been praying for Mohsen's return so she can trill."

I knocked on our door. I heard the sound of steps growing close. Saada appeared in front of me. My mother asked, "Who is it?"

Saada was so surprised, she did not answer.

My mother insisted, asking, "Who is it, my daughter?"

I overheard her steps as she was walking toward the door.

Saada whispered, "It's Mohsen, Mother."

I ran toward my mother to embrace her. I hid my face in her neck, pressing her face in my chest. I felt very happy. Here I was in our home, my mother's face in my chest. Her mouth is touching my chest. I thought, how can she trill?

Her head rotated irritatingly between my arms and chest. She said in a low voice that seemed as though it was coming from both our chests together, "Trill, Saada, trill."

I heard Saada trilling for the first time in my life, her voice buzzing, full of life and energy and youth. My arms around my mother's head trembled as she freed her face and started to trill. I again held her tight.

Finally, my father said, "Enough, Salama. No more trillings. The whole town knows by now that your son Mohsen is back from the Sudan."

After dinner as we were drinking coffee my mother asked, "What do you think of Saada's trilling?"

We did not answer.

Saada shrank, and shyly lowered her head.

My mother added, "It is good. Her trilling is strong, hoarse, and low
. . . and after all, it's her first time trilling."

They promised me that by the end of the vacation they would flood
me with trillings. As if they were providing me with food and were keen
to give enough. Even more. I had two more years left to study. I didn't
know what would happen in those years.

♦ ♦ ♦

The first year passed. At the beginning of the second year, my father
died. If he had died in the summer, I would have gone home. I imagined
my mother crying and mourning. My father was a nice person. In jest,
he once wrote me, "We heard that you got different toys for the children.
For example, the drumming monkey, the violin-playing bear, and other
things. Here, we don't need them. All we need is a toy of a trilling
woman."

Nine months after my father died I finished my studies and returned
home. My mother did not receive me with trillings; she just embraced
me and wept. I kissed her forehead and enveloped her in my arms. She
buried her face into my chest. The room where my father used to spend
most of his time surrounded us and was covered with carpets that we put
on the floor only on Eid and special occasions. I said to myself, "Where
are you, Father, to greet me, as I return with my diploma?"

A week after I returned home I asked my mother, "Why didn't you
trill on the day of my arrival?"

"I cried instead." Then she began to weep. Whenever someone
asked her about her trillings, she would say, "My time for trilling is
over."

It now felt as though there was no life without trillings.

♦ ♦ ♦

Mother, we buried you by the side of our father, during the afternoon
prayers. Today I have an unbearable longing for you. I need your
trillings. Was it not you who used to say, "To know whose wedding it is,
listen to its trillings"?

Today is my wedding day. Saada came with her husband to the
wedding party. But she was sad. She could trill only in a low voice. She
said, with tears in her eyes, "Our mother used to say after she trilled at
others' houses, 'When will I trill at my children's wedding parties?' She
used to specify you by name, Mohsen, for you're her eldest child."

So, you used to say that? Then trill, yes trill, please trill, Mother.

◆

'ALI 'AWAD BADIB *is a short-story writer, novelist, and journalist. His published collections of stories include* as-Safar fi adh-Dhakirah *(Travel by Memory) (1984).*

A Parting Shot

Muhammad O. Bahah

---◆---

In the Friday morning newspaper, in December 1994, there was a small framed announcement on the right side of the second page. Here I found my name and the seal of the High Court of Aden. It must be the notice my wife told me about:

> The case of Saida Ahmad Husayn vs. Nu'man Saif. To Nu'man, who is not living in the Republic: Since Saida Ahmad Husayn has filed a lawsuit asking the resolution of her marriage from you, your presence is required in this court at 8 o'clock on Jan/15/95. You're further required on that day to bring all the evidence that you would like to present in the proceeding. If you are not present on the specified date, a sentence of the dissolution of the marriage will be given and the case will be decided even in your absence.

I looked at the announcement several times. My head spun as if it were disconnected from the rest of my body. For the first time I thought of Saida and my children. She was the solid ground on which I stood, and here she was being pulled from beneath my feet to leave me forever. I never thought that this would happen to me. I was sure that Saida was the type of woman who waits for her husband, the type of woman who does not replace her husband except by the grave.

What happened to her? What happened to the world? Perhaps it is I who stood still and did not move with the wheel of time.

My eyes were drawn to the last line: ". . . the case will be decided even in your absence." It was after midnight—deep night. A few lines from Saida's letter would reveal the end of the tragedy. Our relationship was not in any way normal. Most of the time I was traveling. She lived in the village, waiting without getting tired of waiting. I couldn't be disconnected from her, especially after having five children by her, but I'm

79

used to living my life the way I like. Though I was keen to keep her, it was my psychological attachment to have a woman be my wife. It wasn't at all related to what we call love. It was an inferiority complex, an escape. The last line in the announcement was still a red light, a parting shot carried by the newspapers. A serious, short, clear announcement: ". . . the case will be decided even in your absence."

My eyes grew wide; I hadn't felt such fear until now. I thought, "This morning I'll fly home and tell her, 'Here, I've come back, as you see. I'll give you my love.' I'll leave the airport and knock on my door with a smile on my face. When I see Saida I'll take her in my arms and kiss my children as I've never done in my life. They will surround me running, and their laughter will fill the world. I'll kiss them again and take them out for presents. When the little ones get quiet, I'll look in Saida's eyes with longing, desire, and eagerness. She'll forget that she was upset, but she'll never forget filing the divorce. 'I've returned, Saida, I'm home. I'll admit that the announcement in the newspaper was a justified parting shot. But let me make it up to you.'"

I don't know. Why did I keep reading her letter over and over? Perhaps for the third or fourth time? "To the so-called husband, wherever you are." The handwriting was bad but very clear. I was shocked by the hostile tone. It couldn't be Saida, so kind, always submissive. She who had written before, "My happiness is boundless, unlimited . . ."

I was very pleased, no doubt she was still longing for me, but I was surprised by what followed: "Finally I can hold the pen and write to you, and say what I couldn't for years. Don't be surprised. In the country of the sun everything is possible. I can feel the surprise take over you. You don't believe that this letter is in my handwriting. You can't believe that the person talking to you is Saida. Saida, the poor creature."

How can this letter be from my wife, who was illiterate, who spent her life unable to read a letter?

The letter continued: "I used to look at magazines, and see photos and black ink, but deep inside I steamed like a boiler, eager to read just one word of it. I wished that you wouldn't bring newspapers home; you knew that I wouldn't understand a thing."

She wrote: "While you've been gone I joined one of those classes that are scattered like electric lights throughout our village. You wouldn't even recognize it now. So many things have changed. You can now get light by just flicking on a wall switch with your finger, and water from a tap fixed on the wall. You could say that the whole world is controlled on the walls of homes."

How could she do that! Why didn't she wait for my decision? If I were there I would have taken her head off her body. She didn't used to think this way.

"I didn't wait for you to decide. For the first time I thought for myself. For many years, I was a slave, a slave to your authority. I said this to myself bitterly: 'I'm trying to get out of the oblivion in which you've imprisoned me.' No, you were not alone, there was the talk of others. When we were children we used to believe all that others said. We women used to be a shame for the family, made by men."

What shameless nonsense! Allah's forgiveness! This is heresy and anti-religious sentiment, but I'm driven to read the rest.

"Did I ever try to be rebellious in your eyes, disbelieving all the values and norms imposed on our life? Although you've tried for a long time to make us submissive, they are your values and norms alone. I've lived for years, imprisoned between walls, first behind my father's walls, then behind your walls. I got older and bigger but the walls did not grow. They kept pushing on my limbs until they nearly suffocated me, until I thought there was no hope, no way out."

In my despair, I tried to seek refuge in irony, but the letter did not allow me that small comfort.

"But I had an appointment with the sun—the rising healthy sun. The sun in our village is love. Now I can go out for a life."

What sort of life did she want? A damned one?

"But why am I telling you this? Perhaps you would like to hear many more details about this life. Just yesterday they hired me at the government farm. The only requirement for working there was a diploma. Be free of illiteracy. In the land of the sun—which you would not know anymore, *wasta*—nepotism and knowing people for connections have collapsed."

What a bitch! I wish I were dead before I had to hear all this! Since when do women work?

"I said in the application that even though I'm freed from illiteracy forever, my financial condition is extremely bad. The workers' committee has discussed my request and approved it. The social welfare committee reviewed my case, mother of five children who were planted in my belly. Then you moved away like a coward and a villain. You wouldn't even recognize the children now. All of them are grown, students in school. I'm indoctrinating them to hate you. When they complain about their old, worn-out clothes, I say to them: 'It's your father, the villain, who didn't send any money for you, not even Eid greetings.' Their mouths are open for food, their bodies are eager for a piece of clothing to cover them."

How could I have been so stupid? I wished I had never brought a newspaper home, but I didn't know it would mean anything to her.

"Let them eat and wear the sun that you talked about so admiringly. Again, I didn't care what you thought, or about the years you've spent far away. No more letters and the allowance that you sent once a year and later stopped forever. I dream about none of these things anymore, or you."

My sarcasm froze on my lips, I was speechless.

"News reaches me continuously. You've got lots of money, but it's for alcohol and women."

They're better than you are, a lot better!

"It is not important, but you should read the small announcement that was published in the newspaper that I've attached with my letter for you!"

◆

MUHAMMAD O. BAHAH *is known for his realist literary style. He has written numerous short stories.*

Sanaa Does Not Know Me

Muhammad al-Gharbi 'Umran

—◆—

He counted the days, including the day he left and the day he returned, since he saw it for the first time. He loved it, the minarets, the eyes in the windows. He walked, pondering about its beauty, the arabesque designs of the façades as they were enveloped in the women's curtains. He got used to the alleys, steps, the smooth sidewalks, the silver domes. He wished it were closer.

As he traveled from Dhamar, the road to Sanaa seemed to grow longer. The asphalt was broken along the way, making the driver move more carefully. He remembered a statement that many repeated, about an old traveler who covered the distance between Dhamar and Sanaa with the ghoul of hunger at his side.

He said to himself, "I'll make it before I run out of food." Then patted his jacket where he kept bits of a biscuit in his pocket. He looked out at the road; it was not too far now.

Silence solidified in the eyes of the traveler. The movement of the car lulled him. He remained occupied in his thoughts, over the hum of the wheels of the car, until he remembered the day he met her for the first time in a lecture hall.

The professor was engrossed in his lecture on the history of Mesopotamia and the role of Sumerian women in that civilization of city-states. Then she stood up at the entrance of the hall, seeking permission to speak. Everyone was silent. All eyes turned in her direction. She was alone, like a palm tree from the coasts of Tuhama. She was tall and elegant. Her smile cleansed all the eyes as she looked out shyly from behind her veil. That was in the first year.

The smoke of memory cleared momentarily. He had arrived at the Nageel Yasslah Checkpoint near the military compounds. The guards asked very detailed questions. He feared that they would impinge on the contents of his heart, that they would perhaps observe his eagerness for her. He smiled and his lips moved, whispering to himself, "Only fifty more kilometers to go and then I'll melt into her arms. We have thirty-two days off."

The car started to descend the mountain, passing the villages of the countryside—Khadran, Waalan—and finally reaching Haziz, where black houses stood proudly and challengingly. He wondered how the cars would make it through this mountain pass. For in front of them appeared the lofty horns of the surrounding mountains hanging from the depths of the sky as if embraced in battle around the gentle soul of Sanaa!

The cars did make it through the pass and suddenly, he was there. He sank into its circular streets, spreading his longing among the beloved sights as he entered through the Gate of Yemen. He searched for her among the high buildings. What would he say to her when he met her face-to-face?

He saw the boys with their mischievous smiles selling garlands of sweet-smelling Arabian jasmine at the crossroads. The local roses grew only in the spring. What would he offer her?

She would love the jasmine. He bought several strands of the white flowers to take with him, but he did not find her. He stood still, searching for her at the park near the college of science, but she was not there! He sat near her table, waiting for her in the library in the midst of thousands of books. He preferred to wait. He turned his back to everything else in order to be able to meet her.

Hours passed by. He heard the rhythm of feet, but none sounded like hers. The librarian indicated that they were closing. Everyone looked at the clock and he looked for her. But she didn't come.

The library visitors left, carrying their books and papers. He left with a heavy heart burdened with questions. The streets seemed to spit at him for alienating them, and the poetry building seemed to repel him.

He closely observed and examined everything, looking for her in the newspaper. He could not find her in the glare of the sun, which was about to set behind Aiban, leaving him alone. He searched for her at the Gate of Shaouh, the airport, the ring road, the Bouniah road, but could not find her. He continued to search for her, climbing the western mountain, following the sun before it died. He searched until the sun was swallowed by the sea.

He reached the mountain of Asser as the sun set and darkness fell on everything. His eyes gazed at the city lights. Zubair Street glittered. There was the Sheraton, Habara, and that Hadah street, and Bir Azab and all the rest of Sanaa's neighborhoods. But where did she go? Where did she hide her beautiful *kohl*-lined eyes? Where did she hide her springlike colors? Perhaps she was at Independence Square?

He closed his eyes. Night crept into his soul. He climbed, trying to escape, until he touched the underbelly of the sky. He stretched out his hands and gathered a number of stars and scattered them into his lover's constellation. He shivered from the pain and cold.

He cried, "Sanaa," for the earth under his feet was covered in misery.

◆

MUHAMMAD AL-GHARBI 'UMRAN *is the author of numerous short stories.*

The Veiled One

Zayd Salih al-Faqih

◆

He lived in a deserted neighborhood in a shop filled with garbage. He'd known nothing else since his childhood. But he made a living in this place. Around him lived mostly poor families and one well-to-do family. That was the only rich family in the neighborhood, Zarga's family.

He left every morning looking for work. But he did not find a steady job, for it was like the old Arab proverb, "One day luck is with you, the second against you, and the third day may Allah protect you from evil." He earned his living one day, to spend it on the next. He lived simply in the shop and managed as best as he could. However, whenever there was work he always returned home happy, smiling at the neighborhood children. He would sit with them and tell stories. He carried no hate in his heart, not even for the children of the well-to-do family.

Children came to him on festivals, and he blessed them in their new holiday clothes. He told them stories. The children grew so fast year after year! The young man looked at them with tender love, especially that girl with the blue eyes, Zarga, for she used to come regularly to hear his stories, wearing the most beautiful and colorful clothes. He looked at her admiringly and his heart ached with longing because he was poor and could not ask for her hand, although he had high hopes for himself. One day, Zarga did not come for his story session, so he asked, "Where is Zarga?"

One of the girls who attended replied, "She won't be coming with us anymore."

"Did any of you hurt her?" he asked.

"No, but she moved to another world."

"Did she die?"

The children laughed. One of the girls said, "No, what we mean is that she has moved into the world of the veiled ones. She has become of legal marriageable age."

86

The storyteller laughed and exclaimed, "You worried me there for a moment!"

He started to tell his story but suddenly grew silent. That surprised the children. One of the little girls tapped his knee.

"Why did you stop?"

Then they realized that he had seen Zarga, who was listening from behind the curtain of the house next door. When she noticed that he recognized her, she moved away from the curtain, letting it fall back into place. He knew her withdrawal was not of her own choice but her family's. She was still interested in his stories.

Days passed and the girl grew older, as her dreams grew, too. The young man was still keen to hold the storytelling sessions until the boys and girls grew older and each walked his or her own way. Eventually, every girl put on the veil. He could no longer bear living in that neighborhood without telling his stories. But after having spent such a long time in that neighborhood, it was difficult to move to another place where he knew no one.

Finally he moved to a location that was on the way to the girl's school. This time he bought a grocery shop. He always gave customers the best price and his sales soon flourished. People came from throughout the area to buy from him. Now, he no longer lived from day to day; he became comfortable enough to buy a villa and other amenities for a good life. But there was still something missing, an ache he could not satisfy.

One afternoon a young woman came to the store. She was blonde, blue-eyed, and moved elegantly in her *abayah*. He hardly recognized her and did not believe his eyes when he made out Zarga's childlike features in the young girl's face. She wanted some school supplies. He gave her what she asked for and looked at her with a question in his eyes, but she did not return his attention. This continued for days, yet he was still unsure whether it was her. He simply dreamed of seeing her again and enjoying her smiles.

One day as he was taking her order, she recalled a story about candy he had told before. He studied her carefully. She smiled and made herself known. He sighed with relief and asked, "Is it really you?"

She said, "Yes, of course. Didn't you tell us this story?"

"Yes," he said. And he gave her some sweets for free. She thanked him, gave him another smile, and left.

He thought about her all day, and when she came back from school, she greeted him and he acknowledged her with a smile.

◆ ◆ ◆

Zarga stopped by his store the next day to buy more candy, but she discovered that he was not there. She asked, "Where's the owner of the store?"

"He was hit by a reckless driver."

She asked, alarmed, "Which hospital have they taken him to?"

"Salama Hospital."

She went to the school very preoccupied that day. At break time she held her school case and notebooks and rushed to the hospital to visit him. At the hospital gate the receptionist asked her, "Whom do you want to visit?"

"The storyteller," she replied.

He laughed, and said, "May Allah forgive you, miss. This is a hospital and not Haroun al-Rasheed's storytelling court. Anyway, you can't enter until you give me the name of the patient you want to visit!"

She stood still, perplexed. How could she know him all this time and never ask his name? How could she leave school, skip the rest of her classes only to get such an answer? Where would she put the gifts she had brought for him?

Zarga decided to go back to school. But when she returned, she found it was closed. Just then her father drove by. She dropped her veil so as not to be noticed. She waited outside the gates until her father had passed. Finally she went home, burdened by great fear. She was afraid her parents would ask her questions.

When her mother saw that she was late and hadn't waited for the car that usually brought her and her brothers from school, she said, "Welcome home, daughter. Why did you come late today?"

Zarga said, "Some of the teachers didn't show up for their classes so they let us out early."

Lying to her mother only troubled her more. When her father came home, the first thing he did was to ask her to go to his room. When she entered his room, she felt herself blush out of fear. He told her, "My daughter, you're the most precious thing in my life and I don't want your reputation to be sullied by anybody."

Tears rushed out of her eyes. "I'm sorry, Father," Zarga said.

She was about to tell him honestly what she had done. But he interrupted her confession with an impatient sigh, saying loudly, "Don't make mistakes for which you have to make stupid apologies."

Zarga left the room, crying loudly. Her mother met her and said, "Your father is right. He gave you the chance to go to school despite objections by the family."

"I pitied this man because he is poor. There is no one to help him, and he's all alone. You don't know what compassion is, it's never occurred to you to have pity!" she lashed out.

Zarga entered her room and closed the door. She heaved deep sighs, sobbing. Her mother followed her into the room and asked, "Who are you talking about? Who are you calling a 'poor wretch'? We, your father and I, were upset, for your father didn't find you in school, and now I discover that you were out with a poor man? Who is this poor person?"

"No one, Mother."

Her mother left the room, saying, "Don't leave school again."

Zarga breathed in two long breaths and wiped the tears from her cheeks. Then she smiled and said to herself, "I don't understand these people. They abuse and humiliate me as if I had committed a crime."

She gently moved her bedroom curtains and looked at the clouds in the sky. On the horizon, the green meadow was dazzled by sunlight and spotted by the shadow of clouds and drops of rain. The sounds of birds, frogs, and water greeted her. The mixture of those sounds composed a symphony, a wonderful musical piece, drawing in her mind's eye a rare painting of paradise on earth.

Breezes of hope stirred inside her. She said, "Why don't people look at the beauty of the world and pray to the Creator who put all those things on earth? Poor storyteller. I don't know how he's doing in the hospital. I wish I knew his name."

Zarga rested in her bed, half asleep. She remembered the stories, and then remembered that the storyteller telling them was called Haj Hawash. She woke up and repeated "Hawash . . . Hawash." When she was able to hold herself together, she whispered, "Thanks Allah, no one heard me." She took her schoolbag and wrote down his name.

When she was fully awake, she drank a cup of coffee and told her mother that she was going to visit a classmate to review their lessons, and left. She walked straight to the hospital to visit Haj Hawash. It was visiting time, and this time she was able to enter the hospital. She was unable to discover his room number, however, because she didn't know his last name. So she went from ward to ward, room to room. After a long and tedious search, she found him.

"Haj Hawash! Is it you?" She ran to him, dropping her schoolbag on his bed.

"Is it possible?" Looking at her, his eyes filled with tears of astonishment.

"Possible? Why not?"

"You're the only one to visit me."

"What's important is your health, Haj Hawash. How are you? What a terrible thing to happen. Will you recover soon?"

Disregarding her concern, he replied, "And you remember my name, too?"

She laughed. The man sighed and said, "How I longed to see that face which has disappeared from my sight. How many years now?"

"Did you miss it?"

"Oh, yes, and with such longing!"

"You're exaggerating, for you see me every day as I go to school."

"Oh, I see it as you go to school, but I see only a black veil that hides your face."

"Let's leave all this. Tell me about yourself. How are you feeling? When will you be able to go home?"

"Thanks to Allah, everything is okay. My leg is healing fast."

"How is your business? Who's looking after the store?"

"Actually, things are under control."

"Are you doing all right in this new location?"

"Yes, things got better once I bought the grocery. A lot better. I even bought a villa, saved some money. I've earned the respect of the people in the community. Now they come to me for advice. All that's missing is a wife."

"You haven't married yet?"

"No, I didn't. I wanted a young, beautiful, educated woman who is suitable to my wealth, and my social status. Tell me about your life."

"My life, you know. I'm a student at school now. I just turned twenty."

"I knew all this. What about marriage?"

"A young educated man sought my hand, but I rejected him."

"Why?"

"Because I wanted a husband who owns a villa, with a big reserve of cash in the bank, and many other things," she said with a smile.

"Those are my qualifications," he said.

She was quietly happy to hear this. They looked at each other for a moment, which seemed to be hours. Then Zarga looked at her watch. She was shocked to find that it was late. Frightened about the prospect of getting caught by her father again, she said, "We've been talking so long I've lost track of time. I have to go, or my parents will worry."

He reluctantly watched her leave. But this time, he had a feeling she would be back to hear more of his stories.

◆

ZAYD SALIH AL-FAQIH *is the author of numerous short stories.*

To Return by Foot

Wajdi al-Ahdal

Ever since I reached manhood and the hair of my beard started to grow long, I have made it a point to walk home by foot. It mattered little how far I would have to travel, or whether my destination was at the opposite end of our province. Nor did it matter if it was close by. None of these concerns could deter me from my goal.

Walking home symbolized my silent rebellion against all those who relied on modern forms of travel. Cars, buses, and motorcycles were for those who were dependent upon others. I, however, needed nothing more for transportation than my pair of leather sandals. I gloried in my independence.

I was not the only one who resisted using the convenience of modern transportation. From time to time there were others who kept me company in my rebellion.

Once, a beautiful young woman in our neighborhood—her name was Dahlia—was walking on the same lonely dusty road I frequently used. She drew close to me and asked in a sweet voice, slightly muted by the scarf drawn modestly over her lower face, "Why is it I often see you walking by yourself down this road?" Pulling the scarf tighter, she peered up at me. Her almond-brown eyes glinted with sympathy. "Have you hit upon hard times and can't afford to take a bus or car?"

Frankly, it was difficult to explain to her the many reasons I refused to submit to the temptation of easy transportation. For one, I hated to impose upon my friends just because they owned cars and lived near our neighborhood. In time that would turn me into a manipulator, and I would be living at their convenience, not my own. Also, how could she understand that changing my style of living would require working for more money just to buy and maintain a vehicle, that the end result would be not only to give up walking but to surrender my independence? There is a price for convenience. One that I was unwilling to pay.

I could see in her eyes that it was difficult for her to grasp why anyone insisted on walking while cars raced blindly back and forth. It is ironic to see yourself walking while small boys, with computerlike intelligence, catch the first bus that passes by. As I see their small faces pressed to the windowpane, it seems they have left their childhood behind.

It seems pathetic to admit that I would like to be a child again! Then I understood the taste of innocence, purity, and love that was free of ulterior motives. But now I'm trying my best, even if it is in vain. I brought my attention back to Dahlia. Perhaps the simplest answer would be the best, I decided.

"I don't like to ride in cars," I said with a shrug.

"You mean to say, at the beginning of this new century, when cars and buses are easily available on every street, that you choose to walk? You are crazy, or if not crazy, then at least a fool!"

Not long after that, I saw Dahlia walking in front of me when she abruptly stopped and held her side from fatigue. As soon as she stopped, an expensive black Mercedes pulled next to her and someone leaned out to ask if she would like a ride. She paused and looked at me. I looked deeply into her brown honeylike eyes. I understood a lot from their modest glance. She did not have any money, and she would pay dearly one day. She stared out at me through the windows as the car slowly pulled away. Her look said, "I'll reach home before you do, and I'll never have to walk again!"

My eyes told her, "Oh! I don't think you'll return home after today even if you say so!"

Days passed after that event, and a rumor spread through the neighborhood that Dahlia was no longer a Miss, that she was now a Mrs. I didn't realize how much I loved her until I heard this news. I made inquiries until I was sure the rumor was true. I was crushed, but I became even more resolute in my determination not to rely on cars. My sweet Dahlia paid what she could. I still refuse to trade in my pride and compromise my ideals. You, who listen to what I am saying, what would you pay so as not to return home on foot?

◆

WAJDI AL-AHDAL *(b. 1970) is the author of several collections of short stories, including* Ratanat al-Zaman al-Miqmaq: Majmu'ah Qisasiyah *(The Jibberish of the Age of Miqmaq) (1998) and* Harb lam Ya'lam bi-Wuqu'iha Ahad *(A War that No One Knew Happened) (2001). He is also a novelist and a playwright.*

The Nightmare

Hamadan Dammaj

◆

The man crossed the crowded street, so deeply in thought that he was barely aware of his surroundings. Ever since the night that he woke shivering in the darkness . . . sinking in a lake of his cold sweat, he had become increasingly anxious and unstable. Nothing he tried—not his mother's soothing herbal tea nor his prayers at the mosque—could calm the great dread he felt deep within. It sat in his chest like a heavy weight, always with him. A constant reminder. A constant burden.

His relations with things, with reality, had started to become more and more tenuous. For what he had experienced was no ordinary nightmare. Actually, it was not a nightmare at all. It was nothing like those he was used to. He had witnessed all of its details carefully, more carefully than he was following the details of this sad, foggy day.

After the terrible dream or vision, really, he had tried to turn on the lights in his dark room on the upper floor of the apartment building. He felt around blindly for the light switch and soon realized that his joints were unable to bear him. His body had turned to jelly. He trembled nervously, and then the smell of fear surrounded him. A gasp escaped his open mouth, but his tears remained locked inside. Yes, it was not a nightmare, it really happened.

The smell of truck tires still lingered inside his lungs, and the fragmented images of the ashen clouds still filled his head. He felt fatigued all the time and his frail, thin body had grown even thinner. At work he was unable to concentrate, and at home he hated the silences, hated the pictures that kept appearing in his mind. Most of all, he hated that moment when he slid into the gray fog of sleep.

"But it was not a dream," he repeated to himself. "So why fear sleep?" The thought did nothing to calm his nerves as he recalled the vision. He was returning home from work on a cloudy afternoon like this one. Immersed in his thoughts, he crossed the street with the fast-moving traffic. He did not hear the sound of the truck tires until it was too late. Even those voices that rose and called to him from the other side of the street were meaningless. And the pulse of the muscles of his arms and legs could not stop the accelerated rate of events. The truck's front grill loomed like the open mouth of a terrible beast. His thin body was struck and sucked beneath huge tires that skidded on the asphalt, leaving long dark lines and a suffocating carbon smell. Dark, wispy clouds drifted in front of his eyes. Faces began to appear and disappear, emotions flashed on their visages, etched with signs of fear and sadness. From above, the scene looked clear. People began to crowd together in the middle of the road, like ants surrounding a cockroach that has turned on its back.

When he woke up, alarmed, something inside him was lost. His body felt shallow and light. The room was bright and filled with the smell of burnt carbon. Since that terrible moment this feeling of dread had remained with him. He tried to be especially cautious when he crossed the street. Any ordinary movement, any sound, struck him as a sign of the end. His mother and those at work noticed that he had changed dramatically, he had begun to withdraw into himself. He had become timid and anxious. Even he was able to realize the change that had affected his behavior lately. He no longer took long evening strolls. He was eating less and the slightest noise startled him.

He decided to ignore the thoughts that preoccupied him. He could not live his life this way. He wanted a break from his fear and confusion, especially after yesterday. He had left an oven burning during one of his night shifts, and his boss had warned him that he might be fired if he could not pay closer attention to his work.

He sighed as he looked at the dark clouds that moved quickly overhead. As usual, his attention was scattered and his feet walked lightly over the asphalt. He stepped off the sidewalk to cross the street to his house. A chorus of voices rose from the side of the street, but he could not distinguish them. He realized he heard something terrible moving. There was a roar like the exhalation of a dragon. The muscles of his legs shivered and he stumbled, falling onto the street. The image of gray clouds flashed before his eyes as his mind sought to make sense of what was happening. Through his broken nose he smelled the suffocating scent of carbon. He heard a great roar and the screech of brakes and braced himself, hands over his eyes, for the end.

Suddenly, he was jerked to his feet by a pair of strong hands and thrown back onto the sidewalk. He fell on his back again, the clouds in his eyes once more, but this time the truck rattled past, blasting its horn in annoyance.

"Are you all right?" asked a voice from above him.

He opened his eyes and saw a tall man standing on the sidewalk nearby. The stranger smiled at him and helped him to his feet. The man was still too stunned to speak, so the tall man helped him brush off his clothes, then led him toward a small café nearby.

"You will never believe this," said the tall man, as they sat at a table together. "But I had a dream . . . more like a vision, really . . ."

The man laughed and ordered tea for them both. "Oh, I believe it," he said.

♦

HAMADAN DAMMAJ*'s short stories are published regularly in local Yemeni newspapers.*

Bus #99

Yassir 'Abd al-Bagi

◆

The bus stopped at the main station to carry some passengers to another city. The passengers who boarded were a mix of different ages and nationalities. Some boarded the bus wearily, as if tired from a long journey. Some boarded excitedly, chattering to one another, as though about to embark on a fantastic adventure. The old driver turned around in his seat to make certain that everyone had settled in before he pulled away from the terminal.

He called out to one of them, "You! Young man, sit down."

The young man seemed confused and peered sideways at the foreigners in the row beside him. He sat down and slipped his large briefcase beneath the seat in front of him. By his side sat an old woman with gray hair and crooked teeth. She looked at him and said, "I used to have a son your age, but he's dead now."

The man didn't say a word. He leaned his head on the dusty glass window and closed his eyes.

In the back of the bus sat an old woman with her ten-year-old grandson.

"Grandmother, look, it's Uncle Samir," said the boy, pointing to the man a few rows in front of them.

"Where?" asked the grandmother, looking at where her grandson was pointing his finger. She squinted for a moment, then put her hand over the boy's and gently laid his hand in his lap.

"It is him. Samir, my son," she said.

Years ago, her son had left home for a mysterious destination. Since that time he had reappeared and disappeared many times. Once he said he was living in Afghanistan, but when she tried to write him at the address he'd given her, her letters came back. A year or two later, he suddenly reappeared and said that he had been in Bosnia with his brothers. Then, a few months ago, he disappeared again. And here he was again.

Her grandson fidgeted in his seat and asked, "Oh, Grandma, should I call him?"

The grandmother smiled sadly and said, "No! He's troubled. Forgive me, Lord."

The bus jerked forward. The man looked at his watch and kicked his case gently as if he wanted to make sure that it was there. Next to him, the old woman with the crooked teeth said, "Son, close your window!"

He looked at her, surprised, because the window was closed. She smiled at him and said, "It is a long trip and I'm an old woman. If no one talks to me through this journey my blood pressure will rise."

He said nothing, but simply pressed his head against the window again. She frowned and turned away. "Arrogant," she murmured.

An hour passed. Most of the passengers fell asleep. Outside the landscape rolled by, unchanging, endless. The child snored softly on his grandmother's lap while she watched her estranged son who sat with his head leaning against the window. She asked herself how it came to be that her own son had become a stranger to her. How he could have boarded the bus and looked past her with unseeing eyes. A tear trickled down one cheek and she took solace in her grandson's innocence, in the untroubled way he slept, smiling to himself, perhaps in response to a pleasant dream. She reached out and stroked the child's hair. He woke and asked, "Grandma, are we there yet?"

She kissed him on his forehead. "No, not yet. Our home is still far away!"

He turned toward his uncle and said, "Uncle Samir is asleep. He'll be surprised to see us when we leave the bus." The grandmother nodded.

The bus lurched over a pothole and Samir stirred. He looked at his watch and toward the foreigners. "Stop! Stop!" he shouted, rising out of his seat.

The driver looked at him and said, "Where? We're not there yet!"

Samir muttered, "I've forgotten something important."

The bus stopped. Sarcastically, the driver said, "Okay, get out. I hope you didn't forget . . ."

But the young man did not hear the last words. He walked quickly in the opposite direction of the bus.

The old woman shouted, "That young man forgot his case."

The young boy jumped up from the seat beside his grandmother and went toward the old woman. "Auntie, where is the case?" he asked. "I'll take it to him!"

The old woman asked, "Do you know him?"

The boy said, "Yes, he is my uncle, and she is my grandmother."

The old woman smiled and said, "But it is quite heavy. Let your grandmother carry it for you."

On the road outside, the young man slowed his steps. He pulled a watch from his pocket and regarded it with a strange smile on his face. Then he put his hands over his ears and waited. But nothing happened. For the first time ever, he had failed.

Inside the bus the grandmother became aware of a heavy ticking sound coming from inside the case. She felt a strange vibration that stopped just as quickly as it had begun.

"What's inside there?" asked her grandson.

"I don't know," she replied. She tried to open the case, but the locks were soldered shut. "We'll look when we get home."

"Maybe Uncle Samir will come to find his case."

"Maybe," she said with a smile.

The bus moved, and the grandmother embraced the case as if she were embracing her son.

◆

YASSIR 'ABD AL-BAGI *has published numerous stories in local Yemeni newspapers.*

Oman

Oranges in the Sun

Yahya bin Salam al-Mundhri

◆

Now . . .

Everything is ruled by the sun.

Cars swallow the street, gritting their metallic teeth at the hesitant lame man who stands on the corner. He surveys the wide black street, feels a wave of heat rise from the sad, hot sidewalk.

He clutches a sack of oranges, the ones he bought a while ago at the fruit seller's shop, taking his time to carefully select each one. He imagines how his children will act when he returns home to give them the oranges. They will dance around him, clamor to bestow upon him their warm kisses. They will pass the sack of oranges, and each of them will take one and peel it.

For now, though, he waits to cross the road.

The sun's rays beat down relentlessly on his head and neck. He sweats. His eyes burn. He puts his hand to his brow, trying to shade his face from the brutal sun, but it does little to dim the harsh yellow light.

While . . .

While the sidewalk . . .

While the sidewalk is hot and sad.

◆ ◆ ◆

Cars swallow the road, chew the hot air, and spit out puffs of black smoke. The lame man steps onto the street but draws back immediately.

At that moment his wife stands in the kitchen in front of the rusty tap, watching the water sputter out drop by drop. She washes the rice and with her scarf wipes the sweat from her forehead. Glancing out the window, she spots two of her children playing with a ball. They shout and laugh together, bringing a smile to her lips. Home from school, the other children have spread out a rug beneath a slowly rotating fan and are doing their homework, preparing for tomorrow's classes.

The shouts of the two children in the yard grow louder.

Meanwhile, their father still tries to cross the road. He promised to bring them oranges, the fruit of this month. Perhaps next month he will bring them red apples. He pictures each of them biting into an apple.

The sidewalk stings him.

The hot, sad sidewalk.

◆ ◆ ◆

Horns blare. Memories of his mother and of the accident that crippled his left foot flash before him. His mother was teaching her daughter how to sew and the daughter was teaching her mother how to write. Later his mother told him her heart was racing even before they told her about his accident. Then she fainted.

He tries to banish the memory from his thoughts. He has to cross the road, and he can't. Cars honk. Drivers spit curses.

While . . .

While the sidewalk . . .

While the sidewalk is hot and sad. And everything is ruled by the sun.

◆ ◆ ◆

Car windows are filled with blurred paintings of colored faces. Sometimes the faces revealed are agitated, other times joyful. And sometimes they look like pictures of old friends, dimmed by time but now awakened, lit by waning memory beneath the hot sun.

Thus do those faces appear, jolting his trembling heart and awakening within him moments when he shared their sorrow and joy.

Now memories are merely fleeting images inside passing cars, and he stands on a hot, sad sidewalk in front of yet another street he needs to cross.

◆ ◆ ◆

Tentatively, he steps out onto the edge of the road with his right foot, then quickly withdraws because of a honking car coming his way. It's as if he had put his foot in boiling water and recoiled in pain.

Another opportunity, another trial.

The flow of traffic ceases momentarily, the cars are still far away.

He rallies all the muscles of his frail body and steps onto the edge of the road. Hobbling, he begins his hurried journey across the wide road.

At last, he makes it.

He regains his breath, rubs his eyes, and sits down to relax, staring at the sky. His breathing gradually returns to normal.

Suddenly, his sense of victory disappears. He remembers the sack of oranges.

But . . .

His hands are empty except for streaks of sweat.

He looks at the sidewalk where earlier he stood. The sack of oranges lies there under the sun.

In his sorrow he heaves a deep breath.

He turns away from the street, the cars, the sun, the faraway sack of oranges . . . and lamely walks toward home. His head is bent, his body shivering, his eyes faint, and hands empty.

◆

YAHYA BIN SALAM AL-MUNDHRI *is one of Oman's leading young writers and has published numerous short stories.*

A Crisis at Sea

'Ali Muhammad Rashid

◆

It was about seven in the morning. Activity in the city's alleys had begun to slow. But there was life and vitality inside the houses now that the men of the city were preparing for pearl-diving season.

Captain Abu Ahmad walked through the narrow alleys to his home, wearing his white *dishdasha*. Around his head was tied a faded *ghutra*. He continued along his way, oblivious to everything around him, a tense expression narrowed his eyes. Though he was only in his fifties, he appeared older from deep seams the sun had burnished on his face.

At the end of the alley was his small home, no different from the rest of the houses around it. He walked to the door and knocked several times, but no one answered. He tightened his lips. As he knocked again, he heard his wife ask, "Who is it?"

"It's me, Abu Ahmad."

Seconds later the door opened, and his wife, Umm Ahmad, peered from behind it.

Abu Ahmad greeted her and went straight to the living room where he sat on the straw-covered floor. He leaned his back against the wall.

For a long moment the room was silent.

Finally, Umm Ahmad spoke. "What's the matter, Abu Ahmad? What happened?"

His wife's voice tugged him from his thoughts; it felt like she was pulling him from a bottomless pit.

He mumbled, "Nothing, really."

His wife looked at him with a disturbed expression. Her lips formed a smile as she sat closer to him and said, "You say that nothing bothers you, but you're not your usual self. Tell me what's troubling you. Anyone can see you are carrying the world's burdens on your back."

Abu Ahmad stretched out more comfortably and said, "Tomorrow pearl diving season begins. Everything must be ready. I was in Abu Saleh's café with some of the other captains and divers, and I learned

106

that several of our men won't be sailing with us this year. They've paid their debts, and some have left to join other ships."

Surprised, Umm Ahmad asked, "What are you going to do?"

"I don't know yet. We are shorthanded. Our crew will have to work harder. And I've asked Abu Khalfan to search for more divers before we leave."

Moments passed. Umm Ahmad tried to imagine what her husband was going through. Seeing how exhausted he was, she softly said, "You're tired, now. Rest for a bit. Don't worry yourself. You've got much to do and a long trip ahead of you!"

He sighed. His thoughts drifted away, and he mumbled, "That's true. We have four hard months ahead of us, four months spent between the sky and the sea."

Abu Ahmad, hearing the call for *isha* prayers, left for the mosque, taking his son, Ahmad, with him. Together, they performed the evening prayers.

After eating their dinner, Abu Ahmad sat down to chat with his wife again. "I can't believe Ahmad is already eleven years old. *Mashallah*, he has become a man!"

Alarmed at her husband's comment, Umm Ahmad glanced at him with a mixed look of surprise and concern. She raised her hands to her chest, trying to calm her fluttering heart.

"I started pearl diving with my father when I was nine," Abu Ahmad continued. "Our son is two years older. He must go diving with me as I went with my father."

Umm Ahmad fervently wished that her husband was joking, but she knew he was serious. She tried to hold herself together but couldn't. Her husband's words had drained all her strength. She felt paralyzed and could not speak. Abu Ahmad understood his wife's fears. Whoever went on a long pearl-diving journey bid his family a last farewell, for he knew he might never see them ever again.

He said, "Ahmad is my son. I love him as much as you do. But you know we have to teach him to become a man. We are people of the sea and pearl diving is in our blood. He has to learn the trade and know how to fill my position once I am gone."

Abu Ahmad looked into his wife's eyes to see how she would react to his words. With her eyes, she begged for his mercy and kindness.

"Please try to understand how important this is for Ahmad's future," he added, his words filled with love for his dear wife.

Umm Ahmad let out a slow sigh and responded with a nod.

Trying to reassure her, he said, "Listen, even though Ahmad will be on board, that doesn't mean he'll dive or be a diver's assistant. He'll just sit and watch and learn."

She relaxed slightly and in a quivering voice, said, "You mean he won't dive?"

Abu Ahmad shook his head. "No, he is too young to dive. He will do nothing more than help the cook or serve water and dates to the crew."

Umm Ahmad sighed sadly, "How I'll miss him! We've never been separated since his birth. I don't know what I'll do without him. I pray Allah will give me patience to bear his absence."

"Woman, do you want him to stay home all his life? We're living in tough times. Ahmad must learn how to be strong and capable. Wake him up at sunrise and help him get ready. He must be prepared for the long voyage ahead."

Umm Ahmad tried to hide the tears but couldn't. She turned her face away and wiped the tears with her black headscarf.

The household slept, except for Umm Ahmad, who lay awake all night. How could she sleep, knowing she would bid her son farewell at dawn? How could she sleep, knowing her husband and son would leave in the morning, knowing she might never see them again? She stayed awake until the crowing of the cocks, only realizing it was dawn when the *muezzin* made the call to prayers. She raised her head from a pillow soaked with tears. Umm Ahmad rose from her bed, not believing that morning had already come. She had wished for an endless night. But here was the first ray of morning light filling her eyes, which had been denied sleep for the first time in years.

♦ ♦ ♦

With sunlight streaming through the house, Ahmad awoke and accompanied his father to the mosque. Then they returned for a quick breakfast.

The dreaded moment of departure was at hand. Tears ran down Umm Ahmad's cheeks as she embraced her son. Unable to control herself, she begged her husband not to take him from her, but the words were drowned in the inevitable rush of departure.

Abu Ahmad gathered their gear, throwing it into a rucksack. He quickly checked the pantry to make sure his wife had an ample supply of rice, sugar, flour, and dates, which she would need while he was away.

Finally, it was time to leave. Abu Ahmad embraced his wife and tried to console her. He gently pulled Ahmad away from her, "That's enough, Umm Ahmad. We're already late, we must go . . ."

At that moment, the mother gave in. She kissed her son and said good-bye.

Ahmad shouldered his belongings and walked out with his father, followed by Umm Ahmad's tears.

The alleys were crowded with people. Men from all over town poured toward the ships that rocked gently in the harbor. Women and children waved good-bye, their eyes raised to heaven praying, "*Sabhan Allah . . . Allahu akbar . . .* God is great." Scattered over the water, the ships prepared for their journey east. Their white sails billowed, and the voice of the *niham*, the sea singer, was raised, announcing the beginning of the pearl-diving season as the ships left harbor.

For those left behind, tears mixed with sighs and voices raised in prayers. An hour passed as if it were a century, but no one spoke the truth: that those who sail have no idea if they will return, and those left behind dare not ask if they will ever see their husbands and sons again.

Captain Abu Ahmad's ship sailed out into the gentle waves of the Gulf. Once they arrived in position near the pearl beds, the divers lined up along the side of the ship and made preparations. Each diver was assisted by a *seeb* who would haul the exhausted man out at the end of his task. Making his rounds, Abu Ahmad noticed a man on board whom he did not recognize.

"What's your name?" he asked.

Abu Khalfan intervened. "This is Jassin, he's from my hometown. He signed on the day before we left. I didn't think you would mind."

"Okay. What does he do?"

"He says he's an experienced *seeb*."

"Good! We need the extra hand."

Abu Ahmad turned and gave orders for the sailors to take their positions and prepare to dive.

Days turned into weeks. The men gathered pearls of every shape and size. Some captains sold the pearls to the traders who traveled the Gulf waters. But others, like Abu Ahmad, would sell their pearls when they returned home.

◆ ◆ ◆

One night Abu Ahmad had a severe headache. He felt as if his head would burst. His whole body ached, so much so that he passed out, falling to the ship's floor. The sailors, who'd gathered on the deck to tell stories after a hard day's work, heard him fall and rushed toward the sound. They found the captain lying facedown with Ahmad by his side weeping.

Abu Khalfan rushed to lift the captain to his bed, and sat waiting anxiously. Other men joined him, sitting near Abu Ahmad as he lay unconscious before them. They were near panicking, unsure of what to do. Before dawn, the captain gave his last breath and died.

The divers could do nothing but moan and pray for mercy on him. They tried to console Ahmad, who could not believe what had happened. The boy pushed them away and threw himself on his father's body, crying, "Father, just answer me!"

Abu Khalfan, whose eyes were red from weeping, recited the final rites. He washed the corpse and prepared to drop it, as was customary, into the sea. But before the body was laid to sea, Ahmad rushed to his father's side, one last time, and lingered there for a final moment.

"Ahmad," Abu Khalfan said, as he placed his hand gently on the boy's shoulder. "It's time, son."

Averting his eyes, Ahmad held his breath until he heard the splash.

The sailors realized their situation: they were on a ship without a captain. "*Ya* Allah! What should we do? We're in a real crisis."

In the morning, they gathered to discuss their situation. The captain was dead, so who would run the ship? Who owned the pearls? Here they disagreed, almost violently. Abu Khalfan sat at the bow with some of the sailors—Hussain, Jassin, Rashid, and Yusuf—and discussed how to resolve the situation.

"I think we should divide the pearls equally among us," said Jassin.

Angrily, Hussain said, "Equally? That's not fair! What about those who worked harder?"

Rashid replied, "That's true. We must divide the pearls among all of us, but each according to his work and effort."

Abu Khalfan said, "But the ship and the pearls belonged to Abu Ahmad, may Allah have mercy on him and may he reside in paradise. They belong to Ahmad now. We must give them to him. "

"Impossible," said Hussain. "Ahmad's too young, and a dependent. Besides, we hated the captain. He was unfair. He exploited us and gave us only the crumbs."

Abu Khalfan responded with a fierce glare at Hussain, "What Captain Abu Ahmad did is done by all the captains. At least he used to give you loans and help you when you needed it."

The argument grew more vehement. Everyone talked and shouted.

After a moment, Rashid said, "Please, sit down and be quiet, or we'll never agree. Since Ahmad is too young to take charge, we must choose a new captain. What do you say?"

Voices were raised, some in favor, some against.

"Oh, no, I disagree," said Hussain. "This was to be my last trip. So we should divide all of the pearls and return the ship to the captain's son; what do you say?"

Angrily, Abu Khalfan responded, "That is treason! We must go home as if the captain were with us, then let a judge decide."

"No, no," said Hussain. "We should divide the pearls now, and when we return, we will tell them we were acting on the captain's orders before he died. What do you think?"

Rashid said, "I agree."

Jassin also agreed.

Abu Khalfan said, "I disagree. It's not right to steal a dead man's wealth."

Hussain said, "But is it right that he stole from us while alive?"

The argument continued to escalate until, losing control, Hussain grabbed Abu Khalfan and pushed him. Moments later, Rashid charged into the group. A melee ensued, with the rest of the crew choosing sides. Afterward, they sat down again, grimacing in pain, especially those who were bleeding.

Suddenly Abu Khalfan asked, "Where are the pearls?"

"I'll get them from the captain's room," Hussain answered.

He went to the room and rummaged for the pearl bag, but did not find it. Then he searched the captain's private box and still found no pearls. Angry, he began to tear the room apart with his hands. Finally, exhausted and with no more hope of finding the pearl bag, Hussain looked up to find Ahmad standing in the middle of the room.

Hussain looked at him threateningly, "Where are the pearls? Did you take them?"

Defiantly, Ahmad grinned, "Yes. I put them in my father's pockets before he was buried." Then he turned and walked away.

Only then did Hussain and the other sailors discover what had happened to the pearls. Ahmad had anticipated the problem, taken the pearls, and returned them, with his father, back to the sea where they belonged.

◆

'ALI MUHAMMAD RASHID *is a prolific short-story writer and highly regarded in the Arab world.*

A Voice from the Earth

Ahmad Bilal

◆

Khadija's husband, Ismail, died suddenly, widowing her before her twentieth birthday. Resigned to her fate, she dedicated her life to rearing her sons, Ahmad and Nassar, in the memory-filled white plaster home her husband left behind. Perhaps these memories caused her brooding during long, quiet nights.

One night, she stood by the front window, as was her habit, and let her eyes wander the dark streets. She half expected wicked souls and fearful ghosts to appear out of thin air. Instead, Nassar startled her from her dreams, coming in search of some papers in his father's room. She watched him for a moment then turned back to the window and her sad thoughts.

As he walked into his father's room, Nassar's foot hit a spot that creaked loudly, as if there was a loose board in the floor. He didn't recall hearing the plank before. Tapping the spot with his heel, he explored the source of the sound. When he felt certain he had identified the creak, he eagerly pulled back the carpet and saw a piece of red cloth, the same color as the rug, stuck carefully beneath it. From inside the cloth, he withdrew a thick bundle of parched paper. It looked like a legal document. Carefully, he unfolded the sheets and poured over the contents. Engrossed by the papers, he mumbled aloud as though he expected the furniture in the room to respond to him.

Then, he left quietly and walked through the sitting room where his mother stood. His face flushed, he paused in front of his mother. "I need a minute to read these," he told her, and retreated to his bedroom. There he dropped onto the bed and asked himself with a shocked voice, "Shamsa, the widow, is my father's second wife—is that possible?"

"But why not?" he answered himself. "Doesn't the marriage contract in your hands prove that?" He sat for a moment, his mind spinning thoughts. "Does my mother know she has a co-wife?" he wondered. He answered himself, again, "No, no, I don't think so." And then he fell silent for a moment before his anxiety returned. "But where is this other wife?"

He reopened the document and checked the address. It was issued from the *sharia* court at Al-Seeb. A spark of hope eased his worry, for he had friends at this court who could help him learn about the woman who had also been part of his father's life.

That night he couldn't sleep. The mystery obsessed him.

◆ ◆ ◆

At dawn, Nassar left to say his prayers and to recite some verses of the Holy Quran. Then he ate his breakfast with his mother and brother. From the look on his face, his mother knew he was worried. "You're not yourself, Nassar. What is it?" she asked him.

"It's nothing, Mother. I am just a bit tired because I couldn't sleep last night." He smiled and kissed her brow as he turned to leave.

It was seven thirty in the morning; he called his office to excuse himself from work, claiming an urgent family matter.

Nassar drove to Al-Seeb faster than an arrow. On the main street, he smelled the sweet fragrance of roses and green gardens. Through the trees he recognized his friend Fahed's house and drove toward it. When he knocked on the heavy carved door, Fahed's mother peered through the narrow opening. Upon recognizing Nassar she responded, "Fahed just left."

"Do you happen to know a woman named Shamsa Salem?"

"Of course I know her. She's our neighbor."

As those words fell from the woman's tongue, he froze. She pointed at Shamsa's modest house, which was only another two hundred meters away.

Nassar ran until he stood before the gate, its door wide open. He knocked and a soft voice answered, "Please feel free to enter."

Nervously, he stepped inside the courtyard where he found an elderly woman sitting on a worn reed mat. She extended her hands respectfully before he had even reached her. So Nassar kissed her warm soft hand as if she were his mother.

"I am sorry, my son, that I cannot stand to greet you properly."

"Oh, Auntie, please don't bother rising. I will sit next to you here." He realized from gazing on her thin bent form that she was paralyzed.

As Nassar sat by her side, she offered him a cup of hot green coffee and a plate of dates, without even asking who he was.

Nassar studied her face, discovering virtue, respectability, and decency within the deeply etched lines. He tried to break through his anxiety and say something, but his mind and his tongue failed him. As he finished his cup, she spoke to him.

"Would you like more coffee?"

"No, Auntie, thank you. I come here concerning Shamsa Salem. Do you know her?"

"Yes, I do. I am Shamsa. Why do you ask?"

He fell silent for a moment. Then he asked, "What is the story of your marriage to Ismail?"

The woman let out a long sigh as if trying to extinguish a fire that the question ignited deep inside her. In a distressed tone, she answered, "Poverty is like a black mountain. It seduces no one. But those who travel through such places are surprised by springs dancing within its silent heart. Ismail was one who visited those springs. He was connected by love and brotherhood to my late husband, despite their differences in social standing. When my husband died, poverty nearly tore me apart. Ismail, with his noble and kind heart, decided to be faithful to his friend and to help me. So that his visits to my house would not be the source of ugly rumors, he married me. Few people knew of this marriage.

"Ismail did not marry me for my beauty or wealth or social status," she continued. "I've been paralyzed since childhood. He intended our marriage to bring happiness to my daughter and to give her a chance to grow up in this small house. His life had an aim and a noble meaning. He was a source of help for a poor, unhappy woman. It is he who gave respect to the life of others."

Nassar's nervousness evaporated. He asked, "Would you like to meet one of his sons?"

The woman turned and replied, "Are you Nassar?"

He nodded.

Shamsa hugged him and broke into tears. At that moment, her daughter entered. She was beautiful and imbued with a natural grace. Nassar felt something stir inside him.

Shamsa introduced her. "This is Shaikha, my daughter. She graduated this year from Teacher's College . . ."

The three of them talked nonstop, like singing birds in the beginning of spring. This went on until Nassar was sure the schoolteacher was not yet married. After dining with them, Nassar left, promising to return for another visit as soon as he could.

◆ ◆ ◆

On the road, the shadow of a young girl moved toward him like a crescent in the clear sky. For the first time in his life, he felt love open her mouth and swallow him.

His mother's look of anxiety turned to happiness when he entered the house.

"What is it?" she asked. "What makes you so happy?"

"One feels very happy when he uncovers a pleasant secret."

His mother asked, "Is there a secret you've discovered that makes you this happy?"

"Yes, Mother. A profound secret."

"Will you tell me?" she asked.

"Yes," he replied. "In a moment. First, I'd like to change and prepare for dinner."

He entered his room, but as he was about to undress, he recalled the sound that had come from beneath the plank in his father's room. He said to himself, "Paper alone cannot cause such a sound!"

Quickly, he ran into his father's room. When he got to the spot, he started testing the floor with his feet. Again, he raised the tip of the rug to find that a piece of the flooring was loose. It seemed natural enough to be so. It could have gotten loose after this many years. So he returned the rug to its place.

But as he stood, he wondered, "Why is the wood so loose only in the spot where I found the document?"

He bent and raised the rug again. This time, he removed the entire plank. As he did, he spotted the neck of a clay jar, its top lying parallel to the floor, its neck filled with palm tree fronds. He pulled the jar out and tried to empty its contents. Inside, something glittered, and he shook harder until out fell pieces of gold and jewelry. Astonished, he guessed the whole amount to be worth more than fifty thousand Omani riyals.

As Nassar spread out the gold, he uncovered a piece of paper in his father's handwriting. Reading the paper, he learned that his father had willed a portion of this money to renovate a mosque he had already built, another portion to his wife Shamsa, and the biggest portion to his wife Khadija and their two sons, Nassar and Ahmad.

Nassar crumbled the will in his hands. Fate gave him the treasure alone. Greed blinded him, and he decided to disregard his father's will. At that moment, though, his mother entered the room and found him kneeling in front of the golden heap. Darkness, gloom, and sorrow descended upon him, and the false hope he had built moments before crumbled like an imaginary castle, for he greatly respected his mother.

Khadija was taken by surprise. "Where did you get this?" she asked and kneeled down beside him. "Is this the secret you discovered that made you so happy? No, Nassar—stolen money is an infernal tree with bitter fruit. It is the very *zachum* oil tree in hell! Seek forgiveness, for the Lord's mercy will cleanse your soul and make you the richest man in the world."

Nassar stood with tears in his eyes, overcome by shame. He mumbled, "I was about to steal the rights of others, but it is the will of Allah that has intervened at the right time to save me. Mother, this gold I took from here." He pointed to the jar and then bent down, picked up the will, and asked her to read it. When she finished reading it, she murmured, "*Shamsa bint Salam . . .*"

Nassar explained to his mother how his father had married the paralyzed woman. He told her of the woman's beautiful daughter, and of his love for her. His mother understood. She felt pity for the woman and joy for her son.

"Nassar, divide the gold just as your father said in his note. Each should get his lawful share. And you must get ready, for we're leaving this evening for Al-Seeb."

"But what about Shaikha, Shamsa's daughter?"

His mother smiled and said, "Leave that to me." She left the house.

Nassar considered his mother's orders to divide the wealth and her implicit agreement to allow him to marry Shaikha. Joy ran wildly through his veins.

That evening, Nassar, his mother, and Ahmad drove to Al-Seeb district. They parked the car in front of Shamsa's home. As Nassar got out, he saw Shaikha and greeted her respectfully. When she asked him to come in, he pointed to his mother, who accompanied him with Ahmad. When Shaikha's eyes met Khadija's, she immediately realized that this woman was Nasser's mother. She rushed toward her, kissed Khadija's hand, and embraced her. Khadija, in turn, took her in her arms like a mother hugging her baby. Then they went into the house together to greet Shamsa. Everyone talked and ate fruit. Finally, Nassar said, "Aunt Shamsa, this bag contains some money that Father willed to you."

Shamsa gazed at the bag for a long moment. Finally, she turned toward Nassar and Khadija.

"I am poor, but content. And jewels cannot bring me greater contentment." She raised her tear-filled eyes and said, "That exceptional man still shines like a star in my heart, and by that light I live. This wealth is yours. You're more entitled to it."

Kindly, Khadija replied, "It is your lawful right and not a present."

But Shamsa vowed not to take a penny, and with that, a loud silence fell over them. Khadija finally said, "I would like to announce a proposal for my son, Nassar, to marry your daughter, Shaikha. Please consider this money as her dowry."

Silence again crept over them, as if each had covered his mouth with a piece of cloth.

"It would be a great honor to accept your proposal, but her cousin asked for her hand, and I gave him my initial agreement."

When the words reached Nassar's ears, pain filled him, and he reached to steady himself against the wall. But then Shaikha spoke, pouring hope back into his heart.

"Mother, if I denied what you've done for me and how difficult it was to educate me, I would be unjust. And if I disobeyed you, I would be much ashamed. But still, as a Muslim girl, my religion gives me the right to be advised about my marriage, and I refuse to marry my cousin."

Shamsa turned toward Khadija and Nassar and said, "So be it. Congratulations, Nassar. She is your bride. You are free to marry her." Shaikha and Khadija exchanged smiles, and Shamsa added, "Now then, we must plan the finest wedding party for you both."

◆

AHMAD BILAL, *a published short-story writer, is also a radio and newspaper journalist.*

Ghomran's Oil Field

Su'ad al-'Arimi

◆

Ghomran ran, laughing as the distance to his sister's home shortened. He reached an area he recognized and stopped abruptly, kicking up dust on the rock pathway. Looking around, he spotted the modest villa. Smaller houses had sprouted up around it like mushrooms. He walked toward the large iron gate, deeply inhaling the hot, humid air.

The relentless midday heat baked everything. Ghomran leaned impatiently against the bell until Saidah bint Abdullah, tall and willowy, appeared at the door. Her thick black brows arched in agitation, but when she spotted Ghomran her mouth turned upward in a smile.

"Brother, welcome! This is so unexpected. Tell me, is anything the matter?"

Ghomran looked down at his feet for a moment, then swallowed hard. "No, I won't be staying." He took a deep breath. "I've trained hard in the desert this week. They promised me after I finished today that I could work as a guard at one of the oil fields near the Empty Quarter."

Saidah pursed her lips, surprise registering in her eyes. "So, you'll be moving away so soon? Please reconsider staying in town. Muhammad can help you find another job. One that will let you come home in the evenings."

"No, I've said what I came to say. Now I must leave."

Ghomran turned and left, a sense of relief spread across his body. It was done. Now he could leave his sister with her new husband. He had supported Saidah, the only family he had, until the day of her wedding. Her life was set now. It was time for him to go his own way.

Ghomran arrived at the company parking lot early the next day. Dawn's pink fingers stretched over the horizon. A cluster of silent men stood huddled together near the bus stand, plumes of cigarette smoke occasionally dissipating over bent shoulders. He eagerly joined the group, ready for the unknown.

When the company bus lurched forward, the driver, a burly man with a thick mustache, told them, "We should reach camp by evening. Someone there will tell you your assignments."

Ghomran stared out the window. Sand dunes faded into unknown terrain. He could feel the wild mystery of the wide-open desert calling him to discern its secrets.

Looking around at the tired faces of the men waiting to arrive at the camp, Ghomran wondered how far they were from home. In the group were Asians, Pakistanis, and Africans. Each man's face bore the tired look of long hours of labor in the sun. As the bus stopped to let three wandering black camels cross the road, the passengers shifted impatiently, their bodies jostling against each other as they gathered their suitcases and duffel bags.

The bus lurched to a stop, and the doors hissed open.

"Friends, this is your stop," the driver announced. He gave each weary passenger a knowing nod as he stepped into the heat of the night. The desert would take whatever vigor they had left.

A company official was speaking to the crowd when Ghomran joined them.

"Tomorrow, you will be dropped at your assigned work sites." Surveying all of the poor, tired faces, he repeated the announcement in several languages.

Darkness fell, and calm settled over the camp as the newcomers found places to sleep for the night. Ghomran pulled a blanket from his bag. Wiping the sweat from his neck, he turned on his side and fell asleep.

Morning broke. The desert looked vast, forbidding, and wild. Ghomran emerged from beneath his blanket. He was taking a cautious step forward to explore the area when a gas flare suddenly opened nearby, releasing a burst of flames. The grumbling roar unsettled him; fear tingled up his spine. Behind him, he heard one of the officials approach, and his body stiffened in alarm. "This is your assigned post," said the man. "You're the guard here. Keep a careful eye on the gas wells." He pointed toward the fire. "You're responsible for everything in this location."

Ghomran inhaled a deep breath of burnt smoke then turned to the small prefab concrete unit to which the supervisor was pointing. The official handed him a key and said, "This is to your room. You will have one week off every month."

Ghomran was silent; his tongue was as dry as a piece of wood.

He watched his site all day long, the vast desert stretching out before him. At night he lay awake, aware and cautious, listening to the roar of the gas flares. His concentration deepened as the density of heat rose. He focused solely on the fire; he did not have eyes, ears, or a voice. Instead, his pulse merged with that of the pulsating gas.

Nearly a month passed.

"I don't want to leave," Ghomran said to his replacement.

"But it's your week off."

Ghomran stared at the man. The oasis where he took his break was a day's journey away. He couldn't leave; he was too close to understanding the mystery of the well. He was seeing, listening, and feeling with the pulse of the fire . . . fire, smoke, sand, dust, wind, faces, gas wells. But the pulse was wrong, the rhythm out of kilter.

"Don't you hear that?" Ghomran shouted above the flare's release.

"Hear what?" asked his confused replacement. "There's nothing to be heard, except the fire."

Suddenly, Ghomran bolted away, shouting a warning. Sand fell into faces, cascading into the men's eyes as columns of flames, shaped like tall malevolent genies, roared upward, torching the face of the sky.

People gathered at the barricades, near the instruments and oil tanks necessary to fuel the daily operations. Innocent souls could be hurt, Ghomran thought.

"Fire," shouted Ghomran. "Don't get close!"

He ran toward the spot where the fire burned unchallenged. "*Allahu Akbar*," he murmured to himself. "I swear by Allah, by the figs and olives of the Holy Land. *Allahu Akbar*." He stood alone atop the hill, beneath a sprinkling of stars, which could do little to compete with the bright flames.

Ghomran approached the flare, his steps frantic. "How great is the Creator," Ghomran said. He stretched his hand out past the circle of fire. "Nothing will hurt us but what is written by Allah for us." A halo of flame illuminated his forehead. "*Mashallah . . .*"

He caught the well's gauge and felt the pulse, tightening with all his strength. The fire's mouth was wide. Ghomran embraced the burning gauge. He felt as though his body and face were about to melt from the heat. The burning faces of the genies twisted and leered at him before dissolving into the fire. But Ghomran persisted, murmuring prayers to Allah, until finally he managed to shut down the gauge and quench the fire.

Ghomran fell back against a wall, his arms singed. Maybe it was his imagination. Maybe there was no genie, no dark demon of the fire. Suddenly, his consciousness began to recede, and everything turned black with the night.

The next morning the supervisor asked the guard, "We've been having problems with that gas well, but how did it become so dry?"

The guard shrugged and said, "Only God knows."

♦

SU'AD AL-'ARIMI *concentrates on the short-story genre in her writing. She is the author of the collection* Tuful: Qisas *(A Child) (1990).*

Sounds of the Sea

Saud Bulushi

◆

The sun began its silent descent beyond the horizon. Every day at this time, Muhammad, the curly-haired child, came to my small dark room to take me out for a breath of fresh air. Today, he arrived in a rush, grabbed my hand, and pulled me behind him. Holding my cane, I followed, bent over, to the end of the corridor that led to the main door of the house. Then I straightened up and stepped outside. We walked for some time, and he led me to the corner of an old fallen wall. His small hand kept slipping from mine. I held it tightly, but Muhammad pulled his hand away, leaving my big calloused hand to grope in the open space.

I stopped and listened to his small, rapid steps. I followed him from one corner to another until I collided with a palm tree branch that had been tied over the walkway. It provided a narrow spot of shade, which served to cool us momentarily. Searching with my cane for a place to sit, I bumped into a goat. I yelled, making it scramble away, but it soon returned to share with me what remained of the shade. I didn't like having it so close to me. It scratched its back on the stones, and then it butted against the leaning palm tree, urinated, and finally brushed its flea-infested hair on me.

I tried to chase it away again, but it bleated sharply in my face. Soon it was joined by its kids, which butted their small, newly budded horns against me. I gave up and rubbed its forehead to stop it from bothering me.

Little by little, the sun descended in the horizon. The shadows lengthened, and a chill ran through my body. Sleep rippled through me. The neighborhood's whispers drifted like music from the houses. My senses quivered as I listened to the muted sounds coming from the most distant houses: children cried, women sighed, fathers called names. Laughing whispers came from nearby shadows, mingling with the blare of television sets.

Thus I stayed all afternoon, refusing an urge to lay my head down for a nap. Leaves rustled in the trees. Wind blew across small sand barriers that protected the village from the sea's high water. Young lovers met secretly in the shade. Air conditioners hummed as the sea whispered in the distance. All of these sounds flowed through my being like the throbbing of a beating heart.

I went far away to my imaginary land as if I were intoxicated by the joy of a lover's caress dancing before my closed eyes. In my imagination women came from all corners of the neighborhood and gathered around me. Some greeted me respectfully; some got close and tickled my big belly. They made me laugh and wave my cane. Giggling, they dashed away and from a distance asked, "How many goats are around you, oh, uncle? If you know, we will chase them away."

"And if I don't know?"

"Then we will leave them there."

Before I could count the goats, the women vanished. I called them, but they were gone.

I sighed deeply and wondered, "Are these women truly beautiful? And why had they come out to visit me now?" It was still early for their husbands to have left for the mosque. Then I heard the men—they gathered about like a flock of roosters—making lots of noise in their colorful wide *dishdasha*s. At the corner of the wall they greeted each other and then went to pray. None of them turned in my direction.

I sat cross-legged in the terrible heat, waiting for the sea to offer a cool breeze or even a hot and suffocating one, but the villagers stayed cool while they lay in their soft beds, surrounded by colorful walls, their air conditioners pumping cold air. I could do nothing but listen, listen to people, listen to the sheep and the other sounds of the late afternoon siesta, listen to the life of the neighborhood.

From far away I heard the seductive call of the sea, calling me to wash myself in its waters, to cleanse the long years that extend behind me like a trail of smoke, to be cleansed of dry, meaningless senses and days that secretly slipped away from my hands. The sea opened its arms, and its insistent call tried to seduce me. "Leave this old crumbling wall. Leave those goats and your shadow, which grows colder as night advances. Run away from that child who suddenly grabs your hands and pulls you behind him, back to the room that gets narrower when night falls. Close your ears against unanswered questions.

"'Why, my granddad, is your shadow longer than you are?' he will ask. And will you keep repeating to him, 'Because the sun is setting, my son; it is sunset'? Or will you leave all that and come to my salty waters, which are full of life, my warm clear waters that are able to wash away the patina of old age? Will you return to that from which you were born? Or will you remain between that dark room and that old disintegrating wall until the village children grow up and you can no longer find someone who will guide you every day from your room to the wall? Will you come? Will you come?"

The voice of the sea grew more insistent. It came from all directions, as if the sea had surrounded the neighborhood, and its warm, clear waters—brimming with life—filled all the alleys and yards and mixed with the mud walls. Its waters swept over my body. My ailments were healed, my dormant cells rejuvenated. The gray hair that covered my head turned a dark, inky black.

I stood, dropping my cane behind me, and walked away from the wall. I waded into the clear waters. There, around me, were seven *houris*, those heavenly creatures Allah provides for his believers. The first one wrapped my waist with a silken cloth; the second dressed me with a *thobe* washed in perfume; the third crowned my head with a cashmere turban; the fourth pinned to my waist a gold and silver dagger; the fifth put a shawl on my shoulder; the sixth threw perfume on me and placed burning incense by my feet; and the seventh sprinkled my shoes with sweet sandal perfume.

They sat me on the shore, on a chair covered with a green silk shawl. Above me, the seagulls flapped gray tipped wings. Dolphins leaped gracefully from the sea. A procession of fish scattered eastward toward the horizon. As I watched, the sounds of the neighborhood faded like a long-forgotten dream. In its place was a music I'd never heard before. The music of my new life.

◆

SAUD BULUSHI *is active in the Omani Literary Society. He has published numerous short stories.*

The Disaster

Muhammad ibn Sayf Rahabi

◆

Ornate tiles decorated every corner of the wide hall, as if it were the setting for *The Thousand and One Nights.* Seated behind the high table was the *kadi* with his thick white beard and glasses, ready to hear the day's cases. He glared at those who were seated before him for a few moments.

Young Mahmoud stood like a wounded bird among a cluster of hawks.

The *kadi* shook his head and asked, "Why did you steal it?"

"Sir, I did not steal it."

"But there are witnesses who say they saw you steal it!"

"No one saw me steal anything."

"Then why do you suppose they say that?"

"I don't know, sir."

The *kadi* smoothed his bright white robe, leaned back on his big bench, and raised his glasses a bit, examining the boy standing in the witness box.

"It's better if you confess. You've got to be repentant like the rest. Why did you steal it?"

"I didn't steal it," Mahmoud asserted. "Actually, I took it."

A murmur arose among those seated behind the benches.

"What's the difference between stealing and taking?"

Mahmoud was silent.

"Why is your tongue paralyzed? Has truth made you dumb?"

He remained quiet.

The *kadi* turned to the two court clerks, one on his right and the other on his left, who were recording what the accused said. When he was assured that their pens were still writing, he smiled until Mahmoud saw his shiny false teeth. Looking skeptically at the accused, he said,

125

"Whoever steals small things will next try his hand on something bigger. That hand must be removed."

The *kadi* looked as if he wanted to speak again, but he began to cough so hard that he was unable to continue. When he was finished, he looked up with watery eyes and was heaving and breathing heavily.

"But, sir," Mahmoud protested. "You said it was a small thing. Even though the witness described it as a catastrophe!"

"So you're able to talk after all, and eloquently at that! What you've taken is not small, young man. It was very expensive and beautiful."

"But, sir, it was a discarded pen! Tossed in the trash, like a newspaper after it's been read."

The *kadi*'s eyes opened wide. His face turned red, and he could feel his temperature and his blood pressure rising. He wiped his forehead with a perfumed tissue and shouted, "This session's closed!"

SECOND HEARING

Behind the same wooden partition where each defendant took his turn, Mahmoud waited, still as a corpse. Faces watched him, their expressions unreadable. He withdrew deeper into himself. They were all *kadi*s, and he the lone defendant.

One of them opened a thick book and began to pepper him with questions.

"How much do you earn? What are you doing that forced you to steal what belongs to others?"

Mahmoud shifted uncomfortably and asked, "Do you want to know the hours posted on my time sheets, or do you want to know what I actually receive as income?"

Light laughter rippled through the room, followed by a momentary silence.

"Stop being so smart, and just answer! Otherwise it will make things worse for you—"

"Sir, I support three dependents on my salary, which is supposed to be two hundred riyals a week, according to my employment contract."

"So, you're not thankful?"

"Well, sir . . ."

"Do you deny what you've got in your possession now?"

"No."

"Then, you took it after a long period of waiting and watching and plotting?"

"Sir, I took it from the garbage. I took it after it was thrown away."
"Then you admit stealing it?"
Again, the session was closed.

THIRD HEARING

Mahmoud entered his employer's office. He thought of his job as the office tea boy who came every day to bring tea, coffee, papers, and whatever else was needed to the director. Insults often followed him down the office aisles.

When he returned home, his wife consoled him, saying, "Be patient for the sake of your two children."

He kept quiet in front of his wife, but he would tell his boss, "I hope I don't let you down and you'll consider promoting me soon. You've always treated me well. Do you think . . ."

The boss drank his fifth cup of morning coffee. The remains of the preceding four were thrown away like Mahmoud's dignity.

THE SENTENCE

"Justice is required. It is the balance to which all that is in nature submits. I've read your file and heard the statements of the accused. You took what did not belong to you. I've given this much thought. The law requires that whoever dares disturb the peace in which each of us lives shall be punished so there will be no more thieves among us."

Mahmoud stood behind the wooden partition. A cold fear filled him, and his legs slowly spread wider, shaking as if they were the old oars of a ship in a tempest.

The one who was still reading said, "When the accused stole the pen of the director, he committed a terrible crime against justice. We find him guilty."

Moments later the wooden partition was empty.

Moments later it was filled by someone else.

◆

MUHAMMAD IBN SAYF RAHABI *is an active member of the Writers' Society. He has published numerous short stories.*

The White Dog

Sulayman al-Ma'mami

—◆—

I woke, and as I did, a long list of troubles flooded my consciousness. I was still in bed when the sight of the calendar hanging near the bed jolted me to reality. It was the twenty-seventh of April, a date to add to the pile of days under which I was buried. It was an important day, no doubt. I didn't draw a red circle on the calendar unless there was a reason. It was not my birthday. What day was it?

When she left me, I was ready to die, to breathe my last breath from my bed. Days meant nothing, hours and minutes even less. Only the memory of the dog I ran over the day before still troubled me. It occupied my thoughts and wouldn't go away. It was not because the dog was dead, but because it was white; it was fresher than the clean rays of sunlight in the morning. When I hit it, when I struck the poor creature down, I was on my way to buy a wedding bed. Now that bed serves only to remind me of my failure.

Nassrin was the reason for my despair. Once I told her she was like a candle lighting the night sky, a piece of the moon that flashed through the heavens as it descended the horizon. But I lost her; she evaporated like an innocent dream. I tried to bolster my confidence. I told myself, "Come on, you idiot, you'll continue to be a faithful brother and a good friend to those who care about you." I was upset. I swore by the Creator that I would not sleep except in my new bed. It didn't matter that it was for our betrothal.

That day, I left the house with a host of demons inside my head. I drove my car as fast as I could. Along the way I thought of Nassrin, who was just steps away from becoming my wife when she changed her mind. It was like another stole her from me. She adored romantic figures like the legendary Antar Bin Shadad, whose poetry she memorized. It was as if she thought they were written for her.

She even began to write lines of verse herself. There was one she called, "The Last Moments." I asked her to recite the poem to me, but she said, "No, my poem is for Antar. No one will hear it except him; it's meant for him alone!"

I must have shattered her dreams when I told her that Antar belonged to another time. I wish I hadn't said that because that was when she left me and disappeared in an imaginary world where the past was alive and she could be with Antar Bin Shadad. She left me, sad and confused in a wedding bed that now mocked my loneliness.

These were the thoughts in my head when the white dog leaped out of nowhere. I couldn't avoid hitting it. My car plowed over the animal, crushing its bones beneath my tires. I stepped out of the car and found the creature covered in a pool of blood with tears streaming from its eyes. I was terrified at the sight of the creature snarling as if it were challenging me. I was even more scared when I recalled that I was driving without a license. I left quickly, before anyone came. Driving away I could hear a scornful, mocking voice in my head saying, "Didn't I tell you that you'd always lose?"

I took two sleeping pills that night . . .

Now I'd awoken to find that it's the twenty-seventh of April, a day of obvious portent, though I knew not of what. I sat up in bed and looked at the calendar. I read what was written in small letters inside the red circle, "An appointment with a dancing teacher." When had I arranged that? I couldn't remember.

Never mind, I told myself. I would not lose the opportunity I had just because I did not pay enough attention.

I dressed and drove over to the address I'd written down. There I found the woman.

She said, "Let's begin our first lesson."

I said, "Yes, let's."

"But you look sad."

"You look happy. We're like two opposite poles attracting each other, as they say in physics."

She was not really happy. Sadness circled her beautiful brown eyes. It was the sort of sadness that wanted to say something but didn't and therefore spoke volumes. She was beautiful. Perhaps she was even more beautiful than Nassrin, but not quite as striking. What was the secret of a woman's beauty that so completely seduces men? Are men the weaker creatures? Why do we willingly fall captive? The sun, the sea, the woman—every movement has its own seductive pattern.

She stood. It was time for our first dance.

She stood, and fear consumed me. The music of Tchaikovsky flooded the room.

"Woof, woof, woof."

I knew it was not the real barking of dogs, but an echo of that tortured moment replaying itself in my mind. I looked at this woman who had her hands on my shoulders. I saw her as if for the first time. Yes, I thought. Now I knew her. I'd seen her, heard of her, perhaps read about her. I tried to remove any lingering doubt by listening to what she was saying.

"You didn't tell me your name," I said.

"Then why don't you ask me?"

"I believe I've seen you before."

"I don't think I've seen you before."

"Why don't you think so?"

"Because I'm Abla."

"Abla who?"

"Abla bint Malek."

"Antar's love?" I asked.

"Yes, Antar's love."

"And what about now?"

"He has found a new love. Her name is Nassrin."

"And you?"

"I've survived by moving here, enjoying my time as a teacher."

Oh, God, she was wounded, too. Antar was stolen from her, as he stole Nassrin from me. What time did he live in now? Antar's time or mine?

"Woof, woof, woof."

What if it were real barking? How was it that I had not entertained this possibility before? Perhaps the clan of the white dog has come to seek revenge, or blood money, or to solicit condolences. What would I do now?

"What's the matter with you?" she asked. "You've stiffened like a fish grilled on its back."

"Nothing. Just wait for me to open the window. Perhaps some fresh air will come through." I looked in the yard outside to see where the barking was coming from. Oh, Lord of the Skies, the barking is real! What can I do?

"What's wrong?" she asked. When she laid her hand on my arm it was as though the most fragile piece of silk had been draped there. "Why are you trembling?"

"He's coming to kill me as I killed him."

"Who?"

"The white dog."

"You mean the barking outside? Don't worry. I'll get it to go away, right now. I have a lot of experience dealing with dogs. Don't be afraid. I'll chase it away. Wait and see."

Abla left, and I stood frozen in front of the window. I watched her walk across the yard. Then I saw a white dog follow. They walked side by side until they disappeared.

I returned to my seat in the dining room. An hour passed, but Abla didn't return. Another hour passed, then a third. When the bright rays of the sun came through the window I was certain that Abla would never return. I stood up like someone who had lost his mind and looked around the room. Maybe I'd find something she forgot. Maybe I'd find her handbag or a wallet with her address inside. As my sight dropped by mistake to her bed, I looked away immediately.

She was not there, I thought.

She would never be there.

◆

SULAYMAN AL-MA'MAMI, *author of numerous short stories, publishes his stories in Oman's newspapers.*

United Arab Emirates

The Plight

'Abd al-Hamid Ahmad

◆

That day there was no delivery of the morning newspaper. For the first time in its history, Rehima Dikkan—a small, lazy mountain village—sold out all its papers within less than an hour. Buyers came from not only the Egyptian community but other nearby villages as well. Some were illiterate citizens, and some could read and write only in Arabic.

Walia Browail, the owner of the small grocery store that distributed the paper, was stunned when he opened the paper and saw on the front page a photograph of someone he knew very well. His heart beat quicker as he stared at the picture; he could not believe what he saw. He began to read the article and as he read a smile spread across his face. By the time he'd finished, his surprise had vanished and his smile had grown wider until a low laugh emerged, shaking his round belly.

The news spread to all the readers from Egypt, including laborers and domestic servants. The entire region buzzed with speculation about Khalfan Al-Battran and what he had done. They spoke of "his plight." A steady flow of local servants and citizens came to Walia Browail's store, asking for copies of the newspaper. He smiled at each one and said, "Sorry, there are no more papers." And then he asked each of them, "Do you know why Khalfan got himself into this trouble?"

The news created quite a stir, especially among those who knew Khalfan well. People who couldn't read or understand the language sought the help of others who did. The article was passed about, read, and translated. Everyone knew the news. Those who didn't know Khalfan started to ask questions about him and his past, to discover his secrets. In just a day, Khalfan was transformed into a new being, one who deserved all their attention and curiosity. Khalfan used to live a quiet life. Then his picture appeared on the front page, with his white beard, his deep-set eyes, and skinny face. By his side was a small, perplexed-looking young girl. Her eyes said nothing, as though they were made of cold glass. His picture, which had never appeared in any newspaper, was now being widely circulated. The gossip was not limited to the plight that had befallen him. Tongues wagged for a week after the infamous day when Walia sold all his papers.

Ubaid Al Fattan sat in his living room, passing small cups of tea to his friends. "Khalfan told me he was traveling to Egypt two weeks ago for medical treatment. But . . ." Ubaid raised his eyebrows and asked his listeners, "What in the world made him decide to get married?"

Mohyddin, Ubaid's tea boy, replied, "It doesn't matter what inspired him. The fact remains that he married an underage girl. That's why they put him in jail."

Ubaid laughed as he envisioned his elderly neighbor behind bars. Another neighbor, Hammad, who could never hide the fact that he envied Khalfan, asserted, "This is the price for being rich. He was just a poor fisherman who became wealthy from playing the stock market! He deserves what he gets."

Ubaid responded, "His wealth was given to him by Allah. Why are you jealous of the man?"

Hammad answered angrily, "Allah's gifts shouldn't make one arrogant or wanton. He sold some land and invested his money. So he became rich overnight, and now he's respected by everyone in the community. He can't even read!" Then he added, "Stupid fisherman. Look how his new status made him a big man; that's why he became so arrogant." Hammad continued abusing the man, and finished with, "And he's married four wives. We couldn't do that. Then on top of that, he marries a fifteen-year-old girl. She is younger than his youngest daughter!"

"And that's why he's in prison," added Mohyddin. "It's forbidden by Egyptian law."

For weeks the women villagers found no news more important than Khalfan and his plight. Some even sent their servants to Walia Browail to get further details.

Walia told them, "During the questioning by the police, he said he didn't go to Cairo in search of a wife because he was worried he would be recognized by Arab friends, so he went to a remote village near Luxor. That's where he got married."

Walia added, "Khalfan insisted that he wanted a very young wife. The village people agreed. Perhaps they didn't know the law, or else they figured it wouldn't affect them. These villagers are good at keeping their secrets! So they agreed and gave him Badshah's daughter, but it was quickly discovered. The police questioned Khalfan and charged him. It's against the law to marry someone younger than sixteen years old."

Walia's friends said, "This is a scandal. It doesn't matter that Khalfan agreed to divorce the girl. It didn't keep him out of jail. He has stated over and over that he went for medical treatment and not to get married, yet he got married anyway."

Batheet Ben Hindi, a merchant, replied, "It's true. Khalfan was depressed. He really did go for treatment. But the one who suggested that Khalfan go there is Said, son of Hummad Al-Khateel! He teased him! 'Oh, Khalfan,' he said. 'There is no better treatment than marrying a very young girl. She will open up your heart!'"

When Said was asked if this was true, he protested. "But I was just joking with him. I didn't know he would take my advice seriously!"

In an accusatory tone, Ubaid joined the conversation, "You know how much Khalfan loves women!"

Despite the initial frenzy of gossip that spread about Khalfan for days after the publication of the paper, the news cooled and lost its luster. Soon it vanished altogether when a new scandal appeared: the police came to Walia's store and took him away. He was frightened and in disbelief. He kept shouting, "What did I do?" The police said, "Khalfan's family has filed a complaint against you. They accuse you of distributing false rumors against their father. That is defamation!"

They threw Walia in jail. He called his boss, the owner of the grocery store, and waited for him to come get him, to help him out of his own plight. A plight for which Khalfan was to blame. He didn't know what to do. Should he continue laughing as he had laughed when he first saw Khalfan's photo on the front page of the newspaper, or should he cry now, as he was there alone with no one coming to his defense? He didn't know that Khalfan had the same dilemma! He could neither laugh nor cry. As Walia waited for his boss to free him from his cell, Khalfan too waited in his cell, counting the hours and wishing that his government, his friends, someone, would intervene to set him free!

♦

'ABD AL-HAMID AHMAD *is an active member of the UAE Writers' Union. His fiction reflects the modern-day dilemmas confronted by Emiratis. He is the author of three collections and a novel.*

An Idyllic World

Muhammad al-Murr

◆

I woke up suddenly at eight thirty-five in the morning. Oh, God, I thought, I'm late for work. It would be the first time I was late since I started my job. I dressed in a hurry and dashed out the door, thinking of a lie, a believable one that I could offer as an excuse to the manager. I imagined his angry face, flames coming out of his eyes, his huge physique and big nose. I imagined him kicking me out of his office, firing me from work, from life. As I went out the door, I became aware of something strange.

There was nobody in the street but me. No pedestrians. All the stores were open, but there was no one in them. Where did all the people go? I looked in every direction, but nothing moved. There was no noise, no shouts. There were no cars. Even the dogs and cats had disappeared. The streets were empty. What had happened?

Had the day of resurrection come and gone? And if it had, why then was the world not upside down, and why did I alone remain?

A pain seized my body. I felt lonely and alienated. I was about to cry. Where would I eat, drink? How would I live? I could not ignore the downward spiral of my terrible thoughts until I entered the first restaurant on my way. There was no one in it. I waited, with trepidation, for a waiter to come and ask me what I wanted. But no one came. I walked into the kitchen, quenched my thirst, and took a breakfast roll. I was about to leave without paying for it, but then I was afraid, so I looked at the menu and left some coins. Then I went to the tobacco store where I took cigarettes with shaking hands, left the price, and walked away, astonished. My mind was numb. The same question kept running through my head, "What's going on?"

I approached the building where I work and searched for the guard, but it seemed he too had gone with all the rest. It did not matter, since the gate was open. But did they still need an experienced accountant who had spent long years of his life with his eyes trained on numbers? If they did not need one, I would not stay even one hour. I entered my office and began to go through my files and papers. I walked into the other offices. I hoped to find a note from a colleague, but I searched in vain. Even my closest colleagues had forgotten about me. Even Abdullah, Sulayman—all of them—had forgotten me, all of them had forgotten the days we spent together, forgotten our cama-raderie. What a wicked group they were! They feared for their positions there, even the manager. I have said life is upside down. Yes, I've said that . . .

Perhaps another world will come, I thought. Inhabited by new people.

But the new world would be a world without knowledge, without civilization, without experience.

No, I decided. It will not be without knowledge or civilization, maybe only without experience. That was not as important.

What about the salaries? Current salaries were not enough . . .

I decided to double the salaries, and let the salary of the accountant also be doubled, for I would have much to do.

But what about the manager's salary? Should he get a raise too?

It is simple. I will satisfy myself and the accountant and will not increase the other employees' salaries.

You're very smart, that is very correct, I said to myself.

So how will this coming world look? What will people look like?

Most probably they will be short, with ugly round faces and small noses. They will have innocence in their eyes and their souls will be clean. They will be new souls, no hate, no envy, and no ambitions.

But how will that be so? Souls transfer from the departing to the arriving. They will inherit the souls of those who have departed.

No, everyone who inherited a devilish soul will be fired from work, expelled from the city.

Who will expel them from the city? You're not the governor. Where is the governor? If there's no governor, then you will be the governor.

I asked myself, then who will be the manager?

Of course it will be you. You alone have enough experience in this company. It is you who will decide its fate. Be brave—don't lose confidence in yourself.

But where would I find employees and accountants who have experience? That means I've become the manager and the governor.

Yes, you're the manager and the governor.

But where are the others? Where are your subjects? Where are those short people? They are very late!

Perhaps they have come. Maybe they are outside, dispersed in the street and in the city . . .

Then I must go find them.

I went out, but there was no one outside. I shouted, ran, tore off my clothes, maybe that would draw someone's attention.

Draw their attention. Whose attention? You're the manager and the governor. How stupid, to draw the attention of those little people in your new world.

You ants. I am the manager and the governor. I am the one who is in command here. I will teach you a lesson. You will not behave like your cowardly forefathers. I will make you feel the pain of others. I will make you change your selfish and egotistical ways. I will teach you new philosophies molded out of my experience. You will teach these to future generations.

You deformed dwarfs. I'm the envoy who is bringing you what is good. I am the manager and the governor. I am everything here!

Suddenly, a soft voice interrupted my speech, "What's happening? Why are you shouting?"

"I am not shouting. No, I am not shouting like some crazy person."

"I know that you're not crazy, but you were having a terrible dream."

"Oh! I remember; it was a wonderful dream."

"Oh, come on. Beautiful dreams don't get anything accomplished. It's seven thirty, come on, wake up."

"But why?"

"And you ask why? To go to work."

"Which work?"

"Did you forget, damn it, your work?"

"I did not forget my work, but I was fired yesterday."

"Fired, but how? Who fired you?"

"Yes, I was fired. The manager fired me. What a stupid man. Can you believe that I didn't do anything wrong but ask for a raise for myself and my cowardly colleagues? I said that otherwise we would strike. Don't worry, my love, I know how sweet revenge is. I will find a manager's job that pays a manager's salary."

◆

MUHAMMAD AL-MURR, *a prolific member of the UAE Writers'*
Union, is the author of some fifteen collections of short stories. Among
those published in English are Dubai Tales *(1991) and* Wink of the
Mona Lisa and Other Stories from the Gulf *(1994).*

Surprise at the Airport

Asma' al-Zar'uni

◆

I squinted through the glare of the bus window and was surprised to see a long line at one of the airport gates. A deep sigh escaped my lips as I thought about our upcoming trip and the long hours that my children and I would have to endure traveling home to Dubai. It was all I could do to bear the longing and yearning to be back. I had been away for two months and even though I enjoyed traveling in the United States, my feeling of homesickness overrode everything else. It was time to return home.

As we descended from the bus, a light drizzle bid us a fond farewell. I tried to fill my eyes with the lush scenery before leaving it behind for the glass and steel of the interior of the airport. Suddenly, I heard my husband's rising voice, "This is exploitation! How dare you try to take advantage of us?"

"What's going on?" I asked.

"Can you believe he wants fifty dollars for that short trip from the hotel? That's robbery!"

"It's not a big deal. After all it is our last day here," I gently reminded him.

"This always happens whenever we travel abroad. People think that every person from the Gulf owns an oil well."

I smiled and responded, "The sad thing is that they really believe it. I had a clerk tell me so when I was shopping."

My husband and I collected our luggage. He urged me to hurry when he saw the long line waiting for us in the hall. When we reached the ticketing desk, he went to check in our bags. I searched for a place to sit. It was crowded everywhere. There was an old woman hugging her young son while she dried her tears. A small girl with curly blonde hair was being warmly cuddled by her mother who was leaving.

The girl admonished her mother as she said, "Mommy, don't be too late. And don't forget to bring me a doll and a red dress."

The woman hugged her sadly. Next to her was an old man, with a dense cloud of cigarette smoke forming above his head. How many packs of cigarettes had he smoked today? I wondered.

I was still waiting for my husband. While I was inspecting the faces, I saw a tall dark man, nearly forty years old, holding a baby girl in his arms and another child by the hand. He was looking everywhere, as if he had lost something. His brow was creased into a perplexed frown and he seemed indecisive. When his eyes met mine, he moved like he wanted to walk toward me, but then hesitated. He was waiting for a sign from me to start talking. I wondered what was wrong. An inner urge over-whelmed me and I felt compelled to say something.

"May I help you?"

He walked toward me like a drowning man heads toward land.

"Yes, please help me."

I was surprised. What kind of help could he need? Then I felt con-fused. What if my husband saw me speaking to a stranger—a man? I ignored all this, and unable to contain my curiosity asked him, "What do you want?"

"Not much. But could you watch my two children while I finish checking in with the airlines?"

I was amazed. Why would he leave his children with a stranger? Where was his wife? What was going on? However, he didn't give me time to ask any questions for he left the two children and promptly walked away. I was stunned. The unanswered questions still spun in my head.

The baby started to cry. I played with her and when she did not stop, I looked in the diaper bag for some food. I found a bottle of milk and some candy. I put the baby on my lap and gave her the milk. My daughter played with the other child, who stayed quiet most of the time. The whole time I kept my eyes on the man so that he did not disappear. He was at the pay phone talking loudly to someone in Arabic; it sounded like he was from the Gulf. I tried to eavesdrop. "Mother, I am bringing the children back with me. Please meet me at the airport."

I turned away so he could not tell I had overheard. I was burning inside with curiosity. What was going on? I watched his children for about an hour. My husband was now at the front of the line. My eyes were exhausted from the effort of looking in both directions, that of my husband and the stranger. I was wondering who would make it back first. What if my husband came first? What would I do with the chil-dren? What would I tell him?

My throat was tight with anxiety. Then, when I saw the man approach with a smile on his face, a rush of calm spread through my body.

"Thanks for helping. I will take the kids now."

I could no longer contain the questions buzzing in my head. "I am confused. What's going on with the two children? Why—"

"They are my kids," he answered, cutting off the rest of my question. "I know you want to ask concerning their mother. And now I can tell you since I will be boarding the plane in a few minutes. My wife is from the States. We had the children in Dubai but she now refuses to return with me. She told me she doesn't want to live there and according to American laws, custody would go to the mother. But I don't want them brought up here. So I told her I am taking the kids for a walk, and came to the airport instead." He said this as he started heading toward the plane.

I sat down, stunned. The enormity of what he was doing penetrated my consciousness. How could I have been duped so easily into helping this man? Then I slipped deep into thought, replaying the events in my head. Finally, my husband came to wake me from my reverie. I kept thinking, "That poor woman, how could she endure the loss of her children?"

◆

ASMA' AL-ZAR'UNI, *who has published both fiction and poetry, is vice president of the UAE Women Writers' Union.*

A Bouquet of Jasmine

'Abd al-Ilah 'Abd al-Qadir

—◆—

The sounds within the plane bother her. Fatigue from flying makes her unable to move from her seat. She doesn't know why, but she feels a premonition that something will happen today. The last time Zayed called, he told her that he would be in the hospital, but he didn't tell her why. Then she was surprised yesterday by the handwritten fax he sent her at work:

> I'm afraid . . . maybe it's my time . . . my fate.
> I believe strongly in the cruelty of illness.
> If you don't find me put a jasmine in my place

Since she met him, her life had changed drastically. She felt deep changes resonate through her being, unlike her earlier experience with her first husband. But in a short period of time, merely months, she was able to erase all the details of her previous life and start over with one full of love, kindness, and warmth. She loved everything about Zayed, but she was still afraid of the future.

Although thousands of seconds separate her from him, he is with her every minute, he calls her every hour, sees her every month. But she didn't expect to feel so anxious. She is even more worried when she rushes to see him. She is afraid of traveling. Then the hour of separation, the moment of meeting each other again and adjusting to the moment. Conflicted feelings jumble together in her mind about what is around her, her life, her daughters, her work, and the joy and fear felt with a sense of déjà vu. The mixed emotions she feels between each trip. Her desire to see him dominates everything else and coalesces within her. She cries his name softly.

Zayed too waits longingly to see her. His days become days of waiting and expecting. He spent fifty years in cafés of Arab cities and experienced the strangeness of other countries. But he did not encounter

145

love! Maybe there were moments of love that passed by, maybe he felt attracted to some women who tried to open his feelings, but none of them were able to enter his world.

The hand on his watch hung in the middle.

Tick . . . tick . . . tick . . .

Time bothered him a lot—actually it was killing him.

Tick . . . tick . . . tick . . .

But he will continue looking for her, waiting for the watch to signal her arrival.

She came closer to him, surrendering, *Oh! If only I could live my life by his side.* Calling him every hour and he would write to her notes of love. *I've bargained with the little ones, my children, to sell me half their lives to stay with him, but not too quickly.*

"Before knowing your secret, to know my secret, when will you feel safe?" This is what he will say whenever he writes her.

She had run as fast as possible to reach the plane, to make the trip to him. She wanted the distance between them to shrink, the cities to disappear. She was afraid he might get lost in the crowds.

Zayed is fearful that time will catch up with him. He obliterates all signs of the past—places, cities, and time, whenever he's with her. There are many reasons that they cannot live together. They met each other at the wrong time, in the lost time. He can't be anyone other than who he is, she can't be other than herself. There are others who are tied to them, need them, and are more important than their emotions and feelings and their need of each other.

Today she realizes how necessary it is for her to be by his side. He is in intensive care. He was able to conceal his illness but was obliged to write her about the matter.

I'm in my last station.

I'll always wait for you.

Night has finished, morning comes.

Many nights and mornings came and left but you showed up.

She reread all his letters as she was seated in the plane on its way to him. He loved roses, he loved good news for people, how animated was his style of talking. How much she loved what he loved.

The plane landed. Deplaning, her fear increased. She felt for the first time the emptiness that he would not be waiting for her at the airport . . . and the fear that she has to rush directly toward the hospital.

When she arrived at the hospital, his bed was empty. The room smelled of medicinal cleaning liquids.

She put a bouquet of jasmine over his pillow and wept.

◆

'ABD AL-ILAH 'ABD AL-QADIR *has published numerous short stories. He is an active member of the UAE Writers' Union.*

Bahrain

That Winter

Muhammad 'Abd al-Malik

◆

That winter came heavy, unwanted. The sky was loaded with clouds, and the earth plotted against us. Its black dusty troops awaited the moment of rain. The clouds in the sky gathered together like black smoke.

Auntie Norah looked toward the heavens. She stretched her hand toward the land she had worked for most of her forty years.

"Look," she smiled, and her blue nose ring flashed. "God's water." Around us the neighbors' houses, made of palm fronds, sat in an eerie silence, as if awaiting the inevitable terrible moment. The sky thundered and its black brow broke up in the faraway heights. I heard her pronounce her faith: "How great is Allah! God is great! Even thunder prays to the Lord!"

Then she closed her eyes. Thunder cracked. Allah sent the rain. My grandfather's house was near the sea, the sea that we'd bathed in since childhood. I walked out and washed my face in the rain. Auntie laughed and brought me a towel to dry myself.

The rain fell strong and brave. I heard its steady rhythm as it hit the ground around me. We, the children, started running in the alley. We were very young, innocent, barefoot and poor, singing for the rain:

"Oh, Lord, make it rain harder."

"Oh, Lord, be merciful to your creatures."

It was a time of childhood that would not come back. We were so happy—a happiness that belonged only to the very young. That winter, however, happiness, clarity, and light were absent from Auntie's face. Her cheeks appeared hollow under her eyes, like the columns of ancient ruins in a country road surrounded by open space. She took care of us, without dwelling on the past, on how things could have been. This she only mentioned sadly sometimes.

Auntie always worked hard. She woke at dawn and just before the sun rose in the horizon, in that moment when the night is still alive. She would walk out barefoot, like all the women of the neighborhood, and bring us milk from Abu Khalil's cow. Then we would wake to the sound of her singing; its tune still lingers in my memory: "Wake up for the stranger who throws the apples. The eyes do not weep but for the kiss of a lover . . ."

♦ ♦ ♦

In the evening, we sat in a circle around the fire—we sat close, seeking the heat. She passed out cups of ginger tea with her hard, calloused hand. As the thunder cracked over our palm frond ceiling, it began to rain hard. The ceiling trembled, sending us to fearfully huddle closer to each other. A feeling of isolation from this world surrounded us. We felt that people lived far away from us, that Allah was angry in the distant sky, that something in this universe needed to be changed. When she told us stories of the thunder, her angelic face comforted us. We felt warm and safe. Around us the rain fell through holes in the roof.

That winter, Auntie grew thin. In the beginning I did not pay much attention. Her skin turned yellow and her lips became dry and dirtlike in color. That winter was a sad one. The rains finally left us, as though the sky was tired of weeping. The clouds hurriedly left the north. Inside our hut, my Auntie slept with her hands as a pillow under her head, as is the habit of the poor. She covered her head with a black scarf, with her eyes turned to the sky. She breathed heavily and sighed like a sad song. I could see that she was suffering. I drew closer to her face as she whispered in a feverish voice, "Don't worry son, it's only a fever. Soon it will disappear!"

But I was worried about the "fever" and started to cry like a baby. When she hugged me, I felt how small and fragile her bones were. Her body was hot as fire under her black *abayah*, as if she had become a young woman again. As she held me close to ease my worries, I felt the love of motherhood in her breast. I realized that it could be her last moment. She was crying. I jumped to my feet and picked her up, draping the upper half of her body over mine. She reiterated, "Recovery is from Allah. Where are you taking me, son?"

"To the hospital, Auntie."

Like two strangers entering a strange city, we approached the hospital. Nothing around us seemed normal; even the people were not normal. I was like somebody searching, someone lost. I covered the two miles on foot. In the middle of the road Auntie lost her senses and started to rave.

The terrible specter of death never left us on that road. At al-Sulmaniah Hospital, I walked barefoot on an unfamiliar marble floor. We clung to each other, her head on my shoulder. In a small room we were stopped by somebody begging for charity or bread from passersby. There I learned how the poor stand like dogs in the clean buildings.

We were met by a young physician who wasn't very welcoming. Though there was an empty chair, she did not offer it to us. She kept silent and we did too, out of shyness. Then the physician coldly asked me how things were. I wanted to shout or do something. To jump in the air. Yell. Hit the wall. I felt helpless. I hated all those people dressed in white overcoats. I felt a crime was taking place in front of me, and all those around me were participating in this crime. Before she even bothered to ask me about Auntie, I felt that she had decided to let her die.

My aunt suddenly fainted and went limp in my arms. My heart froze as she began to slide from my arms toward the marble floor, weightless as a piece of cloth. Looking up at the doctor, my pain-filled eyes welled with tears. Then and only then, did the doctor order a wheelchair.

♦ ♦ ♦

Winter fled in a hurry. The clouds left the skies. Auntie was still in the hospital sick with malnutrition and tuberculosis.

Over and over she said, "Take me there." I knew what she meant. "There" where she grew up. "There" was her home, where she wanted to die.

I buried my head in her chest, but I did not hear her sweet, warm voice, that voice begetting love and giving. I saw her disappearing into the white sheets, with her stony gray lips and white chapped skin.

I could not allow her to die here, in this cold place with the people who turned their faces away from us in disgust. I lifted my Auntie from the wheelchair, taking her into my arms like a baby. The doctor protested, but I ignored her. I carried my Auntie back through the long, cold hospital corridors, then out through the door to begin the long walk home.

On the way back to the village, she died. I felt the life leave her body and she went limp and became heavy in my arms, like a sack of grain. I wanted to put her down, to say a prayer over her body, but I continued to walk. As we approached the village, people saw us and began to gather around. They walked with me, offering their sympathy and prayers.

When we reached the courtyard, I knelt and lay my Auntie gently on the ground under the great palm tree. Here she could rest peacefully, amid people who cared about her, about the fact that she had once been alive.

A wind ruffled the top of the palm. She had sat in its shade when she was alive, stitching our clothes and singing. Now my Auntie Norah was dead, but still alive to those who cared about her. Women filled our house, beating their chests and weeping. Her friends embraced me sadly and said, with tears running down their faces, "She was very kind."

I sat without tears, my hands at my side. I looked at these old women, my aunt's friends, and hoped that when their time came, they would have someone like me who could carry them back home.

◆

MUHAMMAD 'ABD AL-MALIK *writes regularly for the Bahrain Writers and Literary Association. He has published numerous short stories.*

Al-Assadiah

Hasan 'Isa al-Mahrus

---◆---

It was an unforgettable day in the life of al-Na'eem neighborhood, as the people of the quarter gathered, expecting a miracle. It was a known fact that the punishment of Allah would befall whoever wanted to cut down the big *sidr* tree, called al-Assadiah, which grew in the middle of the square.

Skeptics muttered under their breath, "This is merely the talk of gossiping women; I swear nothing will come of it . . ."

Others yet responded, "May the Almighty stop those who would delay Allah's will."

Al-Assadiah was a massive tree that dominated the square. It was so ancient that only its upper branches were green; its middle was gray and withered. The lower part, however, that closest to the ground, had the fragrance of *'ud bakhoor*, the spicy incense that locals combined with rose water and poured on its bark. The gray surface of the bark was polished smooth from the many hands that rubbed it as the inhabitants reverently came to touch it, smell it, and kiss it.

The children were not forbidden to climb the tree. In fact, they scrambled up on it and played around it every day. But if anyone were to try to harm al-Assadiah, it was considered a gross sin. Whoever dared such an atrocity would be punished by God. People came from everywhere to visit it. They came in large groups like the devout who make the pilgrimage during the grand *hajj*. There were even sacrifices made near it. People would approach the tree and recite prayers for happiness or success in business or with schoolwork.

Near al-Assadiah, there were three tall palm trees where Sayyid Hassan kept his donkey and wooden cart. Sayyid would relate to anyone who would listen the strange story, where one time he awoke to find his donkey erratically moving around in circles. If he didn't know any better, he'd say that while he was asleep at night, some bastards gave his donkey liquor to drink! How else could he explain his donkey's madness?

155

The tree was special for the local women who believed greatly in al-Assadiah's power to bless them, particularly when their time for bearing children was near. When a neighborhood woman was about to give birth, it was customary that she bring locally made sweets and a traditional dish known as *rushouf*. This specialty dish, usually cooked for pregnant mothers, was enjoyed by many, but especially by the children who would eat it with their fingers. Some women would add coins to the *rushouf* plate for an additional blessing.

Very few would venture close to the tree at night when shadows gave it an eerie presence. Even Sayyed's donkey, when it innocently twitched its ear in its sleep, looked scary. The tree's location close to the graveyard only added to the villagers' apprehension. One of the women said she once heard al-Assadiah moaning at night. The next morning, when she went to the tree, she found marks where a saw had cut into its trunk. There were drops of blood on the ground. Women said whoever cut at the tree must have injured himself and deserved God's punishment.

"The evildoer wanted God's punishment to fall on us!"

"We pray that the evildoer will not even complete this day alive."

"They forgot what blessings the tree bestowed on them."

"May Allah curse any who doubt the blessings of al-Assadiah."

Days passed and sight of the open wound from the saw continued to make the hearts of the women ache. The injury on the tree became an unforgettable story that they repeated to everyone. Whenever they would pass its way, the women would kiss the wound in the trunk and pray for it to heal quickly.

Then one day, the day the women had hoped would never come, a man from the neighborhood passed word that something bad would happen to the tree. The news spread like wildfire throughout the village.

"The landowner is planning to build a new villa in place of al-Assadiah."

"Where al-Assadiah is? What? . . . How could they?"

"Al-Assadiah itself?"

"It's impossible! That's not fair! May Allah curse them!"

"May Allah curse any who doubt the blessings of al-Assadiah."

Within the neighborhood, there was a wall of silence born of shock as the women tried to absorb the news. Many did not believe it. Many even could not sleep that night. The women had faith that a miracle would take place, a disaster, and even more fittingly—a severe punishment for whoever dared to cut down the tree. The news was authenticated when a big truck pulled up in a plume of dust near the tree. Three Filipino workers stepped off the truck, while nearby a new shiny black car pulled into the square. The landowner, dressed in a fresh white *thobe*, appeared. He looked disoriented, confused.

The news spread. Women gathered quickly at a distance. Some observed the event from latticed windows overlooking the mob of people crowding around al-Assadiah. The women shouted abuses at the Filipinos. The Filipinos were surprised, and as the noise from the crowd became louder they began to tremble fearfully. Suddenly, one woman, then another started to throw stones at them. When the Filipinos turned to bolt, the landowner shouted, ordering them to stay in their place. The women responded angrily:

"May Allah kill them so they'll never come back again!"

"May Allah curse these men."

"May He also curse those who came here at night."

"No one can cut down al-Assadiah, no matter how hard they try!"

"May Allah curse any who doubts the blessings of al-Assadiah."

The children were happy, waiting for the green branches that they were never able to reach to fall to the ground. It would be the first time ever that green branches from the upper part of the tree had fallen down.

The noise calmed suddenly when a Filipino worker wrapped the trunk several times with a thick rope and tied the end to the back of the truck. A young woman ran between the truck and the tree, trying to interfere, to stop the sinful act. But the Filipino ignored her and carried on. He climbed in the truck and turned on the noisy ignition. Suddenly, everyone watched intently as they witnessed the miracle, the punishment, the curse of this heinous deed. Faces reddened in grief, some women turned fearfully away, while a pregnant one fainted. The truck rocked forward, the rope tightened, the truck's wheels turned quickly, but the truck stood still; it didn't budge. The driver accelerated, grating hard on the pavement, but the truck still did not move. Prayers and curses filled the square. Some believed even more in the sacred nature of al-Assadiah, while others could not decide. The driver changed his plan. He added a heavy chain to the rope and accelerated. The front of the truck was raised from the ground, the wheels spinning in open air, the motor groaning loudly. Everyone saw thick smoke coming from the motor. Then suddenly, there was silence! The engine had burned out!

The women believed it was the mystical power of al-Assadiah that had done it.

Now, prayers grew louder, clearer, and more demanding. As the Filipinos left the scene, people rushed toward the blessed tree; they kissed it, women wept at its side, people touched their faces to it. Some women sadly asked forgiveness from it. An old woman timidly touched the rope and the iron chain. She thought that al-Assadiah was feeling the pain when she put her fingers at the place where the rope had scraped its trunk. Young men touched the tree for its blessing. Some green leaves had fallen to the ground. Soon these were collected, boiled, and everyone drank the water. What remained from the leaves was used to clean the eyes of the elders. Many sacrifices were promised. News spread concerning the rewards and punishments of the evildoers:

"The truck driver was burnt from the inside," one surmised.

"The landowner was cursed," another guessed.

"A heavenly light appeared and it punished the driver," a third added.

"The roots of al-Assadiah became like swords that stabbed the driver's legs."

"A light came out of al-Assadiah, killing the driver and burning the truck."

"May Allah curse any who doubt the blessings of al-Assadiah."

Two days later, the landowner returned with a bulldozer. This time he looked afraid, agitated. The cigarette dropping ash from his hand looked like a wad of several cigarettes stuck together. People had already gathered to pay homage to the tree that day. They were confident that the landowner would fail once again. Prayers were continuous. The miracle today would be even greater; the belief among the women was very strong. The punishment today would be even greater on the daring worker. None objected, none doubted. The curse would fall on the evildoer. The tree would defend itself as it did before.

The driver walked out and sized up al-Assadiah. He looked attentively at its enormous trunk and again at its surroundings.

"That driver's crazy!"

He jumped into the bulldozer, turned on the ignition, and advanced toward al-Assadiah. He slammed its withered trunk from several angles. As the hearts of the women began to ache, they began to softly cry. After ten minutes of assault, the driver stopped and climbed the tree. He deftly tied a thick rope around its upper trunk, and tied the other end to the bulldozer. The monstrous mechanical beast advanced slowly and cautiously forward, and turned. Al-Assadiah twisted as its tall midsection began to bend closer to the ground. People were afraid; silence covered the sounds of their beating hearts. Suddenly, the roots began to thrust out from the earth, leaving a huge deep hole.

The bulldozer continued to move, pulling al-Assadiah through the narrow alley, in the direction of the dock where shipbuilders awaited the wood. Large gusts of dust made it impossible to see.

Children ran after the tree laughing and pointing to the sky. The women marveled and commented among themselves.

"Al-Assadiah ascended to the sky, in the shape of a line of trees," they said.

"It will come back one day, green and blossoming. And in every house there will be a green branch descending from the sky before dawn prayers."

"May Allah curse any who doubts the blessings of al-Assadiah!"

◆

HASAN 'ISA AL-MAHRUS *is the author of numerous short stories.*

The Dogs

'Abd Allah Khalifah

◆

He pulled open the gray curtains and looked into the alley below. It was empty. Turning, he sat in the creaky wooden chair and picked up his paint palette, studying the blank canvas in front of him. Suddenly a tall lean man came in, crowding his space. The man gritted his teeth and said angrily, "Sagr, what do you want from me? I can't go on fighting you this way."

Sagr laughed and said, "But this is not a fight; it's merely a discussion, a debate. Don't exaggerate."

"I am really in agony over this. I paint however I want to, I paint people realistically or in an abstract manner. I don't care. I always think about our bickering and what you do against me. I can't bear your attacks anymore. I can't live in such discord. But anyway, we are friends, brothers, right?"

Sagr sat down comfortably, picked up the phone, and made a brief call.

"He will come soon," he reported to the painter.

"Whom did you call? Omar?"

"Yes, so we three will have a talk."

"But why? What for?"

"He too is against you, as you know."

"Yes, he is, but that too is a plot of your making."

"You always imagine plots. You don't know what you're talking about. We want to help you develop your talent. You can still paint for the masses, with real art. But you must push yourself, play with your brushes, let your colors shout and get excited. Don't ask for approval from others. Ask of them to accept the chaos and confusion in your paintings, spit in their faces, let their faces bleed. That's what art is! Art goes against the masses, not with them."

"I have heard that before. I don't agree with such nonsense."

160

Omar walked in and sat down. He stared coldly past the gray curtain. Then he turned to his friends. "What happened? Did you guys reach a peaceful agreement yet?"

"Yes, our friend here wants an agreement, a personal peace treaty as if we were in personal conflict," Sagr replied.

"But this *is* personal; you both envy me and don't like me. My paintings get the attention of a huge number of people. Many love them, not for any primitive style, but due to the depth of my vision; neither of you knows anything about the art of painting. Your jealousy and resentment push you to badger me. I refuse to accept your ideas, but I want to settle it so that we can put this behind us."

Omar exhaled a wisp of cigarette smoke. "You still don't have a vision; your style is so mundane! You think that working-class people like garbage collectors deserve art. This belief of yours might get you extra money, but it makes you nothing more than a salesman, not a true artist."

The painter couldn't breathe from the acidity of Omar's smoke. Moving the curtain aside, he opened the window for fresh air. The street was quiet. There was a lone stray dog in the alley, searching through the garbage.

"Say whatever you want, Omar, but you must admit that I draw for these people you despise. I love these simple people. They are my audience, my friends. Anyway, I am not here to add to our feud. I want to put an end to it."

Sagr moved agitatedly on the hard bench and said, "What are you talking about? Your style ruins our efforts to produce art. We won't be happy until we have removed you from the art scene. You simply don't know what art is. With your work you drive people away who would otherwise buy from us."

Omar picked up the argument. "Your paintings are bad; but even so, you are popular. Change your style. Then we might shape something better together for the general public! Let go of your childish ideas and paint like we paint, which is both faster and better."

The painter continued looking out the window. The lone stray was now surrounded by a pack of dogs. It attempted to escape, but they had encircled him.

"What if I don't change my style?"

"We'll make things worse for you. You are really a nice guy and can't imagine how miserable we can make you. We have a lot on our side we can use to ruin you."

"Like what?"

Omar laughed sarcastically, lit another cigarette.

"For example, we will bar you from the upcoming art exhibit."

It was a harsh blow.

"You . . . bar me—"

"Yes," Sagr interrupted. "We are on the Admissions Committee."

"That's impossible, impossible! You'll never pull that off!"

"Why not? With your style, you constitute a stumbling block for us. Either you're with us or . . . we will destroy you."

In the street, the dogs suddenly were at each other's throats. But the stray resisted fiercely. Children gathered to watch, as the snarling of the pack increased.

"We have another weapon. I've got a report in my pocket. It is a solid scientific analysis of your work. It deconstructs every segment of your art. We can destroy you based upon it alone."

"Why all this spitefulness, Sagr?"

"That's life—either you're a small fry among big fish or a big fish among the small fry . . . choose which one you would rather be."

The dog held its ground; although he was bleeding, he did not retreat. Was it a matter of time before he surrendered?

Sagr had brought a book of paintings with him. "Read this book," he said. "Look at these paintings, then you will be able to crank out a canvas every month."

The painter lit a cigarette and started to thumb through the book. Disgusted, he slammed the book on the table and looked at the two men in astonishment. "This is what you call art? You dirty bunch! You are merely stealing the paintings of others, without any hard work. You have no talent!"

Omar smiled. "Even stealing requires hard work. You have to apply yourself."

"No, I won't change! Do as you like, but I assure you, you will not be able to destroy me."

"Taking the high ground won't help. Do you think you can intimidate us?"

"Of course—I can see that I scare the hell out of you both! My vision is stronger than all your threats!"

He spat at them and stormed out of the studio. In the alley, he felt the cold gust of wind in his face. He noticed that the dogs had dispersed. He was about to walk off when he heard a deep growl. It was the stray, licking blood off its fur after fighting off all the other dogs. He stared at the dog, then turned away and walked courageously down the street, dropping his head against the wind.

◆

'ABD ALLAH KHALIFAH *is a prolific writer of many short stories. He also writes for magazines and newspapers.*

The Siege

'Abd al-Qadir 'Aqil

◆

I leaned out the car window and shouted at my young son, Muhammad, to come and join me as soon as possible. My wife opened the door, smiling. "He's coming! In a minute." Muhammad planted a quick kiss on his mom's cheek, said good-bye, and rushed toward the car. It was a sunny, clear day, perfect for a drive. Muhammad, six years old, always asked me to take him for a ride, but my busy schedule often made it impossible. I had set this day aside to make it a holiday outing with my son.

My wife, who didn't like car trips, stayed behind. But she had baked enough meat pies and sweets to hold us as if we were crossing a far-off desert.

I was happy to see Muhammad excited by the prospect of the ride.

"I'll show you the highest mountain at the end of the city!"

"Are we going to climb this mountain?"

I nodded in agreement, and started to spin tales about adventures from my childhood. "When I was your age I climbed this mountain all by myself. But once, I found this passage inside the mountain and got terribly lost, wandering for days. At the end, I was able to get out by cleverly outsmarting a *jinn* and safely returned home."

Astonishment covered my son's face as he listened to my embellished stories. He was not happy until I had answered in detail his questions on what happened with the *jinn* and what all I had seen inside the mountain.

Suddenly, he asked, pointing in front of us, "Is that the mountain, Baba?"

We had reached the road that would lead us there. I turned and had driven for a short distance when I noticed a police car parked on the side of the road. I stopped to find out what was the matter.

"What's going on?"

A policeman turned toward me. I became uncomfortable somehow, noticing how nervous he was. Waving his hand, he gestured at me, saying, "This road's restricted. There's been a murder. Please leave—immediately!"

"What happened?"

"I am not at liberty to give you any details."

I returned to the main road, then pulled over, stopping for a minute while I thought things over. A murder . . . who was the killer? . . . and the victim?

At that moment, Muhammad asked, "Where are we going now?"

As I started to drive on, I said, "We'll go to a beautiful place on the beach!"

I began to tell him tales about a magical fish that could talk and sing for children. When Muhammad started to ask his questions of curiosity, I could not answer because I was asking myself, "How could anyone kill another?"

"How far is the beach?" Muhammad asked me.

"We'll pass through the palm trees on our way to the beach. I used to come here a lot when I was your age."

As soon as I said that, Muhammad began to ask even more questions. I turned off the main road and entered a side street that led toward the beach, as far as I could remember. But I was perplexed when I saw two identical streets, one leading toward the right and the other to the left. I did not remember ever seeing either one of them before. I could not decide which one to take.

Muhammad said, "Let's take that one." I agreed and quickly turned right, to find myself in a narrow alley that allowed only one car to go through. On both sides of the street there were dead palm trees, standing erect with their sad branches drooping down. The land had demanded water, but there was not enough. The earth, parched and full of cracks, conveyed a sense of death. I continued to drive, hoping to reach the beach, or a road less creepy.

"When will we be there?" Muhammad asked.

I could not answer. Shocked, I saw a number of palm trees in the middle of the street blocking our way. Taking a deep breath, I tried to control my agitation.

"How did we get here?" I said to myself.

"When will we be there, Baba?" Muhammad asked again.

"When we get back to the road that takes us to the beach. I must have made a wrong turn. But how is that possible?"

The only way to get back was to drive backward until I could get to a point where I could turn the car around. I felt a pain in my neck as I hit the accelerator. Finally, there was a widening of the road where I could turn around. I tried to go back the way we had come.

"Where are we going now?" Muhammad implored.

"We are returning to the other street that turns to the left, which should take us to the beach."

We traveled for some time, but my heart skipped a beat when I realized we were still not on the main road—once again, we came upon the dead palm trees that blocked our way.

"This is impossible! How did we get back here again?"

"When will we get to the beach?"

"Hush, son. Let me think."

There was no other solution. We had to go back, turn around, and get out of here as fast as we could. Nervously, I tried once more. I drove until I had reached the narrow road and hurried forward. We covered the distance quickly when I saw the dead palm trees once again.

Fear squeezed my heart; I laughed hollowly.

"Let's go back home, Baba. I don't want to see the magic fish anymore."

I concurred readily, "Son, I want to go home, too."

I got out of the car to study our situation. Muhammad followed me. We walked down the dusty deserted street. I was looking at the road we had taken, which was supposed to lead us back to the main street. How was it that every time we found ourselves back at this place?

I yanked Muhammad's hand and returned quickly to the car. Nervously, I began to back out, then I heard my back tire spinning in a sandy ditch. I tried to rock the car back and forth several times to get it out of the ditch, but in vain.

"I want to go home," Muhammad said anxiously.

I was angry and afraid. I shouted back at him, "Me, too. I want to go home, too!"

Muhammad couldn't bear it and broke into tears. I felt bad for shouting at him and quickly hugged him.

"Please, son, keep quiet while I work on this problem. I promise I will get us home as soon as I can."

He gasped and tried to calm himself, but after looking out of the car, his large brown eyes filled with a fresh round of tears.

"Stay here while I try to get the car out of the ditch."

Muhammad stopped crying and decided to follow me as I got out of the car. I studied the wheel, trying to decide what to do. I tried pushing, but it was clear that I needed somebody else's help; little Muhammad could not help. I wished a car would pass or someone would come along to help us. But I had not seen a soul since the policeman. Soon the sun would set, which added to my anxiety. I began to blame myself for even taking this trip and leaving the house.

Muhammad's eyes were huge with fear. He kept looking around and stayed close to me as if some force would reach out of the trees and snatch him.

I started to push again, but all my efforts were in vain. Darkness began to fall, adding to the gloom around the road. I pushed until I couldn't anymore, then I gave up.

"Will we ever get back home?"

"We will stay here in the car just this evening, and early in the morning we will go home. Don't worry, son; try to calm down. I am right here."

But Muhammad wasn't satisfied with my answers. I led him to his seat in the car and we both sat waiting.

"I want Mama!"

Sighing deeply, I asked myself, "How will I find a way out of this mess?"

I needed to reassure Muhammad first. "Son, why don't you lock your door? Go ahead and roll up the window so we don't get any mosquitoes in the car."

He seemed to feel better after doing that. I took out some of the meat pies and passed a few to him. Then I began to tell him once again about the mountain and my escapades with the *jinn*, whom I had out-smarted. Slowly, Muhammad's self-confidence began to return.

I pondered whether to leave the car and walk to the end of the street. Maybe I could find a way out to the main street. But the darkness and deep gloom made me dismiss the thought.

Muhammad finally slept while I remained awake, listening closely to any suspicious sounds. From time to time I looked back, to be sure nothing had followed us.

I had to ask myself, "How do people put themselves in such stupid situations?"

I suddenly froze. I thought I saw something moving in the dark. Or was I imagining things? I began to shake uncontrollably. I put my hand on the ignition, but remembered that our car was stuck, so I dropped my hand back on my lap.

The darkness was dense, the stars were extinguished, the moon was dim. All I could make out was the shape of a girl standing directly in front of our car. She knew I was inside. She was signaling at me to leave the car and go to her. I raised my head and looked hard at her. She disappeared and then returned, beckoning to me. When I turned on the head-lights, she suddenly vanished, and only the dead palm trees were there.

I turned off the lights to save the battery and continued staring into the dense darkness around me.

I decided to lie down, thinking I'd sleep a bit and not wake up until dawn. But my eyes would not close. I remained awake, listening for any noises outside.

I was startled by Muhammad stirring. He wanted to urinate. Scratching my chin, I concluded there was no choice. Quietly, I took him outside and asked him to be quick, while I opened up the trunk and took out a heavy wrench to defend ourselves if we needed to!

We returned to our car, and I locked the doors. I got a strong grip on the wrench in my hand and returned to my vigil.

Once again I saw the girl. But when I turned on the headlights to see better, she disappeared.

I looked at my watch; it was eleven fifty. There were at least five more hours before dawn. How long would all this take to pass?

I closed my eyes. It seemed that I really fell asleep. When I woke up again, I felt that someone was watching us. I looked at my watch; it was twelve o'clock, midnight.

I looked through the darkness as my eyes adjusted to it. I saw the young girl skipping and dancing around the palm trees. She then stood up and looked at me, asking me to come to her.

This time, I felt that she came even closer to us. I put on the lights, and again she disappeared.

I had a sharp pain in my chest. I was afraid I might have a heart attack from the tension. But I was able to hold up, and I started to focus on ways to get out of the crisis—get the tire out of the ditch when it was light enough.

I was startled awake with Muhammad shaking me.

"Can we leave now, Baba?"

I looked at my watch and was surprised to find it was six in the morning. I quickly moved to carry out my plan.

I got out of the car to find some strong wood to pile near the ditch. Then I put some rope under the tires for traction, placed the wood under the corner of the tire, and quickly accelerated until the tires got traction and we moved forward.

Muhammad clapped his hands with joy and shouted to encourage me. I drove backward, turned the car in the right direction, and rushed madly out of that place.

After we had driven a short distance, I noticed I was shaking with fear, worried that dead palm trees would block our way once again. I looked at Muhammad, and we shouted happily when we finally saw the main street that we had entered the first time.

"Baba, let's go home!"

"As fast as we can!"

Just then, I saw a movement from the corner of my eye—standing on the side of the main street was the girl urgently waving for us to stop. It was the same girl from last night.

I slowed down as we reached her. She looked younger than fifteen years old, dressed in a nightgown over her skinny body. She had very short hair and a wicked smile on her small face. She gave me a cunning look and lunged toward us.

As I drove past her, I looked in the back mirror to see her still staring at us, her hand stretched out as if she were beckoning us to join her. I sped away before she could reach us.

◆

'ABD AL-QADIR 'AQIL *is well known in Bahrain for his short stories, published in four collections as well as in magazines and newspapers.*

Qatar

Layla

Widad 'Abd al-Latif al-Kuwari

◆

"Are you an Arab?"

I quickly lifted my eyes from the book I was reading. A little girl with shining brown eyes stood in front of me.

"Are you an Arab?" she asked again.

I smiled and touched her sweet face. "How did you know?"

She laughed at my naïveté, exposing a milk-white smile. She was missing a front tooth. "Because your hair is black like mine—look." She held a strand of my hair with the tips of her fingers. "My name is Layla. Will you play with me?"

I looked at her beautiful face, black hair, and small body. I wondered how old she was. Perhaps six or seven. If I'd had a daughter soon after I got married, she would have been Layla's age.

I found myself going back over the years that had passed since I was an industrious high school student. I was beautiful and popular. Then suddenly, I found myself the wife of a young man I didn't even know. The only thing that distinguished him was that he was the only child of a wealthy businessman who paid my father an extraordinary dowry. One large enough to make my father forget his old dream of seeing his daughter become a doctor.

Though I had objected to this marriage that was imposed on me, I found myself living a happy wedded life. I discovered many good traits in my husband that pushed me to work hard at our marriage, to try to make him as happy as possible.

My happiness would have continued had his parents not insisted we have children, and then insisted that he marry another woman when the early years of our marriage indicated I might be infertile.

Ahmad, though, refused to even contemplate another marriage. He stood by my side. It was the stand of a loving husband. He defended me, sometimes violently, against the fingers of accusation pointed at me.

Eventually, my husband thought something must be done to silence

173

his parents. He decided to take me away from the atmosphere of doubt and accusations that besieged us. He proposed to his father that he take me with him to London. He said, "It'll be an opportunity to supervise our office there and at the same time Nadia could be seen by specialists."

I was very happy about this. Yes, I must be examined by a physician and treated, for I was badly in need of a child to clear the air between me and my husband's parents, and to prove that I wasn't infertile, as they claimed. Besides, I'd adored children ever since I was a child myself. I had always dreamed of having a baby to fill my life and to share with him his laughter and games.

The voice of Layla woke me from my daydreaming.

"Won't you play with me?"

"Of course, my dear."

I ran barefoot over the green grass in Hyde Park to the playground in the middle of the park. Layla climbed onto the swing, and I began pushing it gently. As it rose and fell, I thought of the innocence of childhood, about my lost dreams, until reality pulled me back to earth again.

"Look," Layla exclaimed. "There's Mama coming!"

I slowed the swing before it stopped. Overcome by shyness, I found myself talking rapidly, "Hi! I'm Nadia. I met Layla in the park and agreed to play with her."

When her mother picked her up, Layla held onto her neck and said, "Mama, I like Auntie Nadia. Mama, I want a chocolate bar. Please tell her to come with us."

I studied Layla's mother. She looked gentle and sweet. She was the type of person who was created to give and only give. She answered my questioning look with a big smile and, warmly taking my hand, said, "There's a special place in my heart for anyone Layla likes."

I thanked her. She seemed sincere, like she was speaking from the bottom of her heart.

She then turned to Layla, "Come on, Layla. We must go now."

Layla tried to wriggle out of her Mama's grasp and, looking at me, she said, "We'll come here tomorrow morning to play together. Don't be late, please?"

I promised and kissed her. On my way home, I thought of the little girl who had given me such a happy day and made me laugh as I hadn't laughed before. Though the air was brisk, I felt warmer than I had felt since arriving in London three months earlier. How strange human beings are, I thought, that only a few moments of joy can make them float in the air.

Ahmad wasn't home. After work he usually joined his friends to play cards. I excused him, for lately I had become nervous and agitated. I'd pick fights with Ahmad as a means to release the tension that seemed to increase with every additional day that I had to wait for the results of the fertility treatments we had started.

Ahmad was an ideal husband, understanding and accepting. He found that the best solution was to avoid rather than confront me.

The next day I went to my doctor. After the examination, he reassured me that everything was all right. I thanked him and hoped for the best, although I had started to lose hope. He had assured me from my first visit onward that I would be able to get pregnant, that I was fertile and so was my husband. All that I needed, according to the doctor, was some medication to vitalize my reproductive system. It had now been months since I had begun taking those medications.

I thought as I left the fertility clinic that it was about time I went shopping. My sister had asked me to buy some cassettes. Also, I needed to buy some presents for the family, so I spent all day going from one store to another. When I returned home, I was very tired. I did not even change into my sleeping gown and slept in my clothes.

♦ ♦ ♦

In the morning, the exhaustion of the night before was gone. I had nothing to do all day so I thought, why not go to the park? I remembered Layla, which encouraged me even more. Oh Lord, why hadn't I thought of her yesterday? There I found her among the trees, her mother on one of the park benches nearby.

Layla saw me and ran toward me, shouting, "Auntie Nadia, Auntie Nadia!"

I rushed toward her to shorten the distance between us. I hugged her tightly, thinking how dear she was to me, though I had only known her for a short time.

She asked, "Why didn't you come yesterday? I waited for you all day long!" Then she changed the subject quickly in a way that only children do. "Have you seen my brother?" She pointed to his hair. He was blonde, but it was obvious he was an Arab.

I laughed with her. "What's his name?"

"Loai," said Layla, without giving her mother a chance to answer. "Mama loves him very much."

"But I love you more," said Layla's mother. Her voice sounded sad and worried. There was in it a mix of fear and kindness. I was perplexed by what I sensed in her tone, but since I didn't have anything to say, I welcomed Layla's invitation to play. Hours passed quickly. Later in the evening, as I was about to leave, Layla's mother approached me. "Layla adores you. So what do you think about shopping with us tomorrow? That is, if you don't have something else to do."

"I'd be happy to go with you," I answered.

We agreed to meet the next day.

♦ ♦ ♦

In the shopping mall, Layla insisted that I choose her clothes. I felt awkward, for every mother prefers to choose her children's clothes, but the kind smile on her mother's face melted all of my embarrassment and hesitation. At the children's department, which carried summer clothes, I helped Layla sort through a huge number of skirts. Though I wanted to remind her that summer would not come around for another five months, I retreated before her joy.

I insisted on paying for her clothes, though her mother objected strongly. "I feel as though Layla is my daughter—please don't deny me the pleasure!" I told her.

She gave in as I'd hoped. Then she said, "We've got to go now. Layla's father is coming at five. I wish you could come with us." To cajole me into going back with them, she added, "Nobody can manage Layla the way you do."

Her last remark gave me a sense of pride. I happily spent the evening with them. I didn't feel like a stranger in their house at all. Layla never left my side, except to bring something for me and her mama. I was pleased by her mother's tender kindness, but was made happier by Layla's adoration of me.

The days that passed proved this love. Even my husband, who insisted on meeting Layla after I talked so much about her, said, "I don't blame you; she quickly enters your heart and wins you over."

I spent all my free time with Layla. One evening, as we played with one of her toys, I suddenly felt tired and decided to leave. Layla's mother suggested calling a doctor for me. She was concerned but I refused to bother her. When Layla insisted on accompanying me home, I was able, after some effort, to convince her to abandon the idea. I reassured her that I would come earlier the next day.

♦ ♦ ♦

I found Ahmad at home. He became worried because my face had turned pale, yellowish even. He wanted to be sure I was only tired and that this was a temporary thing. Suddenly, I lost consciousness. I had no idea how much time had passed, but when I opened my eyes I found myself in bed with Ahmad standing by my side and gazing at my face. "Sweetheart, how do you feel? You gave me a fright!" I looked lovingly at him and took his hand. Beaming at me, he continued, "Congratulations, the doctor called to tell me you're pregnant!"

Words would have been useless. The room suddenly looked prettier; even Ahmad felt closer to my heart than ever. Finally, I would become a mother, finally there would be meaning in my married life. The feeling of motherhood captivated me until the next day.

I was awakened by the doorbell. I wondered who could be visiting me at this early morning hour. I ran to the door, fearing that the ringing would wake Ahmad. At the door, I found Layla and her mother. I was surprised, but happy to see them. Her mother justified the visit by saying she had been worried a lot about my health. I did not let her continue. "Please come on in. I'm very happy, more than you could imagine."

I hugged Layla lovingly, for it was she who had thought of the visit. I told her how much I loved her. In the small living room, I told Layla's mother about my pregnancy. Allah knows how happy she was for me, as if she were my own mother. Layla stood in a corner and said nothing.

After making tea, I noticed Layla's silence, which I was not used to. I sat her on my knee and played with her, saying, "Aren't you happy, now that you'll have a younger sister?"

"You'll love her more than me," she answered in a soft voice.

"No, I won't. I swear to you I will not love her more than you."

With those words her eyes lit up again and happiness returned to her face. Allah knows I didn't lie to her, for I meant what I said. When her mother asked permission to leave, I asked her to let Layla stay with me and offered to bring her home in the evening. She agreed, for she knew how much I loved her daughter.

In the evening Ahmad accompanied me to the doctor's. On the way, he suggested we travel outside London for a few days. I welcomed the idea, although I couldn't take Layla. Her mother would object to letting her young one go away for a week.

♦ ♦ ♦

Ahmad and I shared a few lovely days together outside the city. He showered me with tender love and care. Nothing bothered me except that I did not see my "Darling Little One," as I called her.

On the first day of my return to London I found myself at Layla's house. She opened the door and stood in disbelief, staring at me. The little one looked beautiful in her green dress, white shining shoes, and white hat. She kissed me many times. "Auntie Nadia, don't leave me again. I love you. Say 'I will not leave you again.'"

Her mother came to welcome me, carrying her son. I'd never seen her without this young boy in her arms. Perhaps she did love him more than Layla. Had I known what the following days would bring, I would not have judged her this way.

When Layla's mother went to bring tea, I talked and played with Layla. I put my hand on her small hat and removed it, saying that it would not rain today. But my hand stopped in mid-air when I saw that most of her head was bald. I raised my hand in surprise. Her mother stood by the door with tears in her eyes. As she moved toward us, I saw unhappiness and sorrow that I had never seen before drawn on her face.

"Mama says that London water is the cause."

"Wait here, I'll be back," I said, and rushed into the next room to talk to her mother. I closed the door behind me and tried to be as natural as possible. "Is it ringworm? Just say the word, and I'll take her to the best specialist and her hair will be back like new. Please . . ." I could not complete my sentence, for tears were running down my face and my words were strangled.

She wept quietly. "It's cancer—her days are numbered. We don't know how long she will live." She hugged her son to her chest again as if she feared losing him, too.

"It's impossible! She's too young. You must be wrong." I held onto the door so as not to fall. I heard her voice from a distance, wishing I were mistaken, but it was a reality that I was forced to accept. I opened the door and rushed back into the living room with my tears ahead of me. I saw Layla there lolling on the floor, playing with the train set I had brought her from my trip. She laughed innocently. She did not know that death was so close to her. The clothes I had bought for her . . . Summer would come, the clothes would be here, but she would not.

Leaving the room, I closed the door behind me again and wept bitterly. I felt a kind hand on my shoulder. "Allah gave her to us, Allah will take her. We can't question Allah's mercy."

When our eyes met, I felt her suffering. It was the mother who consoled the stranger. It was faith that held her together to bear this tragedy.

I wiped my tears and rushed to Layla. I did not want to waste a second away from her so that when she departed I would have as many memories of her as possible. I put her toys aside, for I felt I had more right than they to be with her.

She said as she hid her face in my hair, "Thanks, Auntie, for the train. Next time get me a bigger one."

She didn't know that there would be no next time. I wished I could give her my life. I wished I could chase away the phantom of death.

We spent many hours together. Ahmad encouraged me. He understood when I told him the whole sad story. "Spend as much time as you can with her. Stay near her. May Allah be merciful to her mother."

Day by day, life vanished from Layla's body. Fatigue showed on her small face, and nothing remained of her hair. "When I get better, we'll play together and go to the swings," she told me. She tore me apart with her hopeful words. The last time I carried her in my arms, her body was very light and had shrunk. She was in pain, gesturing to me silently to help her. Even at the moment she was silent forever, she did not let go of my hand, as if I were her shelter from her illness. Her departure was like a dagger pushed into my heart.

Today as I hug Layla, my daughter, who was born seven months after the death of Layla, I still cry for my "Darling Little One" and will continue to miss her as long as I live.

◆

WIDAD 'ABD AL-LATIF AL-KUWARI *is a pioneer among women writers in the Gulf region. Her short stories appear regularly in newspapers and magazines.*

A Night of Sorrow

Kulthum Jabr

———◆———

There are many papers to go through before I can go to bed. The clock by my side announces that it's midnight. Thinking is tiring. All of my concentration is focused on the papers in front of me. I must get them finished.

The telephone rings. I hurry to pick it up before it wakes my mother. My heart is beating hard; it must be him. I feel something burn deep inside as I think of him. Forcing myself to calm down, I pick up the telephone.

"Hello."

"Lou-Lou."

"Hello, Yousif."

"What are you doing now?"

"I have a lot of work to do and I'm trying to finish it."

"I want to talk."

"All right."

"Now? When you're busy?"

"I'm listening, Yousif."

"I need to talk to someone who will listen to me; I don't want to talk to a clerk sitting in front of a pile of papers."

"It's okay. Just go ahead and say whatever it is you want to say." I keep cool, my nerves frozen by fatigue.

"It's that simple?"

"I'm listening, my love." I press my lips together and swallow my sorrow.

"Huh! But that's not from the bottom of your heart," he replies, sarcastically.

I can't bear it anymore. I understand what he means, and I wait for the moment when he will begin. But he wants me to start. I keep silent until he loses control and starts to confess. I'm not trying to provoke him; it's just that the pain he awakens in me makes me silent in spite of myself.

With a deep sigh, I quietly hang up the telephone and return to my work, distressed. The phone rings again, and before I say anything, he starts again. I can't bear it anymore. I let him do as he likes, and he shouts into my ear.

"Don't blame me for anything. Don't blame me if I stop loving you, because you're the one who started hanging up on me, who shut me out."

A hot tear runs down my cheek as I listen silently. Then he slams down the receiver.

◆ ◆ ◆

I return to my papers, but they disappear behind a curtain of tears. The pain increases in my chest. I work even though tears fall on the papers: tomorrow I have to hand them in to the school principal. She's been waiting for three days. Anyone else would have reprimanded me for the delay, but she respects my hard work. I drag myself to the bathroom to wash my face, look in the mirror, and see my pale reflection. I return to my study to continue working, but my concentration is broken. I just want to lie down now.

I go to my bedroom and slip in between the sheets. I feel the room spinning. His words are tearing me apart. I'm dying slowly, an endless reservoir of tears cleansing my face. For three years we seemed to be the happiest two people in the world, a deep love connecting us. Simplicity and honesty made up the core of our relationship: he wouldn't do anything without me. He would call from his office to tell me that he would be late because of work.

When I went to the supermarket after work in the evening, I would buy things for him too. I used to choose all his clothes for him. He confided in me concerning all that worried him. We were like a couple, though we were not married, nor did we share a home.

I lived with my family in the suburb of Doha. My father worked in the seaport as a laborer; he was able to somehow provide for me, my mother, and my younger brother. My eldest brother, Ahmad, abandoned us after he got married; he wasn't any good, anyway, even to his new wife. My father did ask Ahmad to help, which was the only time he ever asked, for he was a proud man. He had never asked anyone for anything, except in his prayers to Allah. When I finished high school, I worked as a schoolteacher to help my family. Our life improved and my father relaxed, for a burden was removed. My salary was reasonable.

At my friend Mai's party, I was introduced to her cousin, Yousif, who drove me home. Mai worked with me in the same school. She would tell me how much he liked me.

Yousif began calling. He became like a son to my father, more than my real brother ever was. I shared with him his daily concerns. Meanwhile, my salary kept increasing. He loved me and I loved him. I learned that he was very rich and from a high-ranking family, and that perhaps he wouldn't be able to marry me and face his family—they wanted for him a bride from a family "like them." The pain of this discovery made me determined to never tell him of my feelings of disappointment. I didn't ask him or ever allude to marriage; perhaps I knew the day would come for us to go our separate ways. Three years passed like a beautiful dream.

Then I started hearing rumors at school that his cousin was whispering she would soon be engaged to him. The news shocked me. But I bore it with fortitude and kept silent. I felt that he was slipping away from me and my silence became deeper. I continued talking to him as if I hadn't heard the rumors. I expected him to tell me the news, for he was frank and honest with me. I waited.

I never expected him to end our relationship as he did this evening, by hanging up on me, punishing me for having work to finish before the next morning. He assaulted me with his harsh words.

I close my eyes as I recall our love; I feel hot. I must forget everything. I must stop crying and concentrate on what I have to do for tomorrow.

◆ ◆ ◆

Sick with despair, I get out of bed and, returning to my office, I pick up my papers. I work quietly but determinedly, not lifting my head until the *muezzin* calls the dawn prayers and my father's movements announce that he is going to the mosque. I perform my ablutions and pray, then return to my papers until sunrise filters through the curtain. It's six o'clock. I must leave by seven. I am tired, and whoever looks closely will know that under my smile there is pain.

The day passes and I hand in the papers. I take the inspector around to one of my classes. The reports that I wrote please the school principal and the inspector. The school principal welcomes me, shaking hands with me, congratulating me. The inspector likes my hard work. I am not happy to hear the news then. It is only later that I am. The teachers congratulate me, telling me the inspector will send a report to the ministry about my work. This may lead to a promotion.

My emotions are mixed. The sound of joy all around strangles me.

If Yousif were with me, he would have enjoyed my success and congratulated me. I would have liked to share with him the good news.

When I return home, my family is delighted to learn of the developments at school. When I am finally alone, however, I see there is something that I must forget. It is Yousif. I must remember that he left me in a way I would never have imagined. I gather his pictures in my study, some stacked between his letters, collect his small presents, even the chain around my neck with the first letter of his name. I put them all in a deserted corner of my drawer to place them out of my sight forever. I drink a glass of cool juice and recite verses from the Holy Quran, then finally I fall into a deep slumber.

My friends—all of them—ask, "After three years, someone else comes and takes him away from you without any resistance from you whatsoever?" But it was his relatives who took him from me, and he agreed to leave me. I wish him happiness from deep inside me. I don't mention him anymore. I try to forget him by working hard. My promotion arrives. I leave the place where I spent my working life and enter another school with new duties and more paperwork.

Riding on my salary increase, my family moves to a new, more comfortable home; our living conditions improve. I don't think of him anymore.

I hear rumors that Yousif did marry his cousin. Work eats up my time; two years pass. The telephone by my side rings. I pick up the receiver and in a low voice I answer, "Hello?"

There is silence.

"Hello?"

I am tired and cradle the receiver between my ear and shoulder. I'm half asleep and about to hang up, when I hear the echo of an answer, "Hello."

I don't recognize Yousif's voice at first. I don't know what I feel at that moment. I start to reply, but I know it's him: his voice is insistent.

"Lou-Lou, I want to talk. I've got so much to tell you . . . Lou-Lou."

I quietly hang up. Then I turn to go to bed, for I have a lot to do tomorrow, and I have to get a good night's sleep without being bothered.

◆

KULTHUM JABR *is one of Qatar's most well-known writers. She is the author of* Anta wa Ghabat as-Samt wa at-Taraddud *(You and the Forest of Silence and Hesitation) (1978), among the first collections of stories published in the country, and has published numerous collections since.*

The Storyteller

Hasan Rashid

◆

Ahmad amused us on many a moonlit night. He used to take us to distant lands and faraway places with his amusing tales. We'd sit on uncomfortable gravelly sand not caring about the summer's heat. We didn't get bored with those stories. Sometimes he'd forget and tell the same one over again. If we told him we'd already heard it, he'd quickly change the story line or add new elements. If he had continued his education, he would have been a famous writer.

Ahmad was cared for by his widowed mother. Being fatherless, Ahmad felt that all the houses were opened for him, that he was the son of all the families in the neighborhood. He entered any house without asking permission. His mother was a mother to us all. Whenever any of us got sick, she'd leave her house and stay with the family of the sick child.

She was a fine woman, respected by all. I still remember how she used to bake for the whole neighborhood before the coming of Ramadan. At weddings, she used to receive the guests and move among them with an incense burner in hand. On sad occasions she'd transform into a weeping widow.

As for Ahmad, we neither knew why he hated school, nor why, when he attended, he didn't understand anything. We used to do his homework for him because we were eager to hear his stories.

One night he told us that he had just returned from Ramiliah after attending a wedding of a friend, whom no one knew.

"The journey was long, the night was very dark, and in the darkness I forgot my weapons."

"What sort of weapons did you have, Ahmad?"

His eyes glowed as he said, "A gun, a dagger, a sword, a knife, a machine gun, and a pistol."

No one challenged him on that. The distance from Ramiliah to the old Ghanim neighborhood where we lived is quite far.

He continued, "Suddenly I was confronted by thugs. I was unarmed, but I was able to overcome them."

"Who were these thugs?" we asked. "Were they humans or *afreet* and *jinn*?"

Later we discovered that imagination played a big role in that story. Ahmad had seen an Indian movie about bad guys that was shown at Al-Wahdah Theater. He'd played the role of the good guy for us. The one who was able to conquer the bad guys, a gang of outlaws. His sharp observation enabled him to narrate the details of the film. His stories about *jinn* and devils and his victories over them were countless. He said he was victorious because he'd memorized the Holy Quran and the *surah* The Chair. We all knew he hadn't, but we let him go on because we liked his stories. They were our only amusement. Our friend Ismail used to say to him between stories, "Don't lie to us," but we enjoyed his lies and his wild imagination. He was the only one among us who had traveled all oceans, flown on airplanes, and had even seen whales from the windows of high-flying aircraft. He'd tell us about how flocks of birds attacked the plane, how the pilot was able to avoid the whales as the plane got close to the sea and escape back into space.

Sometimes we believed him, for we had never flown anywhere. Despite all the exaggerations, we used to get together every night to hear his stories. Some might think that all of Ahmad's stories were made up; that is true. But those who did not see Ahmad as he played the role of the good guy fighting the enemies, or listened to him as he dove into the depths of the Gulf to catch fish, could not imagine his excellent acting.

So he lived, and so we lived with him, until that sad day. On that day our storyteller was transformed into something strange, a defeated person. It began when other people, who were not exactly strangers, settled in the neighborhood with their children. We discovered that their experiences of life were better than ours; they played football better and swam longer distances. We became friends with them and Ahmad's importance in our lives diminished.

The children also knew more stories than Ahmad. Because we had heard all of his stories, our interest in him dwindled. One moonlit night, we sat together as usual. We saw his shadowy form from the distance and shouted, "Ahmad, Ahmad!" He shyly came to us, and sat silently. One of the new children said something about how while diving, his father saw the ghost Bodriah and was able to challenge it. Here Ahmad chimed in, saying that as a child he'd gone to the sea with his father and saw Bodriah. We all knew his father died when he was a baby, but we kept silent as usual.

One of the boys finally asked him, "Since when have you been a diver?"

Ahmad said, "I can dive for an hour nonstop!"

At that time we did not have watches and we did not know exactly what was an hour, a minute, or even a second. All we knew was that an hour was the period of a class in school. One of the new boys challenged Ahmad, saying, "You cannot dive for even a quarter of an hour."

Ahmad insisted he could stay submerged for even more than an hour, and accepted the bet. He would dive the next day at the beach. The bet was two Indian rupees. The next afternoon we walked toward the spot we knew of with a high rock. Ismail brought his father's watch. It was important that we had a watch—we didn't care much whether we knew how to use it or not. Ismail held the watch, others held the money. Ahmad took off his clothes and gave them to a boy to hold. He plunged into the water. There was much floundering, then suddenly Ahmad's thin body went still.

We shouted all at once, "Ahmad's drowned, Ahmad's drowned!"

One of the sailors from a nearby boat jumped into the sea and pulled Ahmad out. His stomach was filled with water and he breathed with difficulty. Another sailor came over. He looked at us angrily and said, "Who threw him into the sea? The poor boy doesn't know how to swim. Were he not rescued, he would have died."

We looked at each other, shocked. Was it possible Ahmad lied? That he did not know how to swim?

Ismail rushed like the wind to Ahmad's mother. We heard the echo of her cries from a distance. "Why did you believe this crazy boy? He doesn't know how to swim at all!"

His mother brought him around with several blows. Suddenly, Ahmad opened his eyes and began gasping for air. We knew he would be allright.

Later that evening, Ahmad joined us as we sat on the sand.

His first question was, "Where are the two rupees?"

We all said, "But you've lost the bet."

"Says who?" he said looking at us challengingly. "I was ready to stay under water for an hour. It was your mistake. Why did you take me out?"

We looked at each other. Was he lying now or telling the truth?

◆

HASAN RASHID *is active in the literary scene in Qatar. His published collections of stories include* al-Mawta la-Yartadun al-Qubur: Majmu'ah Qisasiyah *(The Dead Don't Visit Graves) (1996) and* al-Hidn al-Barid: Majmu'ah Qisasiyah *(The Cold Embrace) (2001), and he is coeditor of* Selected Qatari Short Stories *(2002).*

A Woman

Huda al-Nu'aymi

◆

He gave my father a huge amount of money. The gold pieces and my father's smile authorized him to bend over my body, to claim my flesh for himself, to call himself my husband.

"I'm Muhammad's wife."

The secretary stopped suddenly when she heard my husband's name. A pale smile appeared on her lips. She pushed a heavy chair into the room without any help, and without wiping off her stupid smile. She asked me to have a seat on a plush chair, seated my maid on another chair, then picked up the phone and ordered a cup of tea for me without asking. Turning to me, she asked permission to announce my arrival to the doctor. When the physician entered, followed by the secretary, she still had the same silly smile.

"Welcome, madam!" said the physician.

Madam. Why does everyone call me "madam"? Was my name obliterated when that man took possession of me? I am eager to hear my beautiful name, Mai. It is a simple name made of three letters. Even my mother has started to call me "Umm Nasser." Has my name formally been changed to "Madam" or "Umm Nasser"? Has it been officially recorded in a document I have not seen yet?

On our first night, he took off his *ghutra* and *agal*. He sat on a red upholstered chair and pointed toward me. "Umm Nasser, come here."

"My name is Mai."

Muhammad was known to laugh a lot. He laughed even louder then, which made him look even more stupid. Had I said something funny?

"You're mine," he said in English.

He continued his stupid laugh, while pouring into his mouth more of the yellow liquid from a dark bottle with a thin neck and wide base.

The word "mine." I remember my friend Summian's teacher told us about this English word at school, that it is a word to indicate possession of things. She asked me to practice using the word in a sentence. So I confidently said, "This pencil is mine," pointing to the pencil in my hand. I meant that it belonged to me, that I had the right to break it, to continue sharpening it until it vanished. Did this man mean that he could break me if he wanted to, or wear me down until I vanish?

I touched my swollen stomach. I asked for help from the maid and the secretary to stand up when the always-smiling physician pointed the way to the examination room. I lay on a hard bed, covered by stiff fabric unlike the silk sheets I had used for the past twelve months. The physician felt my stomach and I did not object, but I hated the sticky liquid she rubbed over me that allowed her to move a cold hand-held device in circles over my stomach. I watched the doctor as she stared at a TV monitor on which appeared a series of incomprehensible wavy lines. I tried to solve the puzzle of the lines, but their undulating movements, along with the motion of the scanner over my stomach, prevented me from asking anything.

I heard the voice of a man—my husband—asking, "Where is she?" The secretary, who looked at him with an even more foolish smile, tried to seat him in the exam room in a comfortable chair. A thick light filtered out from the waiting room. It broke the darkness of the examination room and made some of the circling lines disappear.

"What's the news?" he asked firmly, as usual.

"Twins, sir. Your wife is pregnant with twins."

He cracked his knuckles, then turned sideways, exposing a fat stomach that had been momentarily hidden behind the wide table. He swallowed a handful of the narrow room's air and breathed it back hot.

"Males, of course?" he asked.

The doctor was silent. The small gadget was silent, too. Moments passed as she studied some photos of the circling lines as they came out of a machine by the bedside.

"Doctor?"

"Sir, I believe that your children will inherit their mother's beauty."

He suddenly looked at the floor and his shoulders drooped forward. That proud male chest disappeared, deflated.

The doctor wiped the sticky liquid from over my stomach. I was happy but didn't know why. I'll have two beautiful daughters, one girl and then another one, I thought. I'll be their mother; that's great.

The physician sat in her office and wrote some phrases in English. I looked at what she wrote. I didn't find the word "mine" in there.

She raised her head toward me in surprise. "You're sixteen years old."

"I'll turn seventeen next month."

The physician wrote her surprise down. Moisture glittered under her glasses. She wiped her eyes with a tissue.

She looked again at this swollen stomach that carried two children who would call me "Mama" just like my sweet doll Nana, the blonde doll my grandmother brought to me on her last visit to our home. On that last visit she had coughed a lot, holding in her hand a thick cane. She had bent over, holding her luminescent prayer beads. She handed me the blonde doll and named her "Nana." Nana had buttons, including a secret one under her dress. When the button was pressed, Nana pronounced the word "Mama." Nana stopped saying "Mama" when my grandmother stopped visiting us. I used to be so eager to hear Nana's voice as I was to see my old grandmother's face. I would take out the doll from her hiding place, comb her silky hair, retie her red hair ribbon, then rock her to sleep and put her back in her warm place. My mother saw me doing that once. Angrily, she grabbed Nana out of my hands, pulled off her head, and threw her in the garbage saying, "How dare a bride like you, who tomorrow will be the wife of one of the wealthiest men in this city, play with a toy like this?"

Later I realized why my grandmother had stopped coming. She had died that day, the day Nana was beheaded and her braid fell in a fire of anger. I was upset over the death of my grandmother and the loss of Nana.

And then came the man who drank a lot of the yellow liquid and changed my name from Mai to "mine."

On the road home, leaves rustled in the trees. They were congratulating the twins inside me. I accepted the congratulations with a smile and laughed. I think the maid also heard the leaves because I saw her smiling, too. Perhaps if the madam smiled or laughed, then she did, too. She ordered the driver to turn on the radio to hide her smile, though it was past the time for the daily story of "Teacher Ablah." But songs were usually played at this time. Perhaps the station would play Muhammad Fawzi's song to his children, "Night has Passed."

I will make my twins happy, I thought. No doubt my two daughters will love to listen to the songs of Muhammad Ziaulden and Muhammad Fawzi. I'll play these songs for them every day. I'll allow them to play all the time; I'll buy them Nanas, lots of them. It will be enough for me to have my two N's: Nahid and Nadia. Yes, the first one of them will be a brunette with dark hair, wide brown eyes, and a small mouth. Nahid. The second one will have skin washed by dawn's rays, fair hair, and transparent eyes. Nadia.

I felt happy when I chose the names of the two girls inside me. I was as happy as a person drinking cool water on a very hot day. My stomach was divided into two sections suddenly, one to the right and one to the left. I interpreted this division as my conflict between the twins: Will the brunette be Nahid, and the blonde Nadia? I laughed aloud this time. I noticed the maid who turned to look, but who failed this time to mimic my laughter. So I redrew the face of the madam over my own countenance and listened to the radio.

The poet of love had died. The knight of the word, the master, Nazar Kabani, the poet of love, revolution, and anger had left us. The poet who had shared the thoughts of women and talked about perfumes, combs, silky pillows, the one who sang for women. His heart had become the shelter for those women who sought love, life, and freedom. The one who said the following about women:

I'm a woman—I'm a woman
I come alive during the day
I found the sentence of my execution
I did not see the door of my prosecutor
I did not see the face of my governors
My father is a selfish man
He is sick in his love
He is sick in his discrimination
He is sick in his stubbornness
He gets angry as my chest grows round
He gets mad if he sees a man approaching my garden
My father will not be able to stop the apples from getting ripe
Thousands of birds will come to pick harvest from his garden.

Strange, did Nazar Kabani know my father? Perhaps he knew the man who named me "mine." If he was such a great poet, as the radio said, then why didn't we study his poems in school as we studied the poetry of Al Mutanabi and Abu Furas Al Hammadani?

I thought of my home with its three stories and wide garden as a giant sitting at the end of the road. Here was my balcony that I never used until daylight lightened its spaces.

Finally, the car arrived at the entrance of the villa. Something—perhaps the fingers of Nazar Kabani—played with my braids. The polite driver opened the car door and the silent maid helped me out, accompanied by Nahid and Nadia. I looked for his Mercedes, but I did not see it. Maybe he left to visit his other wife, the one who had preceded me by two years and who gave him a baby boy last night. When I got out of the car, I felt my hair comb fall down. My long braids touched my back and appeared from under my veil but I didn't care. I continued to slowly ascend toward my spacious room, to drop the veil and head cover and the rest of the combs, and rush to the wide window that was covered by heavy curtains. I drew open the curtains and looked at the garden. As I caressed my twins with both hands, I watched the birds picking at the apple tree.

◆

HUDA AL-NU'AYMI *is one of Qatar's many women writers. She is the author of numerous short stories.*

The Checkpoint

Muhsin al-Hajiri

◆

As was customary, the checkpoint moved from one place to another. It did not retain one person, neither was it something very definite. But in it, everything melted, even human beings!

The driver had to stop his car. A uniformed man crossed in front of him. He was tall, his face was all eyes. Those eyes never kept still but appeared to dart from one place to another, once on his cheeks, once on his forehead, on his lips, and for all you know they seemed like they could even leave his face to be seen on his hands or feet!

Does the guard even know how he looks, or was he unfortunate enough to have this faceless face, this bodiless body?

The guard with his thin worn-out body inside an old uniform was kicking the ground with his black plastic shoe, using a voice rough enough to break the eardrums of the driver who was listening attentively to hear what was being said. But the guard's thick lips did not move until he got close to the window. Then he spoke painfully in a harsh tone and with words he seemed to have been repeating over and over since ancient history, "Give me your license."

After that, the guard's eyes moved again, looking at the man as he sat behind the driver's wheel, as if they were capable of pulling out the man's license from his wallet by sheer willpower. The man felt the impact of his stare, and quickly and politely handed the license to the guard, not realizing he was holding it upside down. The guard looked at it for some time and then gave it back saying, "Show me your ID."

Again the poor man quickly produced his ID. The guard firmly held it and examined the photograph, the same face, same color, the same mustache, same eyes, same nose, but the hair? The hair was under a head cover, a red head cover—the driver had wrapped it around part of his head to protect his face from the dusty wind.

"Uncover your head," the guard said like a raging bull that wanted to avenge himself at a bullfight, excited by a red cloth.

"But why my head, sir?" the poor driver asked politely, hoping to calm the fire burning in the guard's eyes.

"Are you arguing with me? Are you trying to give me trouble?"

"Absolutely not—I dare not cause you any grief!"

"Shut up, you! Don't say another word!"

"Curse my tongue for being impolite, sir. But why do you want to see my hair?"

"To be sure of your identity."

"But isn't my photo enough?"

"Not at all."

"What's wrong with it?"

"I can only see your face, but your head is covered—I can't see it."

"Isn't the face what's most important?"

"How do you know? I decide what's important. Many faces look alike, but they are different in the details."

"What do you want, then?"

"Get out of the car, take off your head cover, and don't talk too much."

The driver got out, pulled off his head cover—revealing a luxurious head of hair that fell over his shoulders. It was black, soft, long, very long, reaching past his shoulders. The breeze played with his hair. The guard was very surprised at the length of the man's hair.

"Is this really your hair?"

"Of course it is."

"I doubt that."

"Do you think it is fake?"

"I doubt your manliness."

"What . . . what do you mean by that?"

"I mean, why do you keep your hair this long?"

"I don't know, but one day I'll cut it."

"Why don't you cut it now?"

"What do you mean?"

Grinning menacingly, the guard took out from his pocket a small pair of scissors and played with it between his fingers. "Come on!"

"What is that in your hands?"

"It is a pair of scissors, to cut your hair."

"But I'll cut it at the barbershop."

"Do not waste time, do it now, otherwise—"

"Otherwise what?"

"Your photo on your ID card doesn't look like you. And consequently—"

"Consequently what?"

"You will not be able to go through!"

"But the photo does not show the rest of my body, only my head."

"Do you want me to examine the rest of your body?"

"No, no. Please don't."

"Then, cut your hair, before I make you take off your clothes, too."

"Okay, okay."

An hour later, the steel pole was finally raised, allowing the driver to pass through. The car rushed into the desert, leaving behind it the checkpoint, the tall guard with a face all eyes, owning a pair of scissors, carrying between his hands soft hair with which the wind played, scattering it all over the place.

◆

MUHSIN AL-HAJIRI *(b. 1973) graduated with a B.S. in mechanical engineering from Qatar University. He has published a number of short stories, including "Daughters of Ibis" and the prizewinning "al-Balagh" (The Announcement).*

The Prize

Jamal Faiz

◆

For the second year in a row I received the "Employee of the Year" prize. I had worked hard all year, secretly wishing for this prize, but I didn't want to appear arrogant to my coworkers. Managers looked down on employees who made their desire to win obvious. No, what caught the attention of those in charge was earnestness and diligence, and so I worked hard to be as productive as I possibly could.

The first time I won the prize, Muhammad, my department manager, attended the party thrown by the company in my honor. He was new to the position at the time and had made a point of getting to know each of the employees individually. He seemed to listen when people spoke to him and had the quality of seeing through those people who didn't do their share. Some didn't like his methods, but I felt he would be good for the company.

I stood up, and the other employees clapped as I stood to receive the prize from the company president. I blushed and felt unworthy, but my heart beat with pride. When Muhammad read his speech, he stressed that he was happy the prize had been given to the most deserving employee in his department. He announced to the crowd that if I won the prize next year he would recommend me for a bonus and a promotion.

Well, here I was again: "Employee of the Year." The ceremony would follow in a few weeks, but for now I was content to know that the future held good things.

The next morning, I went to the meeting room like the others. The president, a stern-looking man with a shock of gray hair, gestured for me to come over and sit next to him. I thanked him and said I preferred to sit with my colleagues.

"Nonsense," said the president. "The man who has been awarded 'Employee of the Year' two years in a row deserves a place of honor. I insist you sit by me."

I got up and moved, sitting self-consciously in the place of honor as I looked at Muhammad and the others. The president coughed. They all looked toward him, and he repeated his welcome to me, the employee of the year, the ideal employee. He said he wished everyone would try to be like me and that he was sure I'd serve as an example to others for years to come. He closed his remarks with a joke that brought tears from laughing and people fell out of their chairs, like leaves in the fall. Others shook as if they were under the impact of an earthquake. Everyone laughed, except me, the employee of the year; I remained stone-faced in my seat. I did not find the joke amusing and felt that my new status within the company demanded a certain amount of decorum. The others looked at me as if gauging my reaction. I struggled to maintain my dignity for their benefit.

On the third day after winning the prize, I entered the president's office with an idea for a new project. He received me a bit coolly, but I understood that he was a busy man, and plunged in with my ideas. When I finished, I added with a smile, "Adding new computers will do magic; management will be better organized, and performance will improve."

The president interrupted me, saying, "Leave the file and I'll look at it." He straightened some papers on his desk and did not look up or say good-bye when I left the room.

Over the next few days, I kept asking the president about my new project, but in vain. He would not answer, and his replies became cooler and less civil. Later, he instructed me to follow up on the matter with his secretary.

Three months later, I was forbidden from entering the president's office without permission. He sent a letter stating that if I had any new ideas or correspondences, I must go through his secretary. I was surprised and asked the secretary to see the president, but he refused my oral and written request. I insisted, but neither the president nor his secretary would give me the benefit of a reply. Others in the company began to whisper about my predicament. Though I couldn't prove it, I had the sense that I was being set up as an object of ridicule.

Days passed, and I persevered. I stormed into the secretary's office and pounded my fist on the desk. I asked, "Is this any way to treat your employee of the year?"

The next day I found a pink slip of paper on my desk. It read: "Thanks for all the services that you've given to our company."

Shocked, I realized this was another award, one for those who don't know their place!

◆

JAMAL FAIZ *is an active member of the Qatari Literary Society.*

The Alley

Nasir al-Hallabi

◆

It was midday, and sound filled the alley. The street shook from its power: the honking of horns, the rumble of carts, the braying of recalcitrant donkeys, the whine of motorcycles and bikes, and the hubbub of people crowding at the crosswalks, waiting to continue their frantic pace. Around them newspaper sellers, porters, and beggars hawked their wares, their cries blurring like human static. Abu Sawalif left the college where he was a visiting scholar taking an intensive course in economics. Today's lecture had been about how in certain Arab countries one can find cheerful citizens despite a plague of economic problems.

"Although some of them may appear on the surface to be carrying all the worries of the world," said the professor, "just talk to any of these people—office workers, street vendors, even the garbage collectors—and you will likely find a contented individual."

That day, however, Abu Sawalif was anything but happy as he returned to his luxury apartment overlooking the Nile. He called this daily jaunt back from the college the "trip from hell" because he had to suffer from the rough, broken sidewalks, the impossibly narrow alleys, and the constant traffic jams that resulted from a total disregard for traffic order, and, in general, abuse of every kind.

Abu Sawalif was an engineer. He was used to order and was unhappy with anything less. On the streets he despised any disobedience of traffic laws, and he could not tolerate their violations, especially blatant ones. When he drove his shiny black Mercedes Benz, it was always slowly, in an orderly way, and in the correct lane.

In Cairo, however, his courteous driving went unappreciated. Abu Sawalif was routinely cursed by frustrated fellow drivers who shouted and shook their fists at him.

"Donkey!" one irate driver shouted from his cracked window.

"And you are the son of a donkey!" Abu Sawalif shouted back.

But really he didn't care. He was used to such name-calling; he mostly ignored their taunts. It didn't matter to him what others thought because he was setting an example, imposing order upon chaos, an admirable feat indeed.

Any casual observer could see that Abu Sawalif's car belonged in one of the upscale neighborhoods. As he drove methodically through the alleys to his apartment, the crowd viewed him as something of an anomaly.

But today, as Abu Sawalif was about to leave one of those alleys, a fast-moving silver BMW darted in from the other direction. The driver seemed oblivious to everything around him as he plowed through the stream of people. Finally, he spotted Abu Sawalif and slammed to a halt, blocking the alley. The driver, an arrogant man who wore his headdress pushed stylishly to the side, honked his horn incessantly. Seeing that Abu Sawalif did not budge, he leaned out his window and warned him—ordered him—to clear the alley.

Quickly, Abu Sawalif made his decision. He did not have to abide by this man's orders. It was the man, not Abu Sawalif, who was in the wrong. He got out of his car and approached the driver. "You have to move. There is absolutely no way for me to back up."

"Me?" the man responded. Under his left eye a small scar turned vivid red. "Has your thick blood affected your head? I have to be somewhere fast. Any fool can see that you are the one who must move!" Then he slammed his car door shut and laid on the horn.

Abu Sawalif returned to his car. There was nothing left to do. He turned off the engine. Then he climbed back out of the car and locked it. "Look!" he said to the other driver. "There's no point arguing. You've got to face the fact that you've lost and should back out and go back to where you came from."

"Okay," the other driver replied, getting out of the BMW. "I give up arguing as well, but it's because you are wrong."

The drivers marched off in different directions, leaving the two cars, face-to-face, parked in the middle of the street, totally shutting down traffic in the narrow alley. Though worried about his expensive Mercedes Benz, Abu Sawalif returned to his apartment. He gave the situation some time, pacing between his four walls.

Believing by now that his rival may have moved his car, he returned to the alley to get his Benz. As he reached his car, he was not surprised to find behind it a long line of jammed cars. What really astonished him was the discovery that although the BMW had disappeared, the way his own car was parked gave the impression that he was the sole person responsible for the massive pileup. Mortified, he squirmed as a cold feeling of fear shot from his stomach, tightening his throat.

From inside the waiting cars the other drivers glared at him, anger turning their faces red. With their eyes they told him they wished to cut him into a hundred pieces. Abu Sawalif examined their irate faces and searched his mind for a plan. But there was no way he could apologize and explain that it wasn't his fault.

So he did what he had to do. He got into his car to extricate it from the mess. But as began to move the car forward he found that it wobbled. A thumping noise emanated from the front. He had a flat tire. What to do now? He stopped the car, thinking he'd go to the trunk for his spare tire, even though it meant facing those angry drivers once more.

Finding that Abu Sawalif had stopped again, the crowd grew more enraged. One man approached his car. A few others got out of their own cars. Then they were upon him. They invaded his Benz, punching and shouting at him. Fists flew, pounding on his face and splattering blood on his immaculate upholstery.

Abu Sawalif struggled, throwing his arms up to block the blows and pleading with them to stop. But it was in vain. The men did not stop until blood flowed down his face and he had two black eyes. Finally, their ire appeased, they left him slumped over the steering wheel.

One merciful soul brought Abu Sawalif to the hospital. His body aching and battered, he stumbled in the door of the emergency room. Five minutes later, his face ashen, he bolted back out the door. Shaking his head, he turned and hobbled quickly away, gladly joining the ranks of the pedestrians.

As he disappeared into the crowd, the doctor ran out the door after him, looking for his patient. Perplexed, he rubbed the small scar under his left eye. Why had the poor man left so quickly—especially since he really needed help?

◆

NASIR AL-HALLABI *has written numerous short stories and is an active member of the Qatari Literary Society.*

Kuwait

The Homeland Is Far Away, the Roads Are Many

Layla al-Uthman

◆

The end of the school day meant freedom for the prisoners of the hot classrooms at the public school for girls. At the sound of the final bell, the schoolgirls bolted out of the front doors like racehorses charging from the starting gate. The clamor of children running mixed with the noise of motor engines, all of which harmonized with the tunes emanating from the bus radio.

Laughing, the girls scrambled onto the bus, their braids scattered over their soft shoulders. A few had tears in their eyes, a sign that their school day had been unhappy.

Group after group jumped into the bus until it was packed full. They crowded together, despite the humidity. The bus smelled of sweat mixed with the odor of soiled socks and shoes.

"Okay, let's go!" shouted the school bus driver, Abu Rajeh. He took out a handkerchief to cover his nose. He waited for the rest of the students while the girls chatted, their conversation drowned out by the music that filtered out through the bus windows.

The bus driver shouted at some students gathered around the ice cream man, and they rushed to the bus. He closed the bus doors behind them and turned the key in the ignition. Before he could move, though, he saw a Mercedes blocking the road in front of him. He honked the horn once, twice, but the driver of the car did not respond. The bus driver angrily honked once more, but still the other driver did not move.

It was too hot. The bus driver felt as though he might vomit, nauseated by the humidity and the students breathing down his neck. They shouted as they reviewed their geography. He started to lose his temper, and he turned back toward them. "Shut up, girls—have mercy on me!"

The students laughed, made faces behind his back, and continued talking, though with lowered voices.

He honked the horn three times—*toot, toot, toot*—but the other driver remained as still as a stone wall. Through the car's back window he saw an Indian woman with gray hair with a bored look on her face. He hoped that because the Indian woman had looked at him, her driver was taking notice of him as well. Abu Rajeh kept leaning on the horn, but his hope failed and he sighed deeply.

The Indian woman moved her fingers in a signal that meant "wait a while." But the bus driver was not content to wait. He put all his weight on the horn, forcing the students to put their fingers in their ears. Finally, the other driver lost his temper. He approached the bus driver's open window.

"Hey, you ass! Why are you making so much noise?"

The students laughed, pleased to see their driver being abused.

To cover his humiliation in front of the girls, he talked gently, "May Allah forgive you. I want you to move so we can get out. We're already late."

The other driver waved his hands in the air and shouted, "So what? Be late. What could happen? Do you have a daughter of a minister or of a president with you?"

The bus driver tried to placate him. "My brother, please, it's hot. The girls have families waiting."

But the man refused. "I'm not moving. I swear if you honk that horn one more time, I'll ask my boss to come here tomorrow and have you fired!"

The bus driver sighed, giving in. He turned off the engine and wiped the sweat from his face with his handkerchief. Then he turned toward the students. "Keep quiet. We'll have to stay in this oven until this arrogant jerk decides to move."

Despair showed on the faces of the students as they whispered, "This must be the driver of a rich student."

The bus driver overheard the students' whispering and turned to them. "Rich? Who? Do you know whose daughter?"

None answered him, though their clothes were soaked in sweat and they looked as if they had just been splashed with buckets of water.

♦ ♦ ♦

Half an hour passed before the student emerged from the front door of the school. She looked about fourteen and was well dressed. Even after an exhausting day, her shoes still looked clean and shiny. She had her braid tied with a beautiful white bow.

"Well, she looks like the daughter of someone important," said the bus driver.

"Her father's a rich Kuwaiti businessman," one student answered.

"Well, he's arrogant," said the driver. "Her driver is arrogant too, and so is the daughter."

Some students objected, shouting, "Oh no, Abu Rajeh! She's rich, but very nice. She's good-hearted and kind and . . . and . . ."

He waved his hand to halt their chatter. "Okay, okay. May Allah help us." He had not expected the goodness buried in the hearts of the students. He was surprised to see them wave and smile at the girl. "Ghanimah!" they shouted. As Ghanimah approached the car, the Indian woman with the skinny arms got out to take the girl's backpack and let her into the car. The car windows were closed, and the AC was put on high.

"Let's go!" exhaled the bus driver. The car moved, and so did the bus.

The bus driver turned on the radio again. The news was on. He turned the radio off saying, "Bad news!"

One of the students asked, "Why don't you want to listen to the news?"

"Well, let that be my secret," he sighed. As if the students knew the meaning of that deep long sigh, they started to clap their hands and sing about Palestine. "It is that voice coming from the dark land, from my fields, my sun, coming from the pain of my people." The words of the song brought back memories of his homeland. He missed his country. His eyes filled with tears.

"Why are you crying?" asked one of the girls.

"I'm thinking of home."

"Do you remember it well?"

"Of course. I was ten years old when I left."

The student sighed. "Our parents left a long time ago and we are too young to have such memories of Palestine. They talk about our country the way you do, and we love it."

He nodded his head and said, "Our country is very precious, my daughter . . . the homeland is very precious!"

The voice of one of the students rose with a special tune. "In the name of freedom, oh, Palestine, we will come back. Palestine is an Arab country."

The voice grew louder. The heat increased. The bus driver waved his finger at the students, "Please, hush! No more songs!"

The Mercedes carried Ghanimah close to the bus at that moment. The students turned toward the car and saw Ghanimah's face from behind the window. She smiled and waved, opening her window. The students shouted, each wanting to say a word, but before Ghanimah could answer them, the traffic light changed to green and the car sped off.

The bus driver began to race the car down the long expanse of road. Thrilled, the students sang happily. They passed the car and the students clapped their hands. But when the car began to gain on them, the girls objected, yelling, "*Ya* Abu Rajeh, please beat it."

"Ah, you want me to race a Mercedes? This is an old school bus!"

Their appeal was mixed.

"Please race it."

"But there is a traffic light ahead of us!"

The bus stopped. So did the car. The students looked through the windows, repeating the song, "I left the stars, left the complaining, left the wandering tune . . ."

Ghanimah opened her window, her face clouded by both sadness and hope. Part of the song reached her ears before her driver closed her window.

The students' voices rose, challenging the driver for shutting the window.

Ghanimah smiled and waved enthusiastically. There was quiet contentment in her eyes.

♦ ♦ ♦

At the last traffic light, the school bus and the car went their separate ways. The car entered one of the elite residential neighborhoods while the bus turned into the working class Hawaly district. Life was vibrant here: small businesses, scattered grocery stalls, pedestrians crowding the sidewalks. Men, women, boys, and girls rushed from the heat to their homes. The savory smell of grilled chicken, French fries, and hot bread with thyme permeated the thick air, making the students' mouths water.

One of them said, "I hope Mom is cooking chicken."

Another said, "Today we have stuffed vegetables."

A third sighed, "Oh, I love that!"

Another said, "I hate it."

Many of the students disagreed with her, even the bus driver.

"That's a good meal; it sticks to your ribs."

A student laughed, "I don't want vegetables. I need to be strong. I work out with gymnastics. I want protein, chicken and meat."

"*Bon appetit!*" said the driver and stopped at the first turn.

"Everybody who lives here, get off!" he shouted.

The bus door hissed open. Five students stepped off. Those who remained in the bus waved to their schoolmates.

The busload grew lighter. The humidity in the bus began to lessen as the air started to clear. The noise of the students decreased. They talked about different classes, imitating some teachers, calling others names. In their excitement, they forgot the earlier delay caused by Ghanimah's driver.

♦ ♦ ♦

Ghanimah's car sped through the residential section. Here the streets were quiet. There were no businesses, no groceries, no smell of chicken, no aroma of thyme. Everything was clean. The foreign grass that had been so painstakingly planted was wilting in the unbearable heat. The branches of the parched date trees had turned brown. There was no breeze, no human movement. No songs from any school bus windows! Ghanimah was bored. That song still echoed in her ears. Tomorrow I'll ask them its lyrics, she thought. She remembered the faces of the students, the joy on their faces despite being stuffed onto their over-crowded and stifling bus. She sighed.

♦ ♦ ♦

The smell of delicious food drifted from the door when Ghanimah reached home, but she told her mother, "I don't feel like eating."

Her mother was concerned. She began to list the different dishes, the appetizers, all the while trying to tempt her daughter to eat just a little bit. But Ghanimah kept silent and refused. She looked around the house. Everything was so clean, so beautiful and perfect. Her mother's voice seemed to come from far away. The song she had heard from the bus still echoed in her ears. She didn't know the words, but she couldn't forget her friends' laughter and joy as they sang.

A cloud of fear came over her mother's face. "Ghanimah, what is wrong with you? Are you sick?"

"No, Mother."

"Then why are you so quiet? Don't you want to eat?"

She sank onto the soft plush sofa. "I'm dreaming, Mother, dreaming."

Her mother asked, "Dreaming? Of what? Tell me all your dreams, and they'll soon come true!"

"Not this dream, Mother."

Her mother insisted. "Just tell me. You know I'll try to make all your dreams come true."

"Then let me ride the school bus with the rest of the girls!"

A look of horror came over her mother's face.

Ghanimah waited for an answer.

◆

The novels and short stories of LAYLA AL-UTHMAN *(b. 1943) are well known throughout the Gulf region and beyond and are the subject of two literary studies (one by Abdullatif Arnaut and one by Hatif Al-Janabi). Her recent publications include the novel* Silence of Butterflies *and the collection* Laylat al-Qahr: Qisas Qasirah *(The Night of Defeat).*

The ID Card

Layla al-Uthman

◆

The guard gestured for me to stop. I looked at him from behind the windshield as he extended his hand with its yellow nails and nervously tapped the glass. I rolled down the window. His bad odor invaded the interior as he pushed his face into the car. In dismay I asked myself, don't they ever bathe? I remained still, looking straight ahead.

"Who the hell are you?" he barked at me.

I turned and gave him an icy look. "What do you think? Am I human or animal?"

"Quit fooling around. I'm not joking. Who the hell are you?"

I looked straight into his eyes and said, "I'm a Kuwaiti."

"Is there a Kuwait anymore? Or Kuwaitis?"

I drew out my national ID card and shoved it in his face. "Look, my ID says so."

He threw it back into the car. "I don't care about the ID. Just answer me."

Taking firm control of my nerves, I asked him, "What do you want me to say?"

His shouting subsided. "Which tribe are you from? One of the main ones or a lineage that has branched off?"

"I'm a tree," I said, smiling.

"You bitch!"

I was surprised I had agitated him so.

"Don't call my family names," I responded, trying to keep composure, but his words enraged me. Under my breath I said, "May Allah curse you and your family. And your president!"

He said, "Now, tell me, what do you mean you're a tree?"

"I mean that my main tribal origin and my branch affiliation are the same."

"Then what in the hell is your tribal origin?"

"Kuwaiti."

He banged on the car with his fist. "You may tell me you're a Kuwaiti. However, now you are an Iraqi."

"That may be what you say," I replied quietly. "But we aren't necessarily convinced of that."

"Then when will you be convinced of it?"

"Never. Unless we die and are reborn."

"Let me see your ID again," he ordered.

I bent down to where it had fallen beneath the gas pedal. Finding it, I handed it to him, avoiding touching his hands.

Glaring at me he said, "Now you're an Iraqi, whether you like it or not."

My heart wept over the memories of the time before they invaded my city, swarming in like rats. I didn't care then whether someone was Iraqi, Jordanian, Lebanese, or any other nationality. I was an Arab, with all the Arab blood mixed in my veins. But now I wanted to be nothing but a Kuwaiti national. This feeling tore me apart. I wished that he could understand and leave me alone. Instead, he clenched his teeth, threw my ID on the ground, and stomped on it, crushing it into the asphalt.

I whispered, "Oh my god, my picture!"

He looked devilish as he rejoiced at his deed and said, "Here's your ID, under my foot. Now go and get an Iraqi ID."

I did not answer. My throat constricted with pain and my eyes filled with tears. I remembered how at the government complex I had fought for my family and myself to keep our IDs. The bastard. Now he had crushed my picture, my pride, beneath his foot. But I didn't dare get out of the car to retrieve it.

◆ ◆ ◆

I turned my attention to what lay ahead down the road. There were thousands of checkpoints ahead of me. Suddenly, through my tears, I saw a light burning in the middle of the sky. It was my daughter's face. I could recall her fragrance as she pointed to a small scab on her forehead. "Look, my face is marred."

I gently drew her hand away and said, "Don't play with it, or it'll spread."

With soft hands she touched my arm and said, "How lucky you are, Mama! You never had these on your face."

I answered honestly. "If I could make everything perfect and beautiful for you, I would, because you are my life."

Oh! But if she were here now, she'd see my face, and my life, crushed into the dirt. Still I wished she was with me, looking at me with her sweet smile, obliterating the dust of his feet.

♦ ♦ ♦

The guard shouted. They always shout. "Do you understand? You have to get an Iraqi ID!"

I looked at him, trying to have pity. He had been crushed himself, and now he wanted to crush me. I was unable to respond. My eyes remained fixed on my mangled ID. I kept calm and prayed for help from above. Finally, I said, "If you don't mind, I would like my ID back."

"I told you, get an Iraqi ID!"

I responded with a wan smile. "They will ask for an ID at the next checkpoint. I have to show them this one. What do I do? Tell them you've taken it?"

He realized how stupid he was and kneeled slowly, keeping his eyes on me, perhaps fearing I might attack him. He picked up the card and threw it through the window. It fell in my lap like a child returning to its mother. When I felt it in my hands again, I wiped away my tears. But before I could relish my happiness he grabbed my shoulder and said, "Look! Next time I ask, you say, 'I'm an Iraqi.' Do you understand?"

I didn't answer. My tears ran, cutting the back of my throat like a razor.

He reached in and grabbed my hair, roughly forcing my face toward him. "This time I'll let you go, but next time . . ." Menacingly, he rubbed the machine gun that hung over his shoulder. "This will not let you go. Do you understand?"

My eyes were glued to the machine gun, and I remembered a time I traveled with my father from Lebanon to Damascus. He'd asked the driver, "Do you have the pistol with you?"

Why did my father need a gun? I wondered. Would he kill someone? I couldn't get rid of the question, or let my doubt continue to burn. So one day, I approached him under the peach tree in the garden of the villa. "Why do you carry a gun?" I asked.

Quietly, he replied, "The road is long, perhaps there are bandits—"

I interrupted him, "Would you kill someone? But you are a peaceful man . . . would you become a criminal?"

"If someone threatens my life," he said, "I have the right to defend myself."

"Oh, my father!" I said to myself. "They've threatened our lives. Where is your pistol now, to defend my existence, my country, the frozen tears inside my throat?"

The soldier's voice, once, twice, three times, dragged me away from my thoughts.

♦ ♦ ♦

"Do you understand?" the guard shouted angrily.

I nodded. "Yes, I understand."

Then he ordered me, "Get out of my sight. Go to hell!"

I closed the window and drove away, carrying my mangled ID and my broken soul with me. I turned on the cassette tape, which I switch off at all checkpoints, and listened to our national anthem:

> Your soil we kiss,
> We will never crush.

The choked river of my tears burst. They stomped on our soil, polluted it, bled it, but we kiss it regardless of the smell of the shoes printed on its face. The river was cleaved in half. Tears in my heart, tears in my eyes, I sang:

> You will be protected,
> Oh, my beloved country, Kuwait!

Inside my heart a flag waved. In my mind my father said, "Don't worry." My mother said, "Don't grieve." I felt future weddings and festivals calling to me, "Don't give up." In my imagination my city consoled me and gave me comfort. It would bear witness that I grew from its branches. I would bloom and then from the seeds of the blossom I would produce a harvest.

Despite the checkpoints and the pain in my heart, the road before me grew wider. I glanced at the rearview mirror. The guard still stood at his post, growing smaller and smaller, until he vanished. I smiled as he disappeared.

♦

The novels and short stories of LAYLA AL-UTHMAN *(b. 1943) are well known throughout the Gulf region and beyond and are the subject of two literary studies (one by Abdullatif Arnaut and one by Hatif Al-Janabi). Her recent publications include the novel* Silence of Butterflies *and the collection* Laylat al-Qahr: Qisas Qasirah *(The Night of Defeat).*

Hunger

Muna al-Shafi'i

Haifa observed the mouse's innocent movement, its tiny body. It looked cute, alive with purpose. She asked herself, why then is the very sound of its name so disgusting?

This was its first attempt that morning. It crept quietly forward to snatch the piece of cheese fixed securely between the jaws of the wooden mousetrap. But it failed; it couldn't snatch even a single crumb.

◆ ◆ ◆

For Haifa, too, her first attempt to fetch some bread had been difficult. She'd stood in a long line amidst foul-smelling people. Behind her a youngster cried restlessly, an old man stumbled headfirst, and a young man retreated from the line because the splint around his leg was so heavy he could no longer continue to stand. She searched for the bottom of her *abayah*, which had been trampled beneath people's feet. She straightened herself and adjusted the thin black cloak so it lay properly on her shoulders, then tried to squeeze back into the line.

After hours of waiting, she heard the baker announce, "The bread's all gone!" The crowd groaned and began to disperse as the man slammed shut the window of the small kiosk. Haifa stepped back, then turned to face the unrelenting reality of her daily existence.

◆ ◆ ◆

Haifa looked at the mouse again. She noticed its troubled eyes begging her. It stared at the piece of cheese and its empty stomach growled. She admired the creature's brave conduct. Moving closer, she pushed her chair in front of it. After a few moments, she watched it make a second attempt. It moved more cautiously this time. Its paw preceded it slowly,

215

until its body was squeezed between the trap and the cupboard. She looked at it anxiously, murmuring.

Hunger pushed it toward the trap. It had found nothing to eat for more than three days. She was becoming more and more sympathetic toward this little creature and chided herself for agreeing to put an end to it. How had she been drawn into this plan?

"Will you go shopping?" her mother had asked.

"Yes."

"Then buy me a small trap."

"Trap for what?"

"I noticed a mouse hiding behind that cupboard."

"Okay. I'll take care of it. Don't worry, Mother."

She stood up and moved even closer. The mouse, noticing her movement, sadly glanced at the cheese then changed its direction and scurried inside a crack in the wall. Haifa returned to her chair, relaxed, picked up a book, and became engrossed in reading.

◆ ◆ ◆

Haifa shouted, "Please, brother, have sympathy. My baby is hungry. I just need a can of milk."

"Breastfeed him. Aren't you a woman? This milk is for other children. Move out of my sight!"

Little Ahmad screamed from hunger pangs. Haifa held him more tightly against her chest, gently rubbing his back to reassure him. She stared at the cans of milk stacked in rows on the shelf. Angry and frustrated, she ran out of the store. Choking back tears, she decided to look elsewhere, even if it meant taking more risks and going someplace more dangerous. If only her milk had not dried up after that horrible encounter!

◆ ◆ ◆

She couldn't concentrate on her book. She was obsessed with thoughts of the mouse. Naturally, the mouse would try again. It was starving. The wonderful smell of cheese had numbed its fears. Of course, the trap would win in the end.

"What should I do?" she thought. "I feel terrible just watching this poor thing. Do I break my promise to Mother and let this innocent creature go free?" She couldn't reach a decision that would satisfy everyone involved: her mother, the mouse, and her own conscience.

She heard a scratching sound coming from inside the kitchen counter. Oh God, it's trying again, she thought, and went to look.

The mouse had snuck out of its hiding place, disregarding the trap. It fearlessly snatched half of the cheese, held it between its paws, and pushed it into its mouth as quickly as possible.

♦ ♦ ♦

"Uncle," Haifa said, "I've decided to go to the port at al-Shuaikh today to find some milk."

"What? That's the most dangerous part of the city! It's packed with Iraqi tanks and soldiers. Please, don't go! I beg you."

"Ahmad is starving to death. I have to go."

Before she could hear any more warnings she moved resolutely toward the car.

♦ ♦ ♦

"Thank you so much. May Allah bless you! These cans of milk may save my baby's life."

Eagerly, she picked up three cans from the counter of the small grocery store.

From nearby came a violent burst of explosions.

"*Ya* Allah! What is that awful sound?"

Moments later, more explosions.

"Hurry, miss," said the shopkeeper. "Go home. Get out of here. It's very unsafe. Every day they blow something up. There's a barrage of machine gun fire and sniper bullets coming from every direction, and then there are those horrible screams that shake us . . ."

♦ ♦ ♦

The mouse showed its sharp teeth while it gnawed at the cheese, moving it deftly from its paws to its mouth.

Haifa relaxed. She sat still in her chair, all her anxiety gone, and watched. Satisfied, she smiled. It's full now, she thought. My conscience can rest!

The mouse gave her a parting look and disappeared again into its hiding place behind the cupboard.

She turned back to her book. She forgot the mouse, forgot her decisions, and even forgot the war.

After a moment of silence, a sound interrupted her reverie. Haifa rushed toward the sound and screamed. The mouse fought under the jaws of the trap, its tail lashing from right to left. It bled heavily. All the while its paws dug into the cheese. She hid her face with both hands, tears streaming down her face, and ran from the kitchen.

♦

MUNA AL-SHAFI'I *is known throughout the Gulf region for her award-winning short stories. Her publications include* Dirama ah-Hawass: Majmu'at Qisas *(Hallucination Drama) (1995),* Ashya Gharibah—Taduth *(Strange Things Happen) (2002), and* Nabadat Unthá *(Heartbeat of a Woman) (2005), and she is coeditor of* Arrivals from the North: A Collection of Kuwaiti Short Stories *(2004).*

The Age of Pain

Muna al-Shafi'i

◆

I was staying in a village, far away in time and distance from my home in Kuwait. I liked to spend time strolling through the surrounding rolling hills and green forests, leaving my worries and the darkness of my nights behind.

The chalet I rented rested at the foot of a lofty mountain. In the early morning hours, the misty road was bathed in silence. I sat on the balcony drinking a warm cup of black tea, reflecting on the breathtaking scene, waiting for the magnificent tranquility to fade as life restarts.

As I gazed out at the enchanted land, spinning dreams and reveries, I saw him. He walked slowly, and it was difficult to see the details of his old face or of the cane that preceded his feeble steps. I smiled to myself, looking at this stranger. Suddenly, the walking stick slipped out of his hand, and he fell. A wave of compassion overcame me. I ran down the wet rocky steps with unusual courage, neither caring about the pain in my knees nor stopping to cover my bare arms. I kneeled next to him to help him regain his feet. There were small, faint dark bruises on his right arm.

I insisted that he sit on a nearby ledge, then I joined him by his side. He slumped against his walking stick and murmured words of thanks. A gentle smile showed the curved lines on his face. After a while, when I'd established that he was all right, I suddenly felt a chill run through my arms. A gentle breeze tickled me. I grasped his tired hands between my fingers. I felt warm again; a captive tear welled on my eyelashes. I lost track of what had happened yesterday and the days before it. In my mind, I eagerly traveled back to a distant time.

◆ ◆ ◆

Every day I would bring my grandfather chocolates, the milk chocolate he liked best. In doing so, I ignored my father's orders and my mother's warnings because it made me happy to cheer Grandfather. Before anyone realized I was missing, I would greet him with a morning kiss, sneak him some sweet chocolates, fix the position of his stick on his bed, and leave quickly, waving good-bye. He would smile back lovingly at me, one of his hands gesturing toward me while the other rested motionless by his side.

He used to call me, "Mariam, Hai, Moudi . . . Sarah," until finally he hit upon my name. I would be very happy with that and answer with a smile.

While at school, I would sit, almost oblivious to what occurred around me, repeating to myself the odd comments that were made about my grandfather.

"He beats the children with his stick," my aunt would say.

"He is senile; he does not hear," Uncle would add.

"He doesn't know what he's doing," Uncle's wife would remark.

"Talk to him from a distance; don't get close to that stick," my father would rejoin.

"He forgets everything, even the names of the children," my aunt's husband would add.

I don't know why, but I hated to hear them speak that way. Those words painfully lodged themselves inside my heart and grew into overwhelming thoughts. I wasn't like the rest of the children in our family, not even like my brothers. One day I overheard my teacher whisper to my mother, "Sarah is a marvelous child. Thanks to Allah, she is very smart and more mature than her eight years."

Each afternoon I would forget the family warnings and rush to my grandfather's room. I sang some of the old school songs to him, told him stories about my day. My grandfather listened to me carefully and smiled a pale, tired smile that made me feel I'd washed away some of his worries. I was too young to understand, but I was able to feel love and kindness inside him, despite his eighty or ninety years of age.

For more than a week strange remarks about Grandfather filled our home.

"Your father must move to the outside room," my mother said.

"But it is close to the living room and the outside kitchen," my father disagreed.

"So what?"

"The children's noise and the servants' bustling about might disturb him."

"But it is he who shouts all night long," she argued. "I can't bear his screaming anymore. Every night the children wake up scared."

"I'll think of another solution."

"The whole family has discussed it. This is the best solution, believe me!"

"Tomorrow I'll move him to the courtyard room."

Worried about Grandfather, I began to creep into his room at different times. When no one would notice me missing, I would sit by his side and talk to him. He was so weak and tired by then, only able to stretch his body toward me, murmuring words I didn't understand. Then he would kiss me with kind, quivering lips. I used to chatter incessantly, without giving him a chance to respond. My joy was to talk to him and see him smile. I asked many meaningless questions and observed silent answers trembling on his parched lips.

One day, I asked him, "Grandpa, the school teacher told us the story of the prophet Moses and his magical staff. I hope your cane is like Moses's staff. You could go with me to the sea . . . and . . ."

My grandfather laughed, a strange, loud laugh, then he began to cough. He did not stop until I handed him a glass of water. Then he said softly, in broken phrases, "Sarah my daughter, today's seas are hard. Not even Moses's cane can part them." He pointed with his cane, sighed, and smiled at the same time.

◆ ◆ ◆

I woke at night to the cries of my younger brother and my sister. My small eyes fought back sleep. I heard voices coming from outside my room.

"You saw yourself how he scared the children."

My uncle: "Thanks to Allah, his hands weren't cut by the broken glass. He scared the neighbors with his screaming. Even Umm Abdullah, the old woman, was trembling as she reported to me through the window. 'Look! The pounding of his stick shook the whole house. You have to do something about this!'"

My aunt: "He started with the kitchen dishes, broke them, and then . . . Thanks be to Allah, the guest room was closed tight. Otherwise . . ."

I strained to listen to the rest of their conversation, but sleep stole over me again.

I awoke that morning with an uneasy feeling in my stomach. By the time I reached school I was racked with worry. My concerns about Grandfather distracted me from my work and from playing with the other children. I felt sad and perplexed as I repeated my family's words in my mind.

"His ailments and diseases are many."

"My father tires me out. He is stubborn."

"He would tire anyone."

"His case is unbearable."

"The only solution, as I told you a week ago, is—"

"I remember what you said, the nursing home."

"What would people say?"

"But it is not something shameful."

"He doesn't recognize us, not even the children."

It was true. He had lost his sense of others, except for me. In the afternoon when I returned from school with my brother and cousins, we went as usual to the living room. I found all the elders sitting around the table, their plates empty. What was happening? My uncle, my aunt, my father, my aunt's husband, my uncle's wife, and . . .

A new fear tore at me as I watched the smoke of their cigarettes grow thicker as it wafted toward the ceiling of the big room. They bent toward one another, whispering incomprehensible words. I looked at their eyes. In each face was reflected a strange, glassy look. I crept closer to the table and listened carefully to what they said.

"He's become a burden to the servants."

"My apartment is too small. It's just big enough for me and my children."

"My budget isn't large enough to take care of him.'"

"My children are afraid of him and what he might do with his cane."

"It's the only solution. We should take him to the home for the elderly."

In my young mind I thought, "They have other intentions."

After a while, a few of them left. The others stayed and whispered. I continued to listen. The others returned after a while and sat back down at the table. My father pointed to the closed door that separated us from my grandfather's room and said, "They will come on Tuesday."

"Are you happy now?"

"I'll gather his stuff."

"You've got two days to gather his belongings and bring whatever he needs."

I left them. My grandfather's room was unlocked. I approached the door, pushed it gently. I poked my small head inside. Our eyes met. I saw in his eyes an unknown river in which my gaze swam without relief. I forgot those who were seated outside. Courageously, I entered. Sitting by his side, I embraced him. For the first time my grandfather spoke clearly, saying, "Sarah my girl, Sarah my girl."

I felt his quivering lips. His eyes sank behind silent tears, and fear crept across his brow. He moved his trembling hand toward me. I realized there was something in it and took it from his shaking fingers. It was an old photo, torn at the edges, a picture of my grandmother in her youth. I held it and looked at him. He was weeping.

Inside me I asked, "Did my grandfather hear what my father said?"

But I knew they'd say he did not hear.

"My father isn't aware of what is going on around him."

"My father is retarded."

"He doesn't know the children's names."

"He doesn't recognize the little ones."

I hugged my grandfather. His tears gently dripped down my face. A strange shudder shook my thin frame. My limbs trembled. He sighed a broken sigh. His cane fell from between his fingers to the floor and rolled away. His head dropped down to his chest. I stood in front of him for a long moment, heavy tears streaming from my eyes. I was shocked and could not say a word. I rushed to his cane, picked it up, and held it tight to my breast. I shouted and shouted.

◆ ◆ ◆

A kind hand shook me and I heard a quivering voice ask, "What's wrong? Why, you are shivering. You're half-dressed in this cold weather. Where did you come from?"

Suddenly my tears ran freely. I remembered the death of my grandfather on that sad day. I sat for a while, unable to reply. After a while, I purged myself of that hurtful memory and smiled at the strange old man.

I held up his cane with a trembling hand and said sadly, "What a beautiful cane, sir."

◆

MUNA AL-SHAFI'I *is known throughout the Gulf region for her award-winning short stories. Her publications include* Dirama ah-Hawass: Majmu'at Qisas *(Hallucination Drama) (1995),* Ashya Gharibah—Taduth *(Strange Things Happen) (2002), and* Nabadat Unthá *(Heartbeat of a Woman) (2005). She is also coeditor of* Arrivals from the North: A Collection of Kuwaiti Short Stories *(2004).*

The Return of a Captive

Hamad al-Hammad

◆

Samira ran into the house, waving a piece of paper. "Mustapha is coming back, Mother. He will be home in three days!"

The old woman turned around. "What did you say, my daughter?"

Samira caught her breath. "Mustapha is coming home. I found his name on a list of freed captives."

"Are you sure?"

"Yes, I've rechecked the names many times. I was so happy, I cried."

"May Allah be with you, my daughter. Haven't I said that whoever depended on Him will be protected by Him? Here is Kuwait free again, and here the captives are back. Allah is greater than any tyrant."

Samira turned toward her young son, Ahmad. She picked him up and threw him high in the air until they were both breathless and giggling. Then she hugged her son, dropped her *abayah* on the living room chair, and sat down near her mother.

"They said that thirty captives reached Rafah in Saudi Arabia yesterday. And they will come to Kuwait by plane tomorrow."

"Our house will shine with happiness again, and this time all fear is a part of the past," said her mother. "Allah is the Protector!"

Samira turned to her son and tousled his curly hair. "Tomorrow, Ahmad, your father will return. The sun will finally rise again. You'll be so happy."

Ahmad smiled. He ran to pick up his plastic machine gun and pointed it toward the wall.

Samira leaned back against a pillow. "Mother, I'm tired today. For more than seven months, I searched for food on my own. I don't know how those black days passed."

"Let's forget those days," replied her mother. "The future is ahead of you. Let's thank Allah for everything. We witnessed days of poverty, and we lived days of prosperity. But thanks to Allah, Kuwait is free now, and the government is restored."

Samira stood up. "Oh, I'm so happy today. I want to run through our neighborhood street by street, house by house, and announce to everyone that Mustapha is coming back."

The old woman laughed, "Are you crazy?"

"Yes, I want to tell all our relatives and friends and neighbors. It's like we've become one family."

"Yes, we must. But if you walk the streets, announcing the return of your husband, everyone will say you are crazy."

Samira laughed, "Yes, I'm crazy. What we've been through would make anyone crazy."

Samira worked hard to restore the house to its former luster. She cleared the refuse from the backyard, then she rushed to the supermarket and hastily shopped for bread, baking supplies, and yogurt.

"I want to make a homecoming cake and light candles to celebrate," she told her mother. "And I'm going to write 'Mustapha' in icing on the top."

"It is enough for us to have Mustapha back again," her mother said with a smile.

The telephone rang incessantly. Their neighbors had heard that Mustapha had been freed from captivity. All wanted to know the time of his return.

"Tomorrow, God willing. The bus arrives at Shaikhan Al-Farsi Hall in Saruah at one in the afternoon. But I'll go in the morning to wait for him."

The next morning, Shaikhan Al-Farsi Hall was filled with families of the captives. Women dressed in black stood waiting in clusters while old men sat on low benches, anticipation making their aged faces more youthful. The throats of those gathered were dry; tears remained imprisoned in their eyes. In their hands, the women clutched photos of their captive relatives.

Samira stood in front of the main door. Ahmad clutched her *abayah*.

"Is that the bus arriving?" one of the women asked.

"No, that's not it," replied another.

A voice came from a distance, "Keep quiet!"

Samira imagined Mustapha in his military uniform, his smile wide and welcoming as he stepped off the bus. As he left the house, his last words had been, "I'll be home soon, my darling."

Samira watched the milling crowd. The tired faces of those around her mirrored back her own expression. By her side a lone woman wept.

"They said the bus will come in half an hour," she told the woman.

A trail of dust appeared in the distance.

Finally, someone said, "The bus is coming! Look over there!"

"*Allahu akbar! Allahu akbar!*"

Sounds of women crying filled the hall as bodies pressed closer.

Samira picked up Ahmad. Carrying him on her hip, she ran next to the bus and searched through each window, looking for Mustapha. Not finding him, she ran to the other side. Frantic, she ran to the bus door. A hiss of air announced the opening of the doors. The captives began to file out.

The crowd surged forward, and Samira got lost in it. She shifted Ahmad to her other hip, shouting through the throng, "Mustapha, Mustapha!" But her voice disappeared in the midst of the cries of joy and women's trilling.

The captive men found their families. On all sides of her, people embraced, laughed, cried, and prayed. Still, she shouted, "Mustapha, Mustapha!

"Where is Mustapha?" shouted Samira, as she rushed to the head of the reception committee. "My husband. Where is my husband?"

The man tried to calm her, saying, "I'll call him over the microphone."

The announcement rang through the hall, "Mustapha Said . . . Mustapha Said . . ."

A moment passed as long as a lifetime.

A man covered in dust and glowing with happiness came to the microphone. "I am Mustapha Said."

Samira looked up at him and blanched in distress. "But he is not my husband!"

"This is Mustapha Said."

"He is not my husband. Where is my husband?"

"Perhaps they have the same name."

Blood drained from Samira's face. She grew dizzy and looked for a place to sit down, but the benches were crowded with reunited families, oblivious in their happiness. She looked at the man who was not her Mustapha and saw all that he had been through, all that they'd been through as a country. The blood, the inhumanity, it was all there with her in the station, there in her husband's absence, in the trills of joy that now sounded ugly and discordant in her ears.

She could no longer bear to see it. She held her son and ran outside, fleeing the happiness of others. She ran and ran, outrunning hope, while her son clung to her neck and cried for his father.

◆

HAMAD AL-HAMMAD *is the author of two collections, including* Layali al-Jamr: Qisas *(Nights of Smoldering Coal) (1991).*

New Wrinkles

Badr Abu Raqabah

◆

Fatimah held the mirror, carefully looking at her reflection. She gently touched her cheek, tracing the topography of one cheek. She tried to pull back the skin, make it taut, erase the lines etched so deeply there. But those wrinkles were wrinkles that lived inside her heart, turning it into ashes, breaking it into pieces. They were the furrows of a life lived in the shadows. A life of hard work with few kind words and even fewer rewards.

Age had left its traces on Fatimah's face, etching deep lines into her cheeks, creating a web of creases around her thin lips. Hair, white as snow, fell in silken waves on her shoulders. A metal bridge bothered her mouth when she spoke, giving her words a blurred quality. She wished it was not connected to her worn old teeth that were in constant pain. Her thin body, covered by her wrinkled *abayah,* was dusted with the smell of the past. Her thoughts and feelings flitted momentarily to a remote time when she was newly married and had her husband's strength to support her. How long ago that seemed. How like the dreams of another person's life.

Fatimah carried in her arms a *boghsha,* a large round bundle of colorful cloth in which she wrapped the cotton fabric that she sold to the women in the neighborhood. Every week it was the same. She supplied her customers with inexpensive material, delivering her goods with stories and myths of time gone by. Her weekly visit was an event eagerly anticipated by the women.

The call to prayer found her following the dusty road back to her house. The path before her loomed, long and exhausting. Her slow, heavy steps only added to her fatigue. Languidly, she paced herself until she finally reached the narrow street that led to her small mud house. It sat awkwardly among the high modern buildings, like an animal squatting between towering trees.

She quietly entered her home and laid her merchandise on the wooden table that dominated the narrow hallway. She entered the kitchen and began to prepare lunch for her three sons. Her unemployed sons. Fatimah muttered under her breath, complaining about their laziness and the unlimited opportunities they let slip by.

The smell from the savory pot of *makbous* permeated the house. She ladled the steaming rice, laced with green vegetables and beans, onto a platter. The noses of her sons led them in her direction even before they could have heard Fatimah's faint voice declare, "Come on, before the food gets cold."

They arrived in an unexpected mass. Each eagerly received a plate, one after the other, the older one, then the younger ones. She tried to put a dry smile on her mouth, but she knew that if they truly looked, they would see it was unconvincing.

The youngest, Mahmoud, said apologetically, "But I've already eaten a piece of pizza."

She did not understand what he said to her, but somehow she knew when she looked at him and at his sheepish expression that he was already full. "Don't worry," she said. "What's important is that you ate."

After she finished serving them, she escaped to her bedroom, searching for some peace in its airless solitude. She dropped herself onto a wooden bed that shook with the beating of her fatigued heart. Her thin fingers removed a torn scrap of paper from her skirt pocket. Fatimah focused on the paper, eagerly examining the day's business record. "Um Saad owes thirty-three dinars . . . Umm Khalid still has an outstanding balance of forty and a half dinars, and . . . and . . ." No one had paid her in full. It had been several weeks already. She did not know why she allowed the numbers to excite her. It was always the same sad story.

Fatimah turned painfully from the bad news, dropping the paper on her lap. She noticed her hand mirror—the one with the ivory handle that she'd put away ages ago—lying on the metal shelf next to her bed. She wondered how it came to be there, whether she had absentmindedly taken it out and left it on her shelf or whether one of her sons had found it and left it there for some reason. If so, what could the reason be? What did they want her to see?

She leaned toward the mirror and suddenly her head and feet felt light. She thought then of her husband. But why her husband? Why now? She asked herself, why did he have to leave her so soon in her life? And her sons, such a disappointment for her. She laid the mirror aside, unmindful of the fact that it teetered on the edge of the bed. Out of the corner of her eye, she saw it fall. She heard it breaking, but the sound came to her as though from far away. She remembered the days of her youth when she used to hide the mirror from the eyes of her brothers as she blossomed into a mature woman. Then she was ready to spread her wings and taste what life had to give her.

She shook her head and murmured to herself, "Can we fix what time has destroyed?"

She knew the answer. Her life was what it was. Her work and her children were what they were. All of these things were as inevitable as the tides, as unchangeable as her walks to and from the market.

Turning away from her memories, from the questions that had seized her and held her rapt in her darkening bedroom, she left to watch the sun as it began to set, quietly gathering its golden threads. The sun announced the beginning of dusk, a time in which she would forget the wrinkles on her face, forget the wrinkles in her heart, and, most of all, forget the wrinkles of yesterday so that she could continue on tomorrow.

◆

BADR ABU RAQABAH *(b. 1971) is among the younger generation of Kuwaiti writers. She has written and published numerous short stories.*

Guns and Jasmine

Layla Muhammad Salih

◆

I still remember the day I filled my arms with white jasmine flowers. I remember the first hour of that day when the sun's red and yellow rays colored my bed as they filtered through the curtains at our seaside cabana. We woke up fully relaxed, ready to embrace the dark blueness of the sea.

My memory is still perfumed by the white jasmine that Tarek, my beloved husband, had given me on the first day of that hot, thirsty August.

People were sitting on the sandy beach where the waves glittered in the sunshine. Children were playing, laughing, throwing water on each other. I was near him, gathering sand, and piling it to build a castle, built on love. I pushed a paper boat from my dreams into the sea, a sea rich with traditions of pearl diving, trading, and songs.

That day the sea seemed to laugh when a disastrous wind started to blow. The cabana began to shake as the morning tides rose.

I blame my fate on the changes of the sea and the absurdities it brought about. The storm moved forward shortly after Tarek placed a ring of jasmine flowers around my neck, a garland braided by the hand of love, and tucked a white fragrant gardenia in my hair and whispered, "You're my dreams, endless dreams."

◆ ◆ ◆

As I looked out the window, the round orb of the moon was reflected in the sea. The small cabanas were illuminated by brilliantly lit paper lanterns. At the end of the wharf a small boat sat placidly still. Suddenly there was a quick flash of movement followed by the sounds of gunshots coming from the north. While people were sound asleep, I shivered and stretched my hand to find an empty pillow next to me. Frightened, I jumped from my bed and slung the door wide open. Tarek was standing there, listening to the noise in the distance.

"My love, change and pack your things. We've got to go now!"

"*Ya* Allah, what happened?"

"Don't talk. Move quickly."

The sound of gunshots echoed through the doors. Light was shivering through the electric lamps. I quickly turned several times in the room. My heart quivered as I put on a long wide dress, fastened my long hair backward, and covered my hair with a black head scarf.

Tarek turned to me as he left to get the car and said, "Get Maha and lock the door behind you."

I didn't fully understand the consequences of the moment when we left the cabana to go home. We both failed to understand what was happening on the soil of our homeland. The sky was torn by the claws of night and spread the poison of black fear into our hearts.

The waves lapped on the beach, while artillery rang out and kept pounding around us. The battle started to turn savage on our soil with its sands, houses, and blue sea that moves our hearts. Our sea, the sea of tranquility, peace, and dreams.

I turned on the car radio for news but heard only static. I recited verses from the Quran and bombarded Tarek with many questions. How could this happen? Why was there such a volcano of hate? Why is there a presence of death now, which is stronger than the presence of life?

Soldiers appeared on the dusty road ahead of us.

"Hurry! They are coming toward us!" I shouted.

"You're very nervous. Calm down."

"How is it possible to calm down? I don't know what waits for us on the road . . ."

"I know, my love. This is bad, but what is worse is the sorrow of a lost country."

◆ ◆ ◆

The residents of the other cabanas had also crowded into their cars to make their way home. Suddenly a bomb fell close by and cars were rocked by the force of the explosion. It is the blow of deceit that sets our lives into motion. We were faced with an overpowering army; there were strange faces all along the way. All roads were closed with checkpoints.

Yesterday Kuwait, the pearl of the Gulf, was vibrant. Its coastlines were peaceful, proud, warmed with poems of love. Now it lay wounded with silence creeping over it. Injustice had fallen on us, along with ugliness, and our streets were empty except for military cars, soldiers, and terrible destruction.

Tarek looked anxiously at his innocent little daughter who was very frightened. Maha changed her grip on my right hand to the other, and dropped her small head on my lap.

He wiped the sweat from his forehead and took a long breath. "It seems our street is blocked and traffic is not getting through . . ."

"Why not go back, and enter from the backside?"

"I've got to get in there while I can still help the others."

Tarek wanted to drop us off safely and then find out where volunteers were gathering for weapons, even if he paid for it with his life. He suddenly reached out and touched my hand. He held it tightly, kissed me, and then Maha and said, "See you later . . . good-bye."

I closed the car door and slid to the driver's seat to drive away. All this happened with my full understanding that I was leaving Tarek behind. I, who adored Tarek, loved him, but I couldn't interfere. He had one choice, one decision, which no one else could make for him. I tried to pull myself together, my scattered thoughts. Maybe I could remember the words of our love, our tranquility. But I was scared, very scared.

In our quiet home, the clock's hands pointed like swords to each passing minute. I gathered myself and started to organize our supplies in the pantry and then secured the cabinet with a lock.

I stood up to water my hanging plants, which Tarek loved. I saw his fingers tenderly touching the smallest rose. I looked about and noticed the details of the home that embraced our love until the terrible storm came from the north.

◆ ◆ ◆

On that dark, black, sad night I stayed awake all night waiting. I felt a pang of anticipation as I imagined Tarek's steps coming down the hall. But the sound of the footsteps were of strangers, armed soldiers. They were outside attacking innocent people.

I tried to bring back my dream from the beach, which was dashed by the sound of that first gunshot. Things were happening quickly, as quickly as lightning that ignites a fire in my heart. Was it just hours ago when the tranquil sea was repeating soft whispers, when there was jasmine that perfumed my hand, and the laughter of children echoed as they played in the waves?

I woke up to the sound of the telephone ringing. When I answered the phone a voice told me, "He will not be coming back."

I didn't feel the pain until they brought Tarek, shrouded in a white cloth, to the hospital. His body was swimming in a sea of blood. Cries rang out in the hospital hall, echoing but strong, "*Allahu akbar! Allahu akbar!*"

Among those shouts, I heard Tarek's voice resound inside my head. I could see him and a smile passing over his lips in the paradise of freedom.

♦

LAYLA MUHAMMAD SALIH *is both a writer and a human rights activist. Her most recent publication is* The Lasting Perfume of Night, *a collection of short stories. She is also the editor of a two-volume anthology of literary work by women from the Gulf region.*

Bashrawi

Talib al-Rifai

Since when did people take up this sport of walking? It has become a duty for me. Every evening I must accompany the lady of the house and her youngest daughter to the jogging track.

"Wait for us here!" they say. "Don't go anywhere."

Always I nod and say, "Yes ma'am!"

They turn their backs to me as they walk to the track like some stiff-legged exotic birds, arms pumping. They enter the jogging lanes and join the caravan of late afternoon joggers. Earlier I was in my room, absorbed in figuring out the cost of traveling home—those never-ending calculations—when the voice of Rangani, the maid, called me, "Bashrawi!"

In a loud voice I answered, "Yes?"

"Come here, please," she said in her commanding way.

I stood and left my room to see what the matter was. I found the maid standing at the entrance. She was more imperious than the mistress of the house, with a quicker temper. "Prepare the car," she said. "Madam will leave at six." She turned her back and entered the house as if she did not want to spare any more words for me.

Rangani knew I was Madam's favorite and so she had it in for me. She liked to complicate things whenever the opportunity presented itself. An idea crossed my mind, and I thought, "I'll seek permission from the lady. She knows of my travel plans; I don't think she will begrudge me two hours. They can go in her car or the car of my younger lady."

I carried my hope inside. I stood, waiting, and when she arrived I said, "Please permit me not to go to the jogging lane tonight."

She looked at me, concern flooding her features. "But why?" she asked. "Are you sick?"

"I would like to go to the bazaar to buy some things for my children," I told her. "I am traveling home soon, as you know, and cannot go empty-handed."

235

"Well, I think that would be okay."

At that moment her daughter appeared, and her mother said to her, "Can we go in your car tonight? Bashrawi wants to go to the bazaar."

"Why?" the daughter asked me with a frown. She was not as under-standing as her mother. In fact she intimidated her mother just as she intimidated me.

"He wants to buy things for his family," Madam said, stuttering slightly.

The daughter did not like what she heard. She moved the back of her hand in a gesture of rejection and said, "But I don't want to take my car. Besides, we won't take long. He can go shopping later."

Quickly she disappeared as she had appeared. I was heartbroken, after having begged for help from the lady, but she only gave me a sym-pathetic look and, with a sigh, said, "Please prepare the car."

Sometimes I meet Uthman at the track. He brings his fat boss to the track. The boss gets out of the car with difficulty and ambles toward the jogging lane. He rolls inside his huge *dishdasha*. He walks like the ducks in our village. I wave my hand to Uthman, and he comes over. We exchange news and reflect on our lives.

I don't want to see Uthman tonight. I am thinking only of the shop-ping I must do and won't have time for his gossip. I wish the lady and her daughter would return quickly this evening. I must go to the bazaar. The list of items I want is long. Time is getting short. When will I buy all of the things I want to take to my family? I'm perplexed about how to make everyone happy. Where to get the money for the presents? Even if I swear by the heaviest of oaths, they won't believe that I've brought them all I could. Since I work here, as far as they are concerned, I play with money, pick it off the streets. Oh, I certainly wish that were so!

There is no sign of the ladies among the joggers even though every now and then I catch sight of my youngest mistress. If she accidentally runs into one of her friends, their conversation will continue forever. When she refuses to go jogging with her mother, my lady is accompa-nied by Rangani. It always amuses me to see the way Rangani, with her round body and tight clothes, walks by the side of my mistress as if she were the lady!

"What a predicament!" I said aloud. Only three days before I leave. Everyone there is talking about me, waiting for me. What am I to take for them? My wife, five children, father, mother, brothers, their wives and children, my three sisters, their husbands and children, my handi-capped aunt and uncles. Massa'ad, my youngest son, is two years older since I've last seen him. On the last cassette that came in the mail I heard his mother dictating to him to repeat, "Papa, come back. You've been overseas for a long time!"

That night I could not sleep. My loneliness was unbearable. I was so eager to see them. I cried into my pillow and in the morning I prepared my bags to leave. I remember that when I finished my degree at the university, I applied for a teaching position at the employment center but it never came. I passed the time, helping my father with farming. He was happy that I stayed with him in the village. He praised my efforts, but I was torn apart, feeling that I should be doing more for my family. Then I came up with the idea of working abroad. I made up my mind and decided to come here. I said to my father, "I'll only be gone for two years and then I'll be back."

He objected. "Mere talk."

I asked him, "What do you mean by that?"

"All those who have gone before you said the same," he answered. "But none came back!"

I argued that I would not stay more than two years.

He refused to believe me and was sad when I kissed his hands farewell. He said, "It's written on your forehead that you'll leave."

My father's vision was right. I've spent nine years, ten months, and twenty-six days away. What pulls me to this land that I cannot leave it? Is it the need that surrounds my family? Everyone there waits for my help, expects treasures from this place so far away from them. I sigh and think that I can only do my best. I hope that will be enough. How long should I wait here?

Darkness has begun to fall. At nine o'clock the stores close. Where is the list? What is to be bought? A radio for my father, school shoes for Saleh, a school bag for Hamida, a watch for Razi, makeup for Zanib, the most beautiful of her sisters. And I've got to buy another dress for my mother.

The last time I went home I handed out the gifts right away and carefully watched their faces for reactions. Most seemed pleased, though their thanks came slowly, as though they were shy around me, or as though no matter what I brought it could not match the treasures they'd imagined. This time I hoped to do better. I hoped to please everyone. But if I had no time for shopping, that notion was lost. I scanned the jogging track and was surprised to see the lady and her daughter approaching. My heart leaped and I hurried to prepare the car for them.

"Thank you, Bashrawi," said the mistress, as I opened the door for them. "We have decided to go to the bazaar with you. We'll even help you pick gifts for your family, if you like."

The daughter slid into the car. She said nothing, but I could tell by her pink cheeks and downcast eyes that her mother had given her a lecture.

I closed the door and climbed into the front seat. "I would appreciate any help you could give me, Madam," I said. I started the engine and the three of us drove off together.

◆

TALIB AL-RIFAI, *an active member of the Kuwait Literary Society, is the author of numerous short stories.*

About the Book

The stories in *Oranges in the Sun* capture a distinctly unique vision of the world, embodying the range of emotional and material concerns of the peoples of the Arab Gulf region. Drawn from the increasingly rich literatures of Saudi Arabia, Yemen, Oman, the United Arab Emirates, Bahrain, Qatar, and Kuwait, the stories also reflect the development of the short-story genre in the region. The introduction to the collection provides historical context, as well as a broad overview of the selections.

Deborah S. Akers, visiting assistant professor of anthropology at Miami University, and **Abubaker A. Bagader,** professor of sociology at King Abdulaziz University and Saudi Arabia's deputy minister of culture, have collaborated in the editing and translation of *Voices of Change: Short Stories by Saudi Arabian Women Writers, They Die Strangers: Selected Works by Abdul-Wali,* and *Whispers from the Heart: Short Stories from Saudi Arabia.*